ELEMENTAL'S CURSE

AN ALICE SKYE NOVEL

TAYLOR ASTON WHITE

DARK WOLF PUBLISHING

Edited by Michael Evans

To my children, because even though you're distractions, you're my distractions.

Alice Skye Series

Witch's Sorrow
Druid's Storm
Rogue's Mercy
Elemental's Curse
Knight's War

Alice Skye Short Story

Witch's Bounty

This book is written in British English, including spelling and grammar.

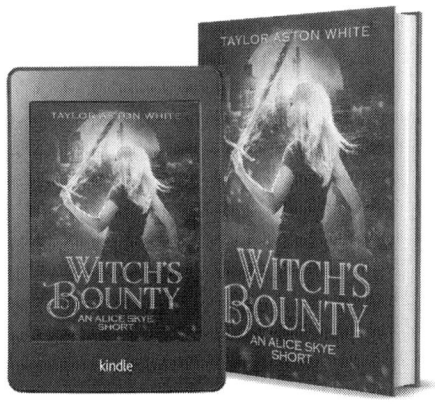

Your FREE short story is waiting...

Witch's Bounty

When the wrong man's framed, and the Metropolitan Police don't care. Paladin Agent Alice Skye takes it on herself to find the real culprit.

Get your free copy of Witch's Bounty at
www.taylorastonwhite.com

BOOK FOUR

He stared at the annoying lamp post outside his window, the bright light flickering every few seconds or so. He couldn't sleep, the insomnia he had suffered with for years howling at him as he puffed on the green cigarette, made from his mother's garden. More like stolen, but she had always said he should show more interest in her homegrown herbs and plants. She probably didn't expect him to smoke them though.

He flicked the ash into the open air, the breeze surprisingly cold considering it was midsummer.

He was tired, yet still sleep eluded him.

He had tried potions, amulets and charms, but nothing seemed to work, so he had learned to live on only a few hours every night.

His room was covered in fresh lavender, courtesy of his mother again. The pretty scent overwhelmingly soothing, yet it didn't make him tired. It did, however, cover the smell of tobacco and mugwort. The combination was supposed to promote vivid dreams, but as he didn't sleep it gave him a slight psychedelic effect he rather enjoyed.

The end glowed orange as he savoured the last puff, the smoke momentarily obscuring his vision before his eyes settled on the suspicious looking man who walked towards the house. He frowned as the man disappeared out of view, followed by a delicate smash.

He wasn't sure if it was real or not, had to concentrate as he distinctly heard glass shattering. The noise slight enough he wouldn't have noticed if his head wasn't half hanging out the window.

"Shit," he muttered to himself, stubbing out the cigarette and quietly opening his bedroom door.

CHAPTER 1

A lice clutched her side as she ran, unable to stop and take a breath as she chased the man through the busy streets.

One of the things she hadn't expected that afternoon was first, to eat her weight in pizza, and second, to have to run over a mile through two tube stations and several alleyways to catch her latest contract.

What were the chances he would be at the same Italian restaurant as her? She would say her luck was changing, but the stitch that stabbed her side seemed to loudly disagree.

"Stop!" she shouted, almost out of breath. That was the last time she let Sam convince her to eat a large pizza on her own. The man was pretty fast as he dodged around commuters and cars, and she would usually be faster, but there she was, defeated by a stomach full of cheese and carbs. With a groan, she forced her legs to move, climbing the fence behind a rundown block of flats a few seconds after him.

She had been officially independent for just over eight

weeks, welcoming her new clients as a private Paladin. At first she struggled to convince someone to hire her, doing the first job pro bono. Even with no pay the client was a pain in her arse, but she got the job done with as much professionalism as she could muster. Well, she hadn't stabbed them when they complained that she had brought back their daughter possessed. She wasn't possessed, she was just a typical pissed off teenager.

It wasn't hard to figure out why the kid had ran away in the first place.

The name hadn't helped either, 'I Spy With My Paladin Eye' sounded like a prank to people who didn't have a sense of humour. Which was a lot, apparently.

Luckily she was successful in tracking a witch who was up on 'grievous bodily harm' charges, who the Supernatural Intelligence Bureau had failed to find, which was ridiculous considering she found him snivelling in the attic of his mother's house.

But at least it gave her the jump start she needed. Her job was essentially exactly the same as before, to track and detain breed that have an active warrant by any means necessary.

However, this time she could offer a lot more services such as retrieving lost items and pets, as well as other things, as long as the price was right. Just not the 'services' like one man asked for. He gave her a one star review after she not-so-politely corrected him, and she called him some descriptive names, but she would deny that if anyone asked.

Without S.I., she took home a larger pay cut. Which was a bonus considering the risk of damage or death was marginally higher than a waitress or personal assistant. But then again, those jobs were a lot less exciting.

"I said stop!" Alice skidded to a halt, breath coming out

in pants as Mr Luton attempted, and failed to climb over a seven-foot brick wall. "You're under arrest."

A black cat sat and watched her beside some rotten bins, its reflective eyes eerily stalking her every time she moved into a closer position. The poor thing was small, severely emaciated with clumps of hair missing. One eye was blue, the other green while he was missing the top part of his left ear, the edge raw. By the angry red colour and obvious swelling it was clearly recent, which made it even sadder.

The stench from the bins wouldn't have been as bad if the cat hadn't decided to rip them open, polluting the air with a mixture of rotten food, milk and what looked like a crusty sock.

"Meow."

She ignored the feline, pulling out her phone and taking a few snaps as Mr Luton turned with a wide-eyed look. She had been hired to find the drug dealer who sold the drug HE2 to her client's son, resulting in his overdose. The police had nothing to go on, so it had taken Alice a few weeks of searching amongst the usual dealers to find the one matching the description, as well as photographic evidence for the police. It resulted in an official warrant for his arrest. As she had already fulfilled her contract and sent over the evidence, actually catching him was just a bonus.

"You again!" he hissed, looking around for a way out before his eyes settled on her phone. "Bitch, did you just take my picture?"

"Meow!"

The cat sat between them, casually licking a paw. She tried to wave it away, worried it would be harmed, but clearly cats wouldn't listen when silently threatened with castration. She should have known, she had threatened Sam with it once, and that hadn't worked either.

"Get on the ground!" She held out her palm, looking as threatening as possible. It would have been easier if she still had her gun, but she hadn't renewed her license since leaving S.I.

Her hair whipped across her face, the wind cool against her skin. The ice and snow had all but melted over the last few weeks, but the chill still remained. She was grateful she had taken her jacket out with her, unlike Mr Luton who she had caught unawares and had ran before he could grab his own coat. So he stood in his jeans and tank top, as if he wasn't in a country that barely reached the mid-twenties even in summer. He had been soaked by a passing car and a puddle a few streets before, turning his white tank top see-through. So not only did she have to deal with his pale-arse arms with the worst tattoos imaginable, she also had to deal with his large burger-like nipples.

"Give me the fucking phone." He took a step forward.

Something brushed against her thigh.

"Meow."

Shit.

She tried to push the cat away, but it just continued to watch her inquisitively before it brushed against her once again. Even a rude hand gesture didn't move the bloody thing.

"Meow."

"Fuck off," she hissed as the cat began to purr surprisingly loudly considering it looked half dead.

"Oi, bitch!"

As if called, the cat walked towards Mr Luton, a slight limp to its back leg.

6

"If you don't get on the ground, I'll have to use force," she warned.

"You?" he laughed, flashing his gold teeth. "You look like you can barely make a fist. Shouldn't you be in the kitchen, doll?" He pulled out a knife, the blade long and serrated.

Well, that was bloody rude.

"Someone is clearly overcompensating for something," she said, steadying her legs. "It's the Mrs I feel sorry for."

A flush coloured his neck. "Give me the fucking phone."

She called her chi, a flame popping to life in her hand a millisecond later. "Last warning."

With a roar he launched himself forward, holding his blade like he had used it many times before. She kicked out, her leg connecting with his stomach with enough force that he folded forward with a wheeze. He recovered quicker than she expected as a fist blurred, the knuckles barely scraping her cheek as she moved out the way.

"*Scintillam!*" she shouted, pushing out her hand as sparks flew towards his face. With a scream he covered his eyes, giving Alice the chance to knock the blade from his hand, kicking it away.

Eyes streaming he blinked at her, mouth twisted into a snarl. "You'll pay for this!"

The cat waddled over, flopping to its side as it begged for attention. "Meow!"

He lifted his foot, his heavy boot sending the defence-less animal flying into the wall with a crack. Alice moved before she even processed the thought, dropping to her knees beside the fallen creature. It tried to roll, the pain too much as it let out a gentle yelp. Mr Luton stumbled into the bins, one hand clutching his eyes. He didn't sense her fist when she smashed it into his face, or the second time when it broke his nose. When he collapsed she locked the handcuffs around a pole, making sure his head faced into the pile of putrid rubbish.

With a quick text she contacted Rose with the details, knowing the feisty Paladin from Supernatural Intelligence Bureau would sort him out, even if she received the bonus and not Alice.

She had other priorities to deal with.

"Meow."

Alice gently scooped up the cat, putting it inside her jacket where it could keep warm.

What the hell was she supposed to do with a broken cat?

Alice sat in the waiting room, glancing at the clock as it ticked loudly behind the desk. She picked at her phone, pressing the large crack that sliced across her screen as she tried to ignore the drooling beast beside her. The dog attempted to bark, the noise escaping in a squeak. It wagged, tongue rolled out in a grin as its owner pretended it didn't sound like a mouse on steroids. It was a large thing, as tall as Alice on hind legs with teeth a wolf shifter would be proud of.

"Lucina Press and Twinkle Toes, please," the receptionist called out.

The woman with the squeaky dog stood.

Alice looked down at her boots, trying to hide her smirk at the ridiculous name.

"Alice Skye?"

"Oh, yeah, that's me." Alice approached the vet, concerned at his worried expression. "Is it okay?"

"*He* will be fine after some rest. He's lucky you've brought him in. Without treatment he probably wouldn't have survived the infection in his ear, never mind the severe malnutrition." He looked down at his notes. "Where did you find him again?"

"In an alley. Have you called his owners?"

"That's what I wanted to talk to you about actually, he's barely six months old and shows signs of neglect. If he did have owners they didn't treat him well, although, it's possible due to no collar or microchip that he's a stray."

"What do you do with strays?"

"Normally they get taken to the closest animal shelter where they remain in a cage until they're adopted. It's rare, but if they show signs they cannot be adopted they can be destroyed."

"A cage? Destroyed?" Alice sighed.

She didn't want a cat.

Had one too many cats at home.

But could she forgive herself at abandoning this one?

"Looks like I'll have to take him then."

The vet smiled, holding the clipboard to his chest. "I'll bring him right out."

Alice nodded as she paid the assistant, cringing at the amount it cost.

Why does something so small cost so much?

How was she even supposed to look after a cat?

Not only did she have to look after herself, she now had to look after an animal that was entirely reliant on her.

When the vet came back he grinned, handing over the black ball of fur with a cone around its neck. The cat attempted a meow, the sound coming out a weird crackly sound. It blinked several times up at her with its different colour eyes, a purr vibrating it's belly.

"Looks like he chose you," the vet said.

"Huh?" Alice murmured as she tried to pull her face away from the cone as the cat tried to nuzzle against her. The plastic clipping her chin.

"They do that you know." With a nod he waved her away.

Alice exhaled, picking him up just under his front legs so he faced her. His eyes looked at her expectantly, his tongue sticking out the right side of his mouth.

"What am I going to do with you?"

CHAPTER 2

"Fuck sake, stick you bloody..."

Sam's annoyed voice carried to the front door as she stepped inside, dropping the cat onto the floor so it could explore.

"Honey, I'm home," she said in a sing-song voice.

"Hey baby girl," came the quick reply. "I'm just in the kitchen."

Alice tossed the broken camera onto the sofa, still annoyed at the cracked lens. Replacements were expensive, something her savings would have paid for except they went on a surprise vet bill instead. She glared at the culprit, his own unusual eyes staring back before she sighed.

It wasn't his fault.

With the photographs emailed she would receive a wire transfer of the rest of the money owed. It wouldn't be enough to cover everything, but it was a start.

Between her and Sam, they barely made ends meet with both their wages. Not with the upkeep of the house, necessities like eating and of course, the rent. It was her childhood home, but as neither parents left a will, and both her and Kyle technically declared dead, the bank became the legal owner. It was Dread who stopped them from immediately selling or renting it out when they passed, using an excuse that it was an active crime scene.

It was vacant for almost two decades, the bank gave up taking Dread to court and left it to become derelict. You couldn't win against the Commissioner of the Supernatural Intelligence Bureau. He had friends in high places apparently.

Or he was just a stubborn old vampire.

So when she finally decided she wanted to move back in Dread suddenly cleared it. Strange that.

She was grateful to him, she didn't know she needed the house to heal, but she did. She wasn't sure if she would stay there forever, but for now, it was their home.

Until they failed to pay their rent, at least.

"Alice..." Sam called through the doorway. "Why do I smell pussy?"

"Yeah, about that..." Alice paused at the threshold. "What the hell happened?"

Sam looked sheepish, an awkward smile on his lips. "Well, I kind of broke Jordan."

"Broke?"

She moved around the table, shocked at the state of their haunted gnome. Sam had attempted to glue the terracotta back together, leaving cracks across his blue coat. For some reason he added an eyepatch, which made him look like a demented pirate. His fishing rod was nowhere in sight, having been replaced with a paddle.

One side read 'Nice,' while the other side read 'Naughty.'

"Seriously Sam?" She couldn't help but roll her eyes. Only Sam would add a sex paddle.

"Did you know I found him in Mrs Shelley's garden yesterday?" he said in reply.

"Really?" Alice took a seat beside him, studying Jordan. "I wonder why he was there?"

Jordan had a mind of his own, randomly turning up in places around the house. They had tried to return him to Al, who was his original owner but he always found his way back. It was creepy to say the least, even worse when Xander confirmed he was haunted. He didn't seem to really do anything other than watch TV, so they left him be. But lately he had been venturing out, scaring their neighbours to the point they had received several rude letters. They thought Jordan was being purposely placed to scare people. While she wouldn't put the joke past Sam, they weren't.

How could she explain to a bunch of mundane humans that Jordan was a sentient being? Albeit, mischievously annoying sometimes.

"Oh, and Mr Polin had a heart attack. Apparently he's going to be okay," Sam continued.

"Isn't that the third person this month?" Everyone seemed to be dropping like flies. "It's strange."

"Not really," he said as he concentrated on gluing Jordan's red capped hat. "You know they're all prehistoric down this street. They gotta go sometime."

"Meow."

The cat attempted to jump onto the table, but the cone clipped the side and he toppled back to the floor. Alice laughed, picking him up and settling him on her lap.

"What the fuck is that?" Sam asked, an eyebrow lifting in curiosity. Shifters didn't keep pets, thought it was morally wrong to own an animal. Which made sense, considering.

"This is…" She couldn't keep calling him 'Cat.' "Poe."

Poe began to purr.

"As in the poet?" Sam gave Poe a wary glance, a frown creasing his brow. "I know black cats and witches go way back, but why?"

"I couldn't leave him." She scratched the bottom of his back, just above the tail until he licked the air. "He can come and go as he pleases."

"You can't keep taking in strays. We already have Jordan, and we've only just gotten rid of Roman." When she just glared he sighed. "Whatever, just don't expect me to change his litter."

With a last scratch she set Poe down, who quickly turned and hissed at Jordan before he sashayed around the kitchen.

Alice watched her new cat before she climbed to her feet. "Don't wait up, I'll be home late."

"Why? Date with Mr Sex God?" he chuckled, holding a piece of Jordan in place while the glue set.

"No." She hesitated at his 'whatever' look. "It's not a date, it's training!"

"Aye, of course baby girl," he sniggered. "Because training takes *alllll* night. Just remember to wear protection, or else we might have little feet running around."

"So funny." She shook her head. Little feet were not on the cards.

She wasn't even sure what was happening with Riley. Neither of them actually confirmed they were exclusive, not that she was looking elsewhere. But he still confused her. They had such raw attraction, but a passionate kiss every once in a while didn't symbolise they would be great in a relationship. Even if just one kiss fractured her feelings into a thousand chaotic pieces.

"I need to call Kyle." A meow caught her attention as Poe purred at Sam. "Make sure you feed him."

Sam growled, snapping his teeth towards Poe. "Fuck sake."

Alice laughed as she climbed the stairs, the sound of Sam threatening the tiny black cat amusing. She knew he would be fine, Sam was the most compassionate person she knew.

Her bedroom was exactly as she left it, her mother's grimoires on the nightstand. One was harmless, the other full of dark spells and magic. It still made her uneasy to see her mother's decorative scrawl explaining how to remove someone's soul and store it in a bottle, but then again she clearly didn't know her mum.

She sat down on her bed, the dark grimoire immediately growling. She ignored it, used to the strange reaction from a supposedly inanimate object. It growled when she was near, almost biting her on several different occasions by snapping itself shut. The more she studied the pages, the more the book began to change. The leather cover appeared to be growing scales, while the spine – which used to be flat, now had several horn-like bumps.

The growl turned into a full snarl when she leant over to grab her mirror, the nightstand vibrating hard enough to cause a perfume bottle to topple over. She needed to contact Kyle, but as she had no idea how to contact him since he refused to take a phone she knew only one person to ask.

She had only used the mirror a handful of times to communicate with Lucifer, and he wasn't happy each time she called. While scrying had been practiced for thousands of years, it was something of which Alice knew little. Being able to see the future, or even the past would be a helpful tool, unfortunately for Alice the only part of scrying she knew was how to call Lucy. Only Lucy, unless she counted the girl she trained in school with, which she didn't.

Alice sat with her legs crossed on her bed, the mirror balanced on her knees as she let out a breath and opened her third eye. She glanced at the glass, watched how it became misty before a splash of colour flashed in the centre.

"Lucifer, I call you through the reflection."

Nothing happened.

"Err, Lucy?"

She tapped the mirror, wondering what she had done wrong when she realised she had called the wrong name. She needed to call Lucifer's Daemon name, not the name he randomly decided he wanted to be called one day when they were negotiating. Daemons usually kept their names secret as they could be used to summon them without their permission. It was only chance she knew his.

"Xahenort, I call you through the reflection."

With her fingertips she touched the edges, feeling the glass pulsate.

"Xahenort, I call you."

She waited.

"Xahenort? You there?"

"Fuck me, did I say you could call me whenever you wanted?" Lucy snarled as his pissed off face appeared in the glass. "What do you want Little War? Did I not warn you about abusing my summoning name? My patience isn't infinite."

"I need to speak to Kyle..."

"What am I, his secretary? You do understand that when you call someone on a mirror it gives you a pain in your head until you answer? A headache, that's what you Skye siblings are, a fucking headache."

"I have no other way to contact him. It's not like you have Skype."

He moved his face closer, his head tilted. "What's Skype?"

Alice closed her eyes, suppressing a giggle. "Never mind. Is he there? I need to speak to him."

"Your pain-in-the-arse brother isn't here," he sneered, his skin pinker than his normal sickly grey, his usually slitted pupils dilated. "He's on an errand."

"An errand?"

She had invited Kyle to stay with her on numerous occasions, but he had always refused.

"Yes, an errand." Lucy grinned, showing her his sharp teeth. "Have I ever told you I regret taking on your brother?"

"Yes," Alice replied drying. "Every time we speak."

"I'm a laughing stock. He barely gives any effort, his control is mediocre, he keeps randomly disappearing and he is one of the worst familiars I have ever had."

"Wait, wait, wait. Did you say familiar?"

Alice felt her body turn cold.

Familiars were magical partners to what she thought was only witches, a being that shared their chi. They were usually a cat, dog or other small domestic animals, as the master would borrow their familiar's aura in spells, substantially expanding their own chi, therefore their magic's capability. As it supposedly caused intense pain and left the creature without an aura to protect themselves, it was ruled as black magic, therefore illegal. The practice of making a person into a familiar was forbidden.

Alice tapped the glass until Lucy growled. "Our deal was for you to release Kyle once Mason no longer held your name. Since Mason was sliced in two I would say I kept my end of the bargain."

"You sound just as bratty as your brother. I'll have you know I released him once he was fully healed. Now offering him an alternative deal on the other hand…"

"You can't do that!"

Can he?

Lucifer chuckled. "Kyle is a big boy, he can make his own decisions."

Shit. Shit. Shit.

"What's the deal?"

"That's between us. Now, I have a date. Unless you give me a better offer I have a lovely lady tied to the bed covered in cream."

"WAIT!" she tapped the glass as if that would make him stop. She wanted to discuss the date thing, wondered if that was why he had made himself look more human. "Can you get him to call me when he can?"

"I'll let him know as soon as he's back from grocery shopping."

"You have him shopping for you? Seriously?"

"Bye Little War, I'll be seeing you real soon." With a wink he disappeared, her own reflection appearing once again.

CHAPTER 3

Alice stepped down the stairs into the basement, stopping at the bottom once she noticed Kace warming up in the centre. She had moved to training at Riley's house at least twice a week, so often that she knew the electric code to get into the side corridor.

It was a beautiful home, one with large, oversized windows that invited the green of the countryside inside while still being decorated in a strong masculine way.

The basement gym was no different, with natural lighting, mirrors and over a dozen houseplants which made the room feel open, not enclosed like it actually was. Various machines and weights were to the left, while the right had benches and the American style metal lockers from Riley's other place. There were seven, each with different stickers, graffiti and dents. She had no idea whose locker was whose, but someone really loved the old black and white horrors.

Jax pounded the running machine, barely breaking a sweat as she placed her bag beside the lockers, her sword knocking against the metal. Kace turned, his expression closed before he spoke too quietly for her to hear, his head faced towards Jax.

Jax immediately stopped running, slowing down until the machine whined. He left the room without a welcoming smile or wave, but a barely audible grunt. Which was progress considering he usually muttered something unpleasant beneath his breath.

Alice ignored the awkwardness, neither of the two men her biggest fans. She wasn't sure if they just didn't like her because she was a witch, or because she was with Riley.

Either way, she had learned to ignore their hostility.

"Where's Riley?" Alice asked when Kace remained, a slight shininess to his naked chest that suggested he had been in the gym for a while. His body was built just like the others, with sleek muscles that weren't just strong, but also fast. Black and red glyphs were tattooed across the left side of his body, the right side bare.

"Not here," he said in a voice like sandpaper. "You'll have to deal with me today."

"Oh, he never mentioned anything," she said, hiding her annoyance as she threw her jacket to the corner of the room. Out of all the guardians, it was Kace she knew the least.

"He'll be here in a while, for now you'll have to deal with me." He narrowed his dark eyes as he looked her up and down. "You got a problem with that?"

Alice bit the inside of her cheek. She had been training with several of The Guardians over the last few months, their fight styles and magic vastly different. But this was the first time with him, in fact, it was the first time she was ever alone with him.

"Just so we're straight, I'm only doing this because you're my Sires Ward." He shot her a cutting glare.

Her temper flared, but she kept it under control. "Well, aren't I lucky."

What an arsehole.

"I'm going to teach you how to throw a dagger." He produced a small knife out of nowhere before he began to flip it. "You threw a dagger at Mason and missed."

"I didn't miss." Technically she did hit him, but she was aiming for his heart, not his shoulder. Not that she would admit it.

The dagger blurred from his hand, the only warning was the slight ringing it made as it soared through the air and stabbed into the wall behind her. It was so close to her head a few blonde strands fell to the floor, the dagger imbedded into a chunk of wood she hadn't noticed. Alice checked closer, realising the smallest cross had been drawn on, with the knife's tip dead in the centre. It had hit the bullseye perfectly, the handle still vibrating from the impact.

Alice turned back to Kace, mouth agape. "Bloody hell! You need to teach me that."

She could have sworn he smiled, the emotion barely lasting a second before it turned into his usual snarl. "Grab the knife."

Alice pulled at the handle, her muscles straining as she struggled to dislodge the blade. Kace sniggered, moving her away so he could pull it out himself with little effort.

"Weak thing, aren't you."

"Seriously, what's your problem?" Alice asked as she grabbed the dagger he held out, gripping it tighter than she needed to.

"What problem?" he replied, clenching his jaw. "All I see is a witch who can't handle her own power. Who gets herself into situations she can barely survive, ones where she needs to be rescued." He stood closer to emphasize his point. "You may be a professional damsel in distress, but you're not *my* problem."

"You're right, I couldn't handle my power." She lifted up the dagger, her hand erupting into blue flames that crackled gently around the metal. "My magic is something I know nothing about, something I'm learning as I go." Alice couldn't help her laugh. "But one thing you're wrong on, I'm definitely no damsel." She spun, releasing the blade. It soared through the air, impaling the wood just shy of the centre cross.

Bollocks.

"You missed." Kace walked up and pulled the dagger. "But not bad. You held too much tension in your arm and shoulders, you need to be relaxed to get a more accurate trajectory." He handed the dagger back. "Go again."

Alice took a deep breath, relaxing her shoulders before she released the blade again, and again, and again. Kace watched with his arms crossed, expression solemn as she repeated the same motion over and over. Her arm ached before she finally hit the right spot.

"Finally." He clapped, the sarcasm not lost on her. "Now hit the cross three times in a row."

It took her twenty more minutes before she hit it three times, her arm aching. The wood was almost unrecognisable once she was finished.

"It's taken you long enough," Kace murmured when he finally moved. Alice hadn't realised that he had stood in the same position, arms crossed for the whole exercise. He hadn't spoken, so she had almost forgotten he was there.

"Yeah, well," she shrugged, fighting a happy dance as he retrieved the dagger.

Something familiar brushed across her chi.

She turned just as Riley stepped into the basement, his stormy eyes settling on her instantly. He could have concealed his chi, hidden his presence from her so she wouldn't have been able to know he was there until she either heard or saw him, like a human. But he didn't. He always stroked his chi against hers, the feeling electric against her senses. It was almost like a flare, a greeting amongst witches, but one that always left her wanting more.

"Kace?" Riley said, his face alarmed when he turned his attention. "Where's Axel?

Kace clenched his jaw, head titled to the side as he stared through slitted eyes. "I don't know, I'm not his keeper. Said he was busy."

"What do you mean he said he was busy?" Riley said through gritted teeth, his eyes swirling to liquid silver.

Alice could feel the tension, not understanding why. "Kace has been teaching me how to throw." She held out her hand for the dagger, clearing her throat when Kace continued to glare at Riley. As soon as the cold steel hit her palm she threw, the blade singing through the air and embedding itself into the centre.

Riley was still watching Kace.

"Guess that's my cue to leave. Sire." Kace didn't glance back as he left the gym.

"What was all that about?" Alice asked.

"You need to keep away from him." Riley pulled the dagger, bringing it with him.

"Why?"

"That's not my story, sweetheart. But he's the most unstable of us all." He closed his eyes before taking a deep breath.

"Riley?"

"Throw this at me," he said once he opened his eyes, the

colour back to normal. "And update me about The Magic-ka." It still amazed her when they changed, how he changed. He would never have shown her before, would have kept it all hidden, a secret. Now, he was open with what he was, with his beast.

"I'm not going to throw this at you." She accepted the knife when he held it out.

"Don't worry, you won't hit me," he smirked, brushing the pad of his thumb across her cheek before he nudged her towards a set of metal drawers. He opened the top one, the inside lined with velvet and contained nine identical throwing knives, the tenth in her hand.

"You've asked me to throw something sharp at you!"

Riley chuckled. "We both know you *can't* hit me," he taunted.

Alice's hand moved before the thought crossed her mind.

Riley caught the blade without effort.

"See, you won't be able to hit me. Do it again." He gestured to the drawer with the other knives. "I'm not the fastest thing out there. You need to learn to anticipate your opponent."

"I've been doing pretty well, considering," she replied as she grabbed another knife.

"Luck runs out, sweetheart. High Lords, certain shifters and even an old Vamp are as fast, if not faster. In that situation you won't be able unsheathe your sword in time."

"I can't run." She started to flip the dagger, watching Riley carefully. She studied his muscles, looking for a slight tense to give up the direction he would turn.

"No, and this is the only situation where you choose not to run. Not when they can catch up to you with your back unprotected. Kace is a prick, but he's right. You need to learn to throw."

Alice let go of the dagger as soon as she saw him tense, the blade soaring past him.

"Fuck!"

Riley chuckled. "It's almost like you want to impale me, sweetheart."

"Shut up," she seethed. She had seen his thigh move, yet he went in the opposite direction than she anticipated. She felt her chi spike in irritation, enough that she felt heat at the end of her fingertips.

Riley continued to chuckle. "You need to surprise your opponent. Throw something at them so they're forced to move. It will give you enough time to grab your sword." He stepped towards her, a smirk painted on his face.

She reached into the drawer and threw the third knife. It missed.

"This is ridiculous!" She didn't want to hit him, but she really wanted to smack the smug look off his face.

Riley picked up the daggers, holding them all in his left hand. "Seven more to go. If you don't hit me, there's a forfeit."

"Wait, you didn't say anything about a forfeit!"

Riley just replied with a smile.

Alice palmed the fourth dagger, throwing it instantly. This time she aimed the opposite direction, ignoring his cues. It grazed his arm, enough to tear his shirt but not skin.

"Six to go. Now tell me about The Magicka? They're refusing to even meet."

"That's because you threatened one of them," she smirked.

"Alice..."

"Fine, they're following me." Had in fact been following

25

her for a while. She had played with some, letting them follow her into busy areas before she disappeared. They didn't like that, so they started sending teams of two to stalk her instead. "They seem pretty harmless."

"The fact they're letting you see them means they want you to be intimidated."

"At least they're not trying to arrest me again."

"Yeah, for now."

The Magicka had been concerned about her ever since she quit Supernatural Intelligence.

They didn't trust her power.

That made two of them.

They had called her a liability, and thought she should remain with The Magicka until such time The Council decided what the bloody hell they were going to do. Stating they were the only people equipped enough to 'handle her,' as if she were a rabid dog. It was Dread who negotiated that she would not spend any time in their hands in exchange for her privacy. Which she was grateful for, especially since it had been months and she still hadn't heard a whisper about the decision.

She was not a patient person.

"It's the not knowing that's killing me. I've been told nothing other than my fate is in the hands of The Council." People who knew nothing about her.

The fifth knife missed, the blade smashing a mirror into thousands of shards that showered across him. He shrugged them off.

Alice let out a sound of frustration. "I know they're planning something, but I'm not sure what. I don't trust them."

"That's the smartest thing you've ever said."

The sixth knife she threw, her anger added a trail of

flame that destroyed its trajectory. It ended up landing on the floor, scratching across the wood. Blood rushed her cheeks as embarrassment burned.

"You need to learn control," Riley said, slight anger shaping his words. "That was your worst go yet. What causes you to lose control, make mistakes?"

Alice took a deep breath, feeling her chi stutter. Before she would have exploded, her flames escaping her grasp. But she was learning.

"You know exactly what makes me lose control." He had used it against her on numerous occasions in training. It pissed her off each time, but it was working.

He stepped forward, her pulse beating in anticipation. "I've seen you lose it to the point I thought you were going to annihilate yourself, then you managed to stop, pulling your power back. What did you do? What changed?"

Alice hesitated, her mouth dry. "I don't know."

"You do." He took another step forward. "You have more control than you give yourself credit for. I can feel you, even now how close you are to losing it, a hair trigger." He rolled his shoulders, watching her through slitted eyes.

She felt like she was being hunted by a predator.

Alice forced herself to relax, remembering Kace's advice even as her shoulders tightened with irritation. Not overthinking, she palmed two daggers and released them both. The first barely missed as he spun in anticipation, the second he caught in his hand.

"Shit!" He released the dagger, blood dripping from his palm as he'd caught it by the blade.

When she heard him growl she turned to the remaining knives, his breath a sudden warmth as it brushed against her neck. His hand went to circle her wrist, to disarm the dagger when she brought up her knee.

With a twist he blocked her, disarming her still, even as she reached for another.

"Enough." He pushed her against the wall, his legs gently pinning hers while his palms were inches from her head.

She panted, excitement running through her blood. She felt him, felt the heat radiate off his body and felt his chi vibrate against hers. She wondered if he felt it too, the unacknowledged electric sensation that caressed across her skin. It was worse since their bath, the only time they had ever lost control with one another. The memory flashed across her mind, the warm water splashing against her skin as Riley's hands...

"I get my forfeit," he said, voice deeper than usual. Almost as if he could read her mind.

"What?" It came out a squeak. "But, I hit you."

"I caught it."

"Yeah, by the sharp pointy end."

"Doesn't count," he smirked as he leant closer.

In a split second she hooked her foot around his ankle, forcing him off balance as she shoved with her whole weight. Her smug victory was short lived when he grabbed her, making her fall with him.

"Ugh." She fell on top, her hands slapping against his chest as her whole weight settled on his. Shock flashed across his face, matching her own before he cracked out a laugh, the sound vibrating beneath her.

"Look, can we..."

"Am I interrupting?" a man said in a scathing tone.

Alice scrambled to her feet while Riley casually, almost lazily, climbed up, his eyes never leaving the tall, skinny man who stood at the bottom of the stairs. Alice remained silent, taking in the stranger's dark hair peppered with white and angrily pinched face. His skin was smooth, a small scar cutting his chin in two.

"Bart, what are you doing here?"

The man growled. "You will call me by my title." He shot Alice a disgusted look, his eyes a warm honey brown that didn't match his tone. "Leave."

She bit back her automatic retort. When Riley nodded she bent to grab her stuff, moving towards the archway as the two men waited for her to be out of earshot.

"You're not returning my calls."

"I have nothing to say."

"I warned you about the rules, Riley."

Alice paused by the stairs when she noticed Kace, who stood by the entrance of the adjoining shower room in the small corridor. He was still shirtless, his eyes closed as he leant against the wall, knee bent and arms crossed.

"Who's he?" she asked, keeping her voice low as she turned to watch Riley's body language become increasingly hostile.

She waited for Kace's reply, getting nothing until she returned her attention to him, his eyes open slightly as he watched her. His red hair was damp, darker than usual and stuck to the side of his face.

"You're like this fire that burns too hot, something that needs putting out." The words were cold, detached as he dropped his foot to the wooden floor with a gentle thump.

Alice stiffened, her heart a jackrabbit against her ribs.

Kace tipped his head to the side, almost if he could hear it. "What does he see in you? Hmm." His iris' swirled, turning liquid silver until she could see herself reflected back. "What does he see that he would risk everything for you?" His voice dropped, ending in a smoky growl.

Alice widened her stance, flames tingling her fingertips. "I don't know what you mean."

There was a heavy pause, his hands fisting until nails dug into skin. "His name is Bartholomew Edwards. He was voted in by the remaining Vectors as the new Archdruid, which also makes him the new councilman."

"Hey, Kace my brother, you okay?" Sythe popped his head over the bannister, his hair sticking out in every direction possible.

Kace clenched his jaw, uncrossing his arms with a nod. "See you around, Alice."

CHAPTER 4

Alice arrived at the crime scene exactly twenty-two minutes after she received the call from Detective Brady. Impressive considering the traffic, even as late as it was. Riley's place was on the outskirts of London, close enough that you could see the city skyline in the distance, but far enough away that the surrounding grounds gave them privacy.

A uniformed officer approached her car, his face annoyed before recognition crossed his face.

Since she had left the Supernatural Intelligence Bureau, the specialised team from the Metropolitan Police 'Spook Squad' had kept her on retainer as a liaison. She was officially a Breed Consultant, something she revelled in, especially as it gave Mickey, the annoying ex-colleague and acting Commissioner a big middle finger. She had kept in contact with some of her fellow Paladins, knew he was a puppet for those higher up. Namely The Council.

"What are you wearing?" Brady grunted when he walked over. "You look unprofessional."

"My ninja outfit," she said with a straight face. "What, you don't approve?"

She wore the same clothes she did at Riley's. Black yoga leggings, black t-shirt and jacket. He was lucky she had worn a plain t-shirt and not one of her funny novelty ones, that would have been extremely unprofessional, especially to Brady.

"Hey, Alice," Jones greeted as he walked over, his overalls tied at his waist as he adjusted the goggles on his head. "Nice ninja outfit."

"See!" Alice turned back to the Detective, a smile tugging her lips. "He gets me."

"Hmmm." Brady walked away, leaving them alone.

"What's his problem?"

"You know what he's like." Jones waved his hand, as if the gesture meant something. "He's sensitive ever since Michelle became pregnant."

"Is it bad?" she said, knowing Jones would understand she was asking about the crime scene and not about Brady's wife. Not that his wife wasn't lovely.

"Well, it's never good." His standard smile dropped from his face. "I've already finished in there."

He walked her to the terraced house, motioning for her to enter through the door. The stench hit her immediately, strong enough she had to make an effort not to gag violently.

"Erm... wow." Her stomach recoiled, bile threatening as she repeatedly swallowed it back down.

"You'll get used to it," Peyton called from the other side of the large living room, his voice its usual monotone.

"Hey," Alice greeted as she stepped further inside, making sure she kept away from the two bodies in the centre. All furniture had been pushed to the walls, leaving only a single red circular rug. At least, she assumed it was originally red. "What do we have here?"

Spook Squad solely dealt in Breed, which meant she was missing something.

"Murder-suicide." Peyton stated, a frown creasing his brow. "At least, that's what it's supposed to be."

"Supposed to?" Alice asked, her face now having an identical frown. Peyton remained silent, his sharp gaze just staring until she figured it out for herself. She narrowed her own eyes at him before she took a calming breath. It was the wrong thing to do, because now the strong smell choked the back of the throat.

"Yeah, the smell is a mixture of backed up drains and a perforated bowel," Jones said from the doorway with a crinkly shrug. He had put back on his plastic overalls including hood, so he made a noise every time he moved.

"How do you know about the bowel without an autopsy?" The man on the left looked peaceful, almost asleep compared to the violent ear to ear slash on the woman to the right. They were close, shoulders and hips touching while their hands were clasped even in death.

"I don't know for sure, but it's just a smell you don't forget."

"That's disgusting. You know that, right?"

"Alice," Peyton interrupted. "I want your input in this. We've found random photographs stuffed down the toilet, hint the backed up drain. We have also found a suicide note in a masculine handwriting stating he couldn't be in a world without Macey."

Alice glanced at the woman again, her throat a splash of red against her skin. "Are we assuming the woman is Macey?"

"I.D.'s confirmed as Macey Black and Rhys Pollen. Their driving licenses were found in the U bend."

"Interesting place to keep them," she muttered as she stepped closer, bending down to take a closer look.

Rhys looked undisturbed, his cause of death not as obvious. His skin was pale, but still held a healthy flush. Macey, on the other hand, looked like she had been dead a lot longer, her skin an ashen grey, her hair brittle and lips chapped. They looked human, no characteristics she could make out that suggested Breed.

Then why was she there?

"How do you know they're Breed?"

It was hard to tell someone's Breed from just a glance, the majority all humanoid in appearance. Even Fae were difficult to tell, as they generally wore charms to make themselves appear more human.

"We don't," Peyton stated. "But the first officer on scene was thrown across the room when he unlocked the door."

"Yeah, that would do it," she smirked as she glanced towards the door, only just realising it was indented into the back wall, hanging off its hinges. "Looks like someone has carved a ward into the frame."

She went to touch the delicate swirls in the wood, pulling back once it sparked at her proximity. It wasn't a ward she had ever seen, the twirls and whirls delicate. There weren't even any elemental anchors that would have been used in witchcraft. Which meant they were Fae. Something she knew little about.

"We need to salt the door, the ward's still active." In honesty, she was surprised the officer hadn't been killed.

Peyton grunted in acknowledgment.

Fae were an unusual Breed, their magic different to witches and druid's. Something she was fascinated with, but also unable to replicate. She found her attention wandering back to Peyton, much to his annoyance. He never once confirmed or acknowledged that he was Fae, and not human like the team believed.

"Jones," Peyton started, his tone coming out cold. "You got an estimated time of death?"

"Well, if I go by my experience I would say from just the look of the bodies Macey looks days old, while Rhys is only a few hours."

"Why do I sense a but?" Alice said.

"But... if I go by Rigor Mortis, they both died within minutes of each other."

"Minutes?"

"Their hands for example," Jones bent to lift both the deceased wrists. They were stiff. "Rigor is the natural contracting and relaxation of body muscles when we all die. It normally starts in the face, working its way down the body."

He gently placed the wrists down before turning to lift up a leg of Rhys', then Macey's.

"Now their legs are yet to even begin, but their Rigor is almost identical. From the look of Macey, she should have already been through the cycle."

"So why is she decaying at a much faster rate?" Alice mumbled.

Peyton looked away as he flicked at his hair in a burst of annoyance, the strands long enough to touch his nape. In anybody else she wouldn't have noticed, however in Peyton she did. She had joked multiple times about having a broom up his arse, how he could stand there rigid as a statue as he efficiently organised the team. But this was different.

She had never seen him fidget before, not once.

Alice nodded to Jones, even as she knew Peyton was

hiding something. He took the tough guy cop routine to the next level, but after the last few cases together she was starting to be able to read him.

"I think the ward may be of Fae origin, but I would need a second opinion," she said, gauging Peyton's reaction. His attention snapped back at her, gaze hard. She would never spill his secrets, but it was clear he also knew more than he was letting on.

"Jones, can you confirm the angle of the cut?" For a throat wound that deep, there wasn't much blood. It covered her front, but barely any drops outside the rug. She would have expected considerably more.

"The Pathologist will need to confirm, but I'm pretty sure she was slit from the back. The slice is deep, yet there is no arterial spray which is unusual." He shrugged, the casual gesture uncomfortable against the backdrop of the scene.

"What about the murder weapon?"

"We have yet to find it," Jones said just as his phone began to ring in one of his many pockets. "We have another team looking to sweep the area once the coroner removes the bodies." His phone began to ring again. "Sorry guys, I need to take this."

Alice ignored him as he left, instead studying the room once more. For some reason the furniture bothered her. Why would he have taken the time to move the furniture, place Macey on the central rug, hide the murder weapon and then spell the door? All before he killed himself too. It was too perfect, too posed.

"The murder weapon isn't here," she decided.

Peyton's blue eyes met hers once more, the intensity of his gaze hard to decipher even as the silence bristled.

She opened her mouth, an accusation at the edge of her

tongue as Brady stomped through the door, his nose curled in distaste as his wide shoulders brushed the doorframe.

"What are we thinking? Inspector O'Neil wants this tied up quickly."

"WAIT!" Alice and Peyton shouted as one.

With an electric snap Brady was thrown across the room, his large form crashing against the wall.

"Shit," Alice dropped to her knees by his head just as Peyton shouted for help. "Hey big guy," she calmly said as she quickly checked over any injuries. "If you wanted some time off, you could have just asked."

Brady tried to sit up, his breath coming out in a hiss when he put weight on his left arm.

"Ambulance is on the way." Peyton helped Brady sit up.

"You never answered my question," Brady said, voice strained.

"Brady, you've just been thrown against the wall..."

"I have a hard head."

Alice would have laughed if he didn't look so pained.

"Now," Brady grunted. "What are the details of the case?"

Peyton didn't give her the chance to answer.

"It has to be upgraded to a double homicide, not a murder-suicide."

"Reasons?" Brady grumbled, straight to the point.

Alice was able to answer first this time. "It looks framed. Why move the furniture?"

"To create an altar to her?"

"But why? He's already tried to dispose of photographs and their I.D.'s, if it was creating an altar to his love, surely he would surround it with images of them together?"

"Also the murder weapon is missing," Peyton added. "According to Jones, he's confident they died within minutes of each other. He wouldn't have had time to kill her, get rid of the blade then kill himself."

Brady sighed, even as his skin turned ashen.

"I'll update O'Neil," Peyton stated just as they noticed the blue flashing lights through the windows.

"And I'll ring Michelle."

After she dissolved the ward.

CHAPTER 5

The instant yowling made Alice pause until she remembered about her new cat. Shutting the door before the bundle of fur could escape she searched for the bloody thing, finding it stuck beneath one of the dining room chairs.

"You've got to be kidding me!" she moaned as she unwedged Poe's cone of shame, although, it was now a cone of flamboyant sunshine. Alice couldn't help her smile when she noticed that it had been artistically styled to resemble a yellow daisy. Sam had cut the edges of the plastic to represent petals, as well as painted the inside a bright yellow. It made Poe, with his different coloured eyes and half-eaten ear look cute, but ridiculous.

Laughter bubbled as she moved into the kitchen, grinding to a halt at the man who stood in the light of the open fridge.

"Erm, hello?" She probably would have reacted a bit differently to a strange man if he wasn't completely naked and bent over in her kitchen. The place where she practiced cooking until she gave up and ordered takeaway instead. Alice carefully settled Poe onto his feet, unable to keep her eyes off the stranger.

"Oh, hello." The man gave a friendly smile when he stood up, a carton of milk clenched in his hand. "I didn't know Sam had a housemate."

"Oh, wow." She couldn't stop her eyes dropping, a flush burning up her neck before she realised what he had said. "I'm sorry, a what?"

"Housemate?" he repeated with a slight hesitation. "Right?"

"Oh..." Alice struggled to contain her laughter. "I'm sorry, who are you? And why are you..." She gestured to his scary, but impressive length between his legs. She had seen way more than she had ever wanted to of that particular area.

What was he, a fucking horse?

"Oh," he moved the milk to cover himself, which instantly made her never want to drink milk again.

Oh, now he blushes, she thought, hiding a snort behind a cough. Alice took an unsteady breath, trying to calm the laughter that threatened to break through.

"Did you just seriously call me his housemate?" She puffed up in fake outrage, an idea popping in her head. "Who are you calling housemate? I'm his wife!"

The colour drained from the man's face. In fact, the colour drained across his whole body. Including, strangely, a place she never thought had that ability.

"Wife? He never said he had a wife!" The man squeaked as a look of utter confusion passed across his pretty face.

"Where's Sam?" she replied tartly, tapping her foot for emphasis.

"Errr, he's in the shower." His eyes darted to the door, his uncomfortableness clear.

"If you would excuse me..." He placed the milk haphazardly on the side before he made his escape, the carton tipping over the edge and smashing to the floor. "I'm so sorry!" he shouted as he ascended the stairs at a run.

Alice stared at the white puddle, her laughter finally breaking through just as Poe attempted to lick up the spill.

"ALICE!"

She poked her head out the door, able to see Sam bending over the top bannister. His hair wet, chest naked with a towel messily wrapped around his waist.

"Oh, hey honey." she pouted. "Am I suddenly not woman enough for you?"

"Fuck sake, really?" he growled. "How am I going to explain my non-existent wife is crazy?!" Sam bared his teeth in a mock threat before he disappeared.

She smirked, able to make out his apologetic voice down the stairs before he slammed his bedroom door.

The milk had spread when she re-entered the kitchen, soaking into the salt, and ruining her pentagram. With a sigh she closed her eyes, a pain shooting across her temple. She had been practicing spells found in her mother's grimoires. At first she had struggled, unable to understand why her mother had dark magic, ones requiring a larger sacrifice than Alice was willing to make. So she experimented, using a mixture of plants and her own blood.

How could bringing a plant back to life be bad? If she only used it on the plant, and not something else. But she guessed that was where it started. As the Councils decision hung over her head, the more she blurred the lines between earth and black magic.

Yet, she would never sacrifice a living creature for a spell, not even the smallest bug.

Alice reached for the kitchen towels as the pain thumped into a full blown head-ache, strong enough she paused to grab a painkiller. Her hand shook as she tried to invoke the charm, the pain radiating across her skull with such intensity before she felt the pressure drop in the room, followed by a high-pitched whistle.

"Put the kettle on, would you, Lucifer said as he appeared in a burst of smoke and sulphur. "Why do you have a puddle of white liquid?"

Her headache disappeared as quickly as it came on. Although, having a Daemon in her kitchen was just as big a headache.

"What are you doing here?" she panicked, fisting her hand as her scar began to pulsate. "You can't just turn up uninvited!"

Shit. Shit. Shit.

His red, slitted eyes narrowed as he frowned. "I did call," he said as he tapped his own head. He looked down at Poe, who stared at him with curiosity. "Oh look, a cat."

"Is that what it feels like?" She now understood why he always looked pissed off when she called him through the mirrors.

"Hurts like a bitch, doesn't it?"

From the second he appeared he had begun transforming. His horns curled beneath his hair while his wings disappeared into two slits down his back. His skin – normally a washed out grey, became pinker as modern clothes replaced his dark leather armour.

Lucy looked down at his new shirt, a grin creasing his cheeks. "Metallica, nice."

She decided to ignore his fascination with his heavy metal band t-shirt. "What are you doing here?"

He knelt, ignoring the milk that soaked into his jeans so he could stroke Poe. "What? You can call me but I can't call you?"

"Lucifer, why are you here?" She watched as her new cat instantly fell in love with the attention. If she thought Poe looked ridiculous before, she was wrong. Because now a warrior Daemon in a heavy metal shirt, was casually petting a heterochromia cat in a yellow daisy cone.

She couldn't make that shit up.

"Your wonderful brother has gone missing. So until I find that skinny runt so I can kick his arse back down, I thought I would pop in and finish the last part of our bargain."

"I thought Kyle could come and go as he pleases?"

A dramatic sigh as he stood to his full height. "Technicality." He waved his hand in disregard as the traitor Poe moaned at his feet. "He knew we had a busy schedule and decided to fuck off anyway." He sniffed, frowning at the milk.

"You still can't be here." The stench of sulphur that had appeared with the smoke had started to dissipate. But not fast enough, not for a shifters nose. She just hoped Sam was too distracted calming his lover to notice.

Lucy pouted, his eyebrow raised. "No, I think I'll stay. I haven't had some free time to walk up here in a while."

Alice went to reply when she heard the tell-tale squeak of the upstairs floor boards.

"You can't go roaming around! I can't let you out around normal people!"

His gaze darted to her and narrowed in irritation. "You

think you can control me, Little War?" The words came out cold, clipped.

Great, now she had offended him.

"Look, I'm sorry. Okay?" she said, trying to control her slow build panic. She could almost make out Sam's conversation now, which meant he could definitely hear hers. "You said something about our bargain?"

Lucy tilted his head, eyebrow raised as if she fascinated him.

"I'm going to tell you about your blade." He smiled as he held out his hand, the fingers long, the nails even longer. "But not here."

She didn't want him there right now, anyway. But, she still hesitated in taking his hand. His smile tightened before he snapped his hand out to grip her arm in a bruising grip. Before she could even blink, her surroundings changed with a static pop.

CHAPTER 6

W hen Lucy's grip relaxed, Alice collapsed to her knees, a dry heave forcing her forward. "You'll get used to it," Lucifer said as he tapped his foot with impatience.

"What the hell was that?" She looked up through her hair, her throat sore from the violent retching.

"This might sound like a far-fetched concept, but I used magic."

"You're an arsehole, you know that right?"

Lucy snorted. "That is what I call a drift. Your body takes a while the first few times. Just be happy you didn't actually puke, that would have been embarrassing for the both of us."

"You can teleport?" She groaned as she climbed to her feet, her legs shaking slightly at the weight. "Where are we?" She blinked to clear the blurriness in her vision, her brain taking a few more seconds to notice her surroundings.

Directly in front of her were several rows of floor to ceiling bookshelves, close enough together they created a tight path between. A bitterly cold mist teased her ankles, the haze thick enough she could barely make out the floor, her feet almost disappeared. The room was dark, the only light from the free standing torches that flickered, creating eerie shadows across the brick walls. From what she could make out, the books were all leather-bound and nondescript.

"Have you hit your head or something? We're in the library, Little War."

"The library?"

"This is where they keep the prohibited books and grimoires," he said with a grin. "You know, the ones they pretend don't exist."

"No we're not," she stated. "I've been to the restricted section before, and this isn't it."

"It is if you're not invited."

"Invited?" Alice felt the blood drain from her face. "If that's true, that means..." She heard the distinctive hiss just as she turned to face hundreds of dark eyes. She leapt back, knocking into Lucy just as the giant spider launched forward, one of its long legs spearing out to slash before the end disappeared into a burst of smoke an inch from her nose.

"Ah, a Somnlin. Old school, I like that." Lucy pushed past her to stand closer to the hissing spider. "I haven't seen one of these in a few centuries at least."

The spider hissed once more, its acidic spittle hitting the floor with a fizz before it spun into a blur, all long legs and fangs spinning like a tornado. After a few seconds it stopped, to reveal a man twice the size of Lucifer, his eyes just as dark as the spider's had been. His hair was black, so dark it absorbed the limited light and long enough the two plaits finished by his waist. He wore leather trousers with his chest bare, druid glyphs patterned across his left pec, red against the sickly grey of his skin.

Very slowly, the man grinned, revealing several rows of distinctively sharp teeth. Wings cracked as they emerged from his back, loud enough she could hear the bones grinding against one another as they clicked into place. They grew so large the edges scraped against the ceiling, leaving little grooves in the concrete high above.

Lucy stood rigid, fists clenched.

"It's not real," she whispered, unable to take her eyes off the Daemon. Shivers went down her spine as she watched, unable to see even the smallest movement once the wings were fully extended. Not his breathing, a pulse or a twitch even as he continued with his cheek splitting grin, the dark eyes not swaying. If she didn't know better, she would have thought he was a statue.

She found herself just as still, almost tense before he punched out in a burst of speed that made her flinch, his fist turning to smoke before it made contact with Lucy.

"Who's that?" she asked when Lucy still hadn't moved away a minute later, even as he stood there while the Somnlin attempted again and again to do damage.

"It's no one," he finally said, his voice the quietest she had ever heard.

"That no one sure looks like your biggest fear." That's what a Somnlin was, an apparition of your biggest fear. They couldn't cause physical harm if you believed they couldn't, which was hard to believe when they did attack. You felt every cut, every graze even though it wasn't real. Although, it seemed it couldn't pass an invisible barrier into the room. "Who is he?"

"I don't have any fears," he replied with a sharp snap,

shaking his head. "Now let's get this over with before we're caught."

The Somnlin Daemon tilted its head, his grin still stretching his cheeks as his eyes followed Lucifer as he approached the books.

It was uncomfortable to watch.

"Why are we here Lucy? Why this library?"

"Because on my own I would have been expelled from the room." He turned with a forced smirk. "The place is spelled against my kind. Which I personally find offensive." He mused to himself. "I wonder if they would respond to a particularly threatening letter involving several hot pokers and an iron maiden?"

"So you needed me to get inside? You used me?"

"Oh, get off your high horse," he replied, the acerbic edge back. "I've brought you here because it completes our bargain. If it helps me too, so what." He shrugged, his eyes scanning across the rows of books. "Now get out Aurora and let's get on with this."

"You mean my blade? The one I didn't bring because I wasn't given a warning before my molecules vanished into the stratosphere then forced back together?"

"You didn't bring it?" He gave her a pointed look. "Well, this is fucking useless. I don't know when we're going to be able to get in here again."

"You said you knew about my sword, if that's true why are we here?"

He huffed with impatience. "I only know that it's Fae, not druid or witch. I think so, anyway."

"You think? You made out like you knew what it was!"

"Careful, Little War." His warning was clear. "I never specified how much I knew. But, I recognised the runes when they flashed across your steel."

"You know about the runes?" She had been studying her blade, jotting down every rune that appeared across the metal. Unfortunately, they changed every time, and she still didn't understand what they were. "Wait, why would it be in my family if it's Fae?"

"How am I supposed to know?" He cocked an eyebrow.

A book dropped onto the floor with a bang.

Lucy frowned at the book before another one flew off the shelf. Then another. "Stop it, you fuckers!" he growled as he turned aggressively in a circle. "I'm working here. We won't be long then you can get on with whatever the fuck you lot do."

Alice was dumbstruck. "What are you doing?"

"Telling the ghosts to fuck off?" He looked at her like she was the crazy one. "Now we need to find a book that specialises in Fae weapons before we run out of time. Now shoo, go study."

He ushered her further into the shelves.

"Oh, and be careful." His voice called over the rows of books. "They may have certain spells on them to protect the contents. Don't be surprised if they try to bite."

Alice heard his chuckle fade as she walked deeper, the room larger than she initially thought. The smell of must, dust and paper was strong as she touched a fingertip to one spine, feeling an unusual current emit from the thick leather. The books looked old and worn, their leather cracked and peeled. None that she could see had any indication what was inside, the jackets completely bare of any information other than a small gold triangle printed at the bottom. She squinted to get a closer look, the light from the torches not carrying this far down.

"Lux Pila."

A ball of light popped from her palm, floating above to

give some more light. A face appeared between the book-shelves, eyes pure white that disappeared in a blink.

LEAVE!

Alice froze, unsure what she just heard.

YOU DON'T BELONG!

A scream inside her head.

Her lungs began to constrict, the glacial mist began to climb up her legs, the cold restraining her muscles.

"Please," Alice begged as she felt the air from her lungs begin to freeze.

YOU ARE NOT WELCOME HERE!

Alice closed her eyes, concentrating as she felt her aura pulsate and her chi stretch. With a single thought bright blue flames encased her arm, fighting back the cold as it crackled and hissed. She felt the welcoming warmth, careful to not touch anything around her.

How did you do that? The voice asked, confused.

Alice felt the presence before she even opened her eyes, the pale face an inch from her own.

"What are you?" she asked, keeping her voice low, calming. She really didn't want to piss her off again.

The woman's delicate face scrunched up, her eyes pure white that glowed with no iris or pupils. She was all one colour, from the flowers that had been plaited into her waist-length hair to the dress that brushed her ankles. No flush coloured her cheeks. No shadows shaded her features. It was if she was a cartoon.

A cartoon that frowned.

You didn't answer our question, she asked without moving her lips.

"I'm a witch. I used magic."

No you're not. The woman began to float slowly, her

toes brushing the ground. *You don't taste of witch. You taste of...other.* She stopped when their noses almost touched.

"Other?" *What the fuck did she mean?*

We are Whisp, she said with a head tilt. *We protect. What are you? Other.*

Alice had never heard of a Whisp.

"I don't know what I am," she said with honesty. "I'm looking for a book that would help with my... otherness."

We protect, we are the keepers of knowledge long forgotten. Her pale eyes stared at the flames that danced along her arm.

Alice thought for a moment, knowing she only had a short amount of time. "Do you know of The Elementals?"

A book fell to the ground with a thump. A white ball floated from the gap in the bookshelf, the sphere attaching to the woman's dress.

Your companion is growing impatient. He tastes of death and regret. His kind is not welcome here.

Balls began to float from her back, heading towards the entrance where Lucifer waited. As each ball detached, her form began to ripple until Alice was able to see the bookshelves behind her.

Alice chanced a peek at the book that lay open on the floor, just as she heard the first snarl from Lucy.

Shit. "What is it?"

It is what you seek. More balls began to float away. *We have never come across someone such as you.*

"WAR?"

Read. You must read.

Alice picked up the book, feeling the power vibrate up her fingers as her eyes settled on the open page.

. . .

The Twins of Gemini despised each other. It is not noted when they began to despise, not when true immortals drunk from the Well of Life, forgetting their past and therefore forgetting the beginning.

I, as the keeper of lore must not drink, even as immortality rots my mind beyond reparation. So I must start at the beginning, at least, the beginning of my fractured memory.

The Twins of Gemini, as immortals drank from the well. Each time resetting their immortality, each time they forgot their enmity. But they did not forget for long.

They wielded their powers like weapons against one another, even though they were equal, identical. It ripped a seam between the realms, allowing the wild magic to leak, showing them the world beyond made of dirt and life.

Lorelei, the first twin, was fascinated by the mortals that lived on Earth Side. Fascinated enough she left Asherah of Far, jumping through the leak creating a door between the realms of her own construction.

Her sister, Aerwyna followed and watched. Silent as her twin honoured the mortals with the ability to manipulate the elements. It was a gift beyond recognition. One not meant for the mortals.

Not to be beaten, Aerwyna gifted the same humans something stronger, the ability to amplify their new powers by the use of blood and death. As in life, is death and therefore the circle is equal. What her sister, Lorelei neglected to understand was she could not just give them magic, that was not meant for them, with no consequences.

Unfortunately, The Creator found out, and before his overdue drink of the Well of Life he wanted to punish the sisters for their betrayal of their own realm. For once the fissure had opened between the worlds, the wild magic would continue to leak forever. He found the mortals who were blessed with wild magic, and cursed them.

He forced them to take more power than they could hold, and many died until only four remained. With spirit he connected the four, then divided them into the remaining elements. Fire, Water, Air and Earth. They needed to be punished, so he separated them from one another.

With his final words he told the twins if their creations ever joined, they would bring about the demise of the world they were so fascinated with. Together, they would bring war, pestilence, famine and death to those around them.

Lorelei returned to her court in Asherah of Far, upset of the pain she had brought the mortals. Aerwyna, angry with what her sister started decided to stay Earth Side for a while longer, so she could observe their new creations. She went to the cursed mortals, angry at them for accepting the gift from her sister, blamed them for their own punishment.

Aerwyna spun stories, encouraging The Elementals to join together and purge their realm in spite. Earth Elemental became known as Death, Fire became known as War, Water became Pestilence and Air became Famine. The Four Elementals became The Four Horsemen, the mortals who would bring the apocalypse to the world made of dirt and life.

She gave them each a weapon, ones strong enough to handle the magic that their bodies were too weak to truly control.

As they were destined to bring the end, and she would make sure that knowledge would come true.

Word reached Lorelei of what her twin was doing, and knowing she would be further punished she returned through the door she made between the worlds to confront her sister.

With a burst of power, she banished Aerwyna back to Asherah, binding her to their realm.

But it was too late, her precious mortals had been corrupted. But with that corruption came hope, as the elements seemed to share and dilute down the family lines, changing into something unexpected.

So before she returned to her home, knowing she would too be bound, unable to return to the world she loved she gave the mortals one last gift. She exposed the stories her sister had twisted, explaining what could happen if all the strongest of The Elementals came together. She shared her power for the last time, allowing only one from each Elemental to gain the spark The Creator cursed them with, reigniting every generation when their predecessor passed. It was up to them to protect their own, to protect their world from themselves.

Just before she returned to her own realm, never to step foot on Earth Side again she renamed herself as The Goddess, the one who gifted magic to the mortals. With a last smirk, she renamed her sister The Crone, the one who cursed the mortals.

"Little War, what is taking you so long?" Lucifer pulled the book from her palms as the Whisps huddled around him like moths around a light. He studied the book in his hand with a scowl, flipping through the pages.

"My sword was a gift from The Crone," she said in shock. "Something that was supposed to help destroy the world."

Lucifer slapped the book shut.

"You've always called me Little War?" She looked up at his face, the Whisps throwing shades across his features. "Why? What makes you so sure that I am?"

"Because you're not the first Elemental I have met, and you're not going to be the last. I have lived for longer than I care to admit, and not once has the prophecy come close. But then again, I had never met one such as you, either. You're not yet War, not yet." He let out a breath, pushing the Whisps away. "Our bargain is complete, Little War. Tell your brother I'm looking for him." With a grin he burst into smoke.

"You have got to be shitting me!" Alice swiped at the air.

The Whisps circled above, a beacon of light. With a loud crack they became one, illuminating the ceiling to show crystal chandeliers that glittered between the wooden beams that weren't there before. The mist evaporated beneath her feet and bursts of colour appeared on the walls.

"You better have a good fucking excuse for being here, Alice," a voice snarled.

T he hall was dark, his parents' room open and empty. His sister's safely shut. "Dad?" he whispered as he crept downstairs, his senses on high alert. "Are you up?"

Glass glittered across the floor in the living room, the front door smashed.

"Dad?" he whispered again, slightly nervous. He slipped his feet into his trainers before carefully stepping over the glass. His foot slid on the stream of liquid that lead into the kitchen, black against the wood. He pushed the door, it heavier than it should be as if something was blocking it from the other side. Nudging it with his shoulder he squeezed inside, the dark liquid shiny on the tiled floor.

He stared at it for a few seconds, wondering if it was all in his head. It wouldn't have surprised him, last time he smoked mugwort he swore he saw a pink orangutan hanging out in the corner of his room. He knew logically there wasn't an orangutan, but it had freaked him out for a few hours before he had passed out.

Was this the same? Was it all in his head?

Confused, he lent down to touch it, shocked at how warm it was against his fingertips.

A groan.

His head swung to the noise, his heart a rabbit in his chest as panic started to grow.

Another groan, slightly louder.

He moved the door, a cry erupting from his throat at the sight of his father face down, blood a pool beneath his head.

CHAPTER 7

Alice spun, an excuse caught in her throat as Xander stood there, arms folded. A muscle twitched in his cheek, jaw clenched as anger radiated off him in waves. Behind him was a large oak door, one that wasn't there only moments before.

"Come on." He moved towards the exit, expecting her to follow.

When a cold hand touched her spine she caught up with only a couple strides. She followed him through a maze of corridors, each holding different doors before they stepped into what looked like a cloak room. As soon as she stepped through the threshold a thick, circular door slowly closed. The metal clunked as the numerous mechanisms locked into place, and the runes decorating the outside glowed purple.

"Hey, what are those..." The words died on her tongue when her back smashed against the cold metal, a heavy arm pinned to her chest.

"I see training is useless," Xander growled, adding pressure. "What's the point in all this if you couldn't even block me?"

"It's not like I expected you to attack," Alice replied through clenched teeth. She had been training, knew she should never fight someone stronger. Riley had taught her to expect everyone to be stronger, and to only engage when it was the last option. The unexpectedness of Xander's lunge caught her off guard, and if he kept up the force on her chest she was sure to feel them crack.

"Why wouldn't I when you broke into the restricted archives?" He left the question taut between them. "What were you looking for?" He pushed even harder, her ribs straining under the pressure.

Alice choked in a breath. "The same thing I've always been looking for... answers." Flame erupted up her arm, faster than she had ever been able to call it. The blue licked up Xander's sleeve, catching the dark fabric.

With a snarl Xander pulled at his shirt, pulling it off just as it turned to ash. It had forced him to step back, allowing Alice to catch her breath as her chest ached.

She would definitely have a bruise.

"Did you really need to manhandle me?" she said on a cough.

"You shouldn't break into places you're not supposed to be. You're lucky it was just me and not the others. Your trust is still in question." His tone hardened. "Now, how did you get inside? It's spelled that only druids have access."

That peaked Alice's interest. "Why only druids?"

"Druids have looked after powerful and prohibited artefacts since the beginning of time," he replied with an annoyed grunt. "We keep dangerous items away from those who would use them for harm. The restricted section is full of books and grimoires full of dark, dangerous magic. What could you possibly be searching for?"

"I wanted to know more about my sword. But the answer wasn't what I expected."

A slight frown pinched his eyebrows when he replied. "If you have the answers, where's the book?"

Alice opened her mouth to reply, but nothing came out. *Shit.*

"You shouldn't have been there."

"It wasn't intentional."

"You could have..."

"I needed to know..."

"No, you didn't," Xander argued, shoulders tight with frustration. "And now a Daemon has his hands on ancient knowledge not meant for him."

Alice narrowed her eyes. "How do you know he was a Daemon?"

"The only thing good about spirits, is they're great spies."

Alice thought back to the white woman. "The Whisps, are they spirits?"

"Of a sort." He didn't give her a chance to ask more questions. "Now tell me everything about this Daemon friend of yours."

"He isn't a friend," Alice began to pace as the pulsating purple runes hummed behind her. They seemed to want her to move away from the door, which she was happy to do. "He was keeping his side of the bargain."

"You made a deal with a Daemon?" Xander let out a hollow laugh. "I'm beginning to believe it's impossible to keep you alive long enough for whatever The Council have planned."

"Do you want me to admit I fucked up? I fucked up!"

Her chi tingled as it stretched, ready to react with her burst of anger. "But I still don't regret it." She didn't have a choice, and if she was given the option again, she would save her brother. Every time.

"You act like you're invincible."

"Says who? Every time I lose control I know there's a chance I may not be able to call it back." Her voice cracked as she tasted smoke. "You wouldn't understand the decisions I've had to make. The risks." Her voice rose to a scream.

"Look at yourself. You're losing control now," Xander mocked with a sneer. "I've seen your strength, I've seen what your power can do and its beyond anything I have ever seen. Yet you're like a little immature girl with your bad judgments."

"You act like I can't make mistakes. It's not like there's a bloody walkthrough for me to follow!"

With a pop Tinkerbell appeared, the blue ball of arcane crackling with excitement at being called. At that point she hated the bloody thing, even as it shot at Xander, sizzling out before it could even do damage.

"Do you know what?" she began, even as Tinkerbell popped into existence once more. "Magic isn't predictable. You can't defend against everything." She went to push past him when he gripped her arm.

"I can clearly see that." He grunted towards Tinkerbell. "But you can at least be prepared for the unexpected. That's the whole reason you're training with The Guardians. Our control is concrete. We have to be, or people die."

"I'm not the same as you."

"No, but you're just as different." He pulled her to face

him, his pale eyes staring into hers. "You can't hide what you are, Alice." Pain flashed across his features, too fast for her really to see. "You need to embrace the power before it consumes you."

———

She would have smirked if she wasn't in such a bad mood. The vision of Xander, bare chested in the bitter cold was a sight to behold. She didn't even break a smile when a woman walking to her car fell over air when she couldn't stop staring.

"You have no shame," she commented as he paused beside her.

"Is there anything I should be ashamed of?"

Did Xander, the man who was constantly pissed off just make a joke?

"I must be hearing things," she mumbled. "Because surely you don't have a sense of humour?"

"Careful Alice..." he growled.

Alice began to laugh, the noise escaping in a snort just before she felt the pressure in the air drop.

She recognised the sensation just as the air shimmered. "Watch out!" She shoved Xander back as something large crashed by their feet.

Xander pulled out a blade, ready to strike when she stepped in between.

"Wait."

The man climbed to his knees, palms flat to the earth as blood poured from the slashes across his arms. With a click he uncurled one wing to its full, impressive length, while the other remained at his side at an awkward angle. They were larger than she remembered, the primaries a deep midnight blue that slowly changed to indigo before it lightened to a soft grey on the inside. She knew who it was even before he looked up, a feral expression painted across his face.

"It's Kyle." She carefully approached, conscious of the sharp spikes on the arch of his wings as his red eyes flickered between them.

"He's fighting for control," Xander said as the druidism glyphs tattooed around Kyle's throat and wrists glowed against the darkness.

"We need to get him out of the street," Alice said as she looked around, hoping his wings were dark enough they would blend into the night from a distance. Daemons were hunted and destroyed to the point the general populace thought of them as myths. They were lucky the library wasn't particular busy in the evenings, but that didn't mean there weren't people around. "Kyle, retract your wings."

He would be less conspicuous without the wings.

In a flash he climbed to his feet, chest pumping as he looked around, confused. "Where are we?" Kyle asked with a hoarse growl.

"In a way too public place," Xander replied with an equal snarl.

"Bollocks, I missed," Kyle sniffed, frowning at his crumpled wing.

"What the fuck do you think you're doing out in the open like that? You're going to get yourself caught."

Kyle dismissed him with a wave of his arm, flicking blood across the pavement.

Xander puffed out his chest. "WHO THE FU..."

"Enough," Alice pushed between them, turning her attention to Xander. His pale eyes were sharp, the wraparound sunglasses he wore to protect his eyes braced on his head. "I'll deal with it."

"He's put you both in danger."

Violence was thick in the air, the tension so strong she could feel it. She knew it took every instinct in Xander not to react, his beast trained to kill and destroy beings like her brother.

"Please," she begged, voice quiet.

"You can't save everyone, Alice," he said, fury apparent in the tension across his body. "Some people are going to destroy themselves whether you help them to or not."

"He's my brother," she said as if that was explanation enough.

"And he's a Daemon. He can't fight his nature forever." Xander shook his head. "I know that better than anyone."

"Yeah, well good thing I'm here to help him."

"Ali, he's right," Kyle agreed, much to her shock. "But right now we don't have much time. I don't know if they followed me." His eyes flickered between green and red, his wings forgotten behind him.

"You literally just appeared from thin air, how could they follow you?"

Kyle looked around, his eyes scanning the darkness. "We can't talk here."

"Who's after you?" Xander asked.

Kyle paused, wary. "I don't know, but it's not me they're hunting."

CHAPTER 8

For such thin slices, the bleeding wouldn't stop. Alice dropped the third towel into the sink, Kyle's blood soaked through before she reached for another, her scar aching at the proximity.

"What happened?" she asked as she added more pressure to his forearm.

He flinched every time she touched him, his eyes the same green as their mother's,

but threatening red at the corners as he watched the two other men in the kitchen carefully.

Xander stood in the doorway, arms crossed with a dagger clutched in his hand while Sam sat directly behind her on the counter. He leant forward, his long hair swinging as his leopard dissected every scent in the room, muscles coiled ready to leap to her defence.

Out of the three predators in the room, she couldn't decide which one was more dangerous at that exact moment. The Daemon, the beast or the leopard.

"Kyle," she said, tugging on his arm so he returned his attention to her. "What happened?"

"He got chopped up with a knife, what do you think happened?" Sam murmured, his voice a throaty growl.

"And how exactly is that comment helpful?" She looked back over her shoulder.

"It's an observation, I never said it was helpful," Sam shrugged, dropping to his bare feet before he padded to her other side. "This room is too full. Xander, you need to leave."

Xander grunted. "It's my job to protect against creatures like him."

"He's wounded." Sam pointed, the tip of his nail elongating as he channelled his leopard. "All you're doing is taking up oxygen."

"Sam!" Alice checked the cuts on Kyle's arms, happy they finally began to clot. "Stop it, or you both can leave."

"I shouldn't have come here," Kyle said, eyes darkening just as his voice deepened. "I can't risk them getting to you."

"Who?" Xander asked, ignoring the overprotective growl from the leopard.

"That's what I've been trying to find out." Kyle tugged at his arms, checking the wounds before rolling down the sleeves of his t-shirt, at least, what was left of it. "When I first escaped, I had nowhere to go so I would sit on the roof of the house. It was there I first noticed them. They always came in pairs, just watching."

"And you didn't think that was suspicious?" Xander asked.

"No, I thought they were the friendly neighbourhood watch," Kyle snapped back. "They just stood there for weeks. They didn't make one aggressive move." He let out a shallow laugh. "It wasn't until one impaled me that I made the connection that they were the same people."

"Xander, you're such an arsehole," Sam muttered.

He ignored the insult, his attention on Kyle. "You're just as inexperienced as your sister."

"That's it." She pointed to both Sam and Xander. "Both of you out!"

"No, he *is* inexperienced, but he also has an excuse," Xander taunted, his glasses back in place but she still felt the burn from his glare. "What excuse do you have, Alice?"

She shot him a baleful look. "What the hell is that supposed to mean?"

"You're a fully trained Paladin, and yet you never noticed the two men, on separate occasions following you."

"What is this? Attack Alice day?" She angrily threw the last towel. "I know about The Magicka following me."

"Strange, I wasn't aware The Magicka were allowed to carry weapons."

"Yeah, but..." Alice froze.

The Magicka were a board of witches that governed her breed, directly below The Council. They were the highest members of the magic world, with the majority being tier two or above in their chosen field. She knew about how the Department of Magic & Mystery had been following her, but she also knew they never carried weapons other than wands.

If it wasn't The Magicka, then who were they?

"Shit," she whispered quietly to herself. "Shit. Shit. Shit."

The last time she had been followed there had been an attempt on her life. But she hadn't been attacked in months, had assumed the price on her head died along with Mason.

But if they were still around, it wasn't Mason who had hired them.

"I need to update The Guardians," Xander said, looking at Kyle. "Do you have any more information?"

"Whoever they are, I can't find any literature on them. All I have to go on is the mark of a sun."

"A sun?" Alice asked with a frown.

"Yeah, a stylised sun engraved on their weapons. You recognise it?" Kyle frowned.

"Maybe..." She closed her eyes, trying to remember. She could have sworn she had seen something like that before.

The pop in the atmosphere was their only warning.

"You're having a party, and didn't invite me?" a deep voice chuckled.

Alice looked up, her reaction too slow as Lucifer launched himself across the room and lifted Kyle up by the throat.

"You little fucker. I've been looking for you everywhere," he said with a growl.

"This one had a symbol, the same symbol as the throwing star over there." Alice gestured to the side table pushed against the wall.

Xahenort hissed, the noise loud enough to make her flinch.

"I haven't seen this mark in a millennium," he turned to her with a full grin. "I hope the person who attacked you is dead?"

"That's it!" she said as she remembered where she had seen

the sun insignia before. "Hey, Lucy!" She threw the closest thing at his back to grab his attention, a mug.

Lucy dropped Kyle and spun, eyebrow arched at the shattered remains of the ceramic.

Alice opened her mouth to speak when a ball of arcane shot across her kitchen, the intense heat melting the plastic off her cupboards before it hit Lucy square in the chest.

"Oh shit!"

Lucifer turned to face Xander, his face contorted into rage as his horns pierced through his dark hair. Two wings erupted from his back, the spikes scraping artex off the ceiling to rain dust down on them.

"WHO THE FUCK...?"

Alice leapt forward just as Xander threw another ball.

"ARMA!" The aegis shield erupted around her with a pop, trapping both her and Lucifer inside. The ball of arcane dissipated as it touched the surface, shooting silver specks across the usual opaque green and blue.

"ALICE!" Xander paced widely beside her, as close as he could without touching her shield.

"You need to trust me," she said as she caught Xander's sharp glare. "I have an idea, but I don't think you're going to like it."

Because she was going to have to go against everything The Guardians of the Order believed in. What she used to believe in.

She was going to have to make a deal with a Daemon. Again.

"Fuck sake!" Sam said with a horrified look, while Kyle looked around the kitchen, opening cupboards and drawers in a panic.

She returned her attention to the very pissed off Daemon, blurring the others completely from her mind.

"WHAT IS THE MEANING OF THIS?" Lucy snarled, fangs bared.

"You really need to stop appearing unannounced," she calmly replied, trying not to flinch as the red arcane crept up his arms in threat. She clenched her hand, the scar along her palm pulsating stronger the angrier Lucifer became.

It was such a pain in the arse.

"It hurts, doesn't it," he said, voice deeper than normal. "It's the bite of one of mine. I can sense it." He licked his lips, smoke floating from between his lips.

Shit. He was freaking out on her.

"I need to make another deal," she said quickly, trying to distract him before he decided to eat her, kill her, or something equally as horrible.

The smoke cut off.

"A deal you say, Little War?" he grinned, his wings snapping flat to his back. They arched above his head, the spikes testing the strength of the shield high above.

"NO!" a muffled voice.

Bang. Bang. Bang.

"ALICE STOP!"

She ignored whoever hammered against her shield, not wanting to drop the eye contact with Lucifer.

"What are the terms?"

Lucifer seemed to be the only person willing to give her answers. At least, give them on a condition. If he didn't know, he knew where to find them, and that is exactly what she needed.

"You better hurry up, Little War. Your brother is working hard to send me back to The Nether."

"The Nether?" she asked, quickly looking for her brother who was drawing a chalk circle around her shield while mumbling to himself.

"He calls it Hell. He's sending me back to Hell."

Hell was real?

"The throwing stars you took last time, they had a sun engraved on them?" At his nod she continued. "I need to know more about them, specifically the people behind them."

His eyes narrowed as a smirk curled his lip.

"You know what I want, but what will you take in exchange?"

The chanting in the background became louder, which meant she needed to make the deal. Now.

"I will give you my knowledge, in exchange for a power drain."

"Wait, what?" She had expected him to ask for something ridiculous before finally coming to an arrangement.

"I'll syphon your chi. All of it."

"But..."

"Tick tock. Do we have a deal?" He grinned with a shrug. "You'll refill, eventually."

Bang. Bang. Bang.

Shit. She had been syphoned before, the pain unbearable but he was right, she did recover.

"It's a deal." She held out her hand, not expecting the sudden weakness of her muscles when his palm touched hers. Her chi melted away, leaving her feeling heavy, empty. The shield surrounding them cracked, dwindling as she felt the last of her reserve disappear.

"You really don't understand what you are. If it wasn't for your heritage, that would have killed you." Lucifer released her just as her legs gave out. "Good thing I knew that."

"Who are they?" Alice asked, her arms shaking as she tried, and failed to climb to her feet.

"Your equilibrium will be off for a few minutes while your aura tries to fill the absence of your chi. You'll feel... hollow for a while."

"Lucy!"

"They're called The Knights, and I haven't heard of them in many millennia." He knelt on one knee, bringing his head eye level. "As far as I understood they disappeared long ago with their King."

Bang. Bang. Bang.

"Our deal is complete, Little War. I look forward to working with you again." With a wink he stood up, smoke appearing from the floor that climbed up his legs.

"Wait! I need more information than that!"

Smoke crept over his stomach. "You never specified the amount of information, inane decision on your part."

"You bastard!"

The smoke paused, stopping at his shoulders. "That's all my knowledge at this exact moment, as you asked for." His eyes settled over her shoulder, the red glowing. "I may have more information in my records, but right now I'm about to be forced back. Please tell that little shit brother of yours, I'll be waiting." With a smile full of teeth, he disappeared.

Arms instantly encased her as her shield disintegrated, the magic resonating back and finding nothing. Panic constricted her chest as her aura tried to reconnect her chi, her breaths coming in shallow pants.

"What the fuck, Alice?" Sam helped her to her feet, his eyes the deep amber of his leopard as he gently touched her, reassuring his animal she was okay. "You really need to stop hanging around with Xahenort, or Lucifer, or whatever his name is now."

Alice waited a second to calm down as her body reacted

71

at the loss. "It's not like I invited him." That time, at least. "Anyway, I'm fine."

Probably.

"I'm going to be punished for that." Kyle brushed the chalk from his hands onto his jeans, just as Xander stepped into her eye line.

"Don't start..." Alice began, noticing Xander's angry face. Not that he wasn't constantly angry.

"What have you just done?"

"What have I done?" she repeated, anger and frustration raising her voice.. "I did what was needed. You believe I'm this weak woman who constantly needs rescuing. I'm not a damsel, and I'm not in distress. I know exactly the consequences of my decisions."

"That's..."

"No, I'm not done," she snapped. If she had magic left she was confident her fingers would be glowing. "You've told me you've seen my strength, the same strength I've been honing with Riley, you and the others. I've proven myself on more than one occasion and yet I still don't have your respect."

"Respect?" he laughed. "You've just made a deal with a creature made from dark magic."

"Yes, I did. And in those five minutes I got the name of the organisation behind the sun and didn't give up anything I wasn't willing to lose." She watched the muscle in his cheek twitch as he remained silent, allowing her to vent. "I never asked for any of this, I never asked to be saved. Don't say I'm this damsel in distress who needs rescuing from the dragon." She slapped her hand against her chest. "I *am* the fucking dragon."

"Don't you see? You've just given away the one thing that can get you out of situations. Your magic."

"It's not for long, and aren't you all constantly telling me I can't rely on my magic?"

"Alice..."

"No, I think you've said enough," she said as Xander subtly stiffened. "You don't have the right to criticise me or my actions when you understand nothing of what I've had to do."

With a clenched jaw Xander bowed at the waist before he headed towards the front door, an odd jerkiness to his movements.

"Wow, that was badass!" Sam grinned, pumping the air in victory while his other arm remained wrapped around her shoulders. "His salty tears were delicious!"

"Ali, I haven't got long before I need to go back," Kyle said, a slight frown pinching his eyebrows. "He mentioned his records, I'll try and search them for more information on The Knights."

Alice collapsed onto a chair, the adrenaline fading.

"Can someone really have this much bad luck? Because of course, only I could gain the attention of a band of vigilantes or some shit." she groaned. "And not even the thousands year old Daemon knew they still even existed."

"The Knights," Kyle began, "you've heard of them?"

Alice sighed. "Once."

"Where?"

"It was at an exhibition." Surprised laughter burst from her as she thought how ridiculous it all was. "The Knights were created by King Arthur himself."

"Hold up," Sam began. "We talking the round table and stuff?"

"I don't see what the shape of his table has to do with anything?" Kyle said, deadpan.

"Allegedly, King Arthur feared The Elementals and sought his Knights to rid them from the earth."

Alice thought back to the poem, the one she had memorised.

"With steady breaths, they ride towards the dawn. Mortals cower in the dark, defenceless, prepare to mourn. Shadows move across their souls, as darkness, corruption and power grows. The four elements, magnets against mortal breath. Generations of lies, of wrath. Power in its truest form, made physical with greed. Are they saviours who wish to lead? Famine destroys along the path, against Pestilence in his wrath. Death stares and waits his turn, as Wars flame's turn to burn. The apocalypse they bring to earth, destroying it for all it's worth."

Kyle remained silent as Sam's warmth wrapped around her.

"That's one creepy poem."

"Sure is, it's the predication of the apocalypse."

Sam let out a low whistle. "Not every day you get a prophecy written about you."

Alice rolled her eyes. "Sam! Don't get all jealous on me now."

Only he would make a joke out of the situation.

Kyle ignored their tease with a confused frown. "Our ancestry states we're descended from the original Draco's. If we're going by their beliefs, that makes you War, the second horseman."

"I'm sure a lot of people are descendent from them." She closed her eyes, resting her head against Sam's chest just as he began to purr, the steady vibrations comforting. He set his chin on her head, his fingers playing along her hair. "Doesn't mean I'm War."

"That's not how magic in a family works, and you know

74

it. It's the same as eye colour, just because a parent has blue doesn't meant the kids will." Kyle knocked his knuckles against the warped cabinet. "But another generation may inherit it instead."

Sam's fingers released her hair. "Do you know something?"

Kyle turned his back, his attention out the window. "Why do you stay here?" he asked, his voice quiet. "Why do you stay here when just out there our mother was murdered?"

"Kyle..."

"And just in here," he interrupted. "Was where they killed father. I can still see the blood, wet on the tiles."

"That was a long time ago," Alice said, her voice breaking. "This is our home."

"Home?" he chuckled. "It's the place where we lost everything." He turned, his eyes flashing red. "I was a slave for close to two decades, treated like nothing because I wasn't the one they wanted."

Alice reached forward, ignoring his flinch as she wrapped her hand around his wrist. "I'm sorry for what you went through."

He tensed, dropping his eyes to the floor. "Embrace what you are, Alice. Use it against the people who seek to enslave you. Treat it as a gift, and not an inconvenience." His hand shook, briefly touching her own before he dropped his arm. "You are War, act like it."

CHAPTER 9

A lice had never been so happy to see a dead body. Not in a weird way, but the idea of working on a case was the perfect distraction. Even the faint stench of decay was slightly less unpleasant than she remembered, which really made her doubt her mental stability. Who smiled at the scent of death? Someone who needed a distraction, especially with so much shit going on.

She had no idea what it was to be War, if she even was. Add that to The Councils impending decision, she was a mess of apocalyptic proportions, literally.

"I really need a break," she mumbled to herself, pinching her nose between two fingers as she let out an exaggerated sigh. She needed to release some pent up energy, physical energy considering she only felt the faintest of chi as it began to refill. She had never felt so uncomfortable, her aura almost cursing her as it tried constantly to recuperate from the loss. Lucifer was right, it made her feel hollow. Empty.

"Good for you to get here," Brady grumbled, greeting

her with his permanently creased frown. "We don't have the scene long before clean up needs to be called in."

"You invite me to the nicest places," Alice smirked as she followed the Detective down the path to a country style detached house. A white picket fence surrounded the property, which was the last house on the long road. Roses, begonias, bluebells as well as several shrubs were pruned to perfection by the porch. The place was cute and well-kept apart from the smeared mud in front of one of the windows, as if someone had slipped on the wet earth while trying to peek inside.

"So, are you going to give me the details?" she asked, secretly scanning him for any casts or bandages. "You're always so vague on the phone."

"Jones will explain," he replied, looking at her from over her shoulder. "Stop it, I'm fine," he grunted, lip lifting into an aggravated snarl. "Just a few bruised ribs, nothing bad."

"I'm glad you're okay." Brady was a private person, very rarely revealing something personal about himself. It was why the team enjoyed it when he brought his wife, Michelle. Without her, they wouldn't have known Brady was allergic to strawberries, or was a huge Sci-Fi fan.

Brady stopped them at the front door, beside the yellow tape that kept the neighbours at bay. "Now you've had reassurance I'm fine, we can get back to work." He gestured for her to enter.

"You staying out here?" she asked, confused.

"I am, so let me know what you find."

Alice blinked, slightly dumbfounded as Brady stared at her with an expressionless face. "Okay." That wasn't how they usually did it. "Why?"

"You'll see in a moment."

"Well, that doesn't sound ominous at all," Alice

muttered as she walked past the threshold into the ransacked living room. With a low whistle she studied the overturned sofa, smashed tv and piles of ripped up paper. "Someone clearly has anger issues."

"Most of this is books," a woman said as she zipped up an evidence bag with a single hair inside.

"Books?" She guessed that was what all the paper was. "And no one saw or heard this happen?"

"Apparently not," the woman said as she stood up, her white plastic overalls squeaking as she moved. "You the witch? Jones is waiting for you downstairs in the basement. We can't finish up until you're done."

"Basement?" She hated basements, they were creepy and full of spiders.

"The door's just through the kitchen. I hope you have a strong stomach."

"Thanks," Alice muttered as she found the door open in the kitchen. "Hello?" she shouted down. "Jones?"

No response.

Alice began to climb the rickety wooden stairs, a burst of light at the bottom from the specialised lights installed by the forensic team. It made the space beyond pitch black, the light concentrating on the body that lay peacefully just to the side.

"Jones?"

As soon as her head passed the threshold she stumbled, catching herself before she could fall.

"What the?" She sat on a step, disoriented as she clutched her ears.

White noise buzzed through her head, overwhelming all her senses. Jones appeared a few steps down, his mask placed awkwardly on his head as he tried to speak, his lips moving but no sound came out.

"I CAN'T HEAR YOU!" she said, unable to hear her own voice either.

With a dramatic eye roll he held one gloved hand out, tugging her down the steps and over the body at the bottom. The further down she went, the lighter the static in her head became, until the only overwhelming sensation was the stench of decay.

"What was that?"

"That's your job to figure out," Jones said with a smirk. "Cool though, right?"

"It's..." Alice covered her mouth and nose with her hand, the smell overpowering as Jones handed over a spare mask before replacing his own. It didn't stop the smell, but it helped enough she wouldn't decorate the floor with her breakfast.

"Yep. Whatever the spell is, it's keeping the smell inside."

"I couldn't hear you on the stairs."

"No, we figured that out pretty quickly. You can only hear what's down here, directly in the basement. Brady was shouting at us from the top and we couldn't hear anything." He shrugged, as if ignoring Brady wasn't a huge deal. "It's as if something is blocking us. What do you think could do that?"

Alice thought for a moment. "Maybe a seclusion spell?" She had heard of them, but had never been able to obtain one herself. Mainly used for important meetings for people not wanting to be overheard, they were little objects that created a private bubble. She knew it was for sound, but hadn't realised the extent the amulet could contain smell too, at least, partially. "We need to find the anchor amulet."

"A what, what?"

Alice looked around the large concrete room, the same

size as the house above but open. The basement was used as storage, with two large freezers, a floor to ceiling shelf that would give a hardware shop a run for its money as well as a single bike. There were no windows, no coal chutes or vents and only the one door which made the room stuffy and unpleasant, which didn't help the smell situation.

She had never heard of a seclusion spell that could contain a room, yet, she realised, it wouldn't need to cover the whole room, just the door. Alice braced herself for the white noise as she climbed back up the stairs, stretching onto her toes to be able to search above the doorframe.

"Found it!" she said, unable to hear her own voice again.

As she stepped down she crushed the disk beneath her boot.

The spell dissipated instantly, the smell breaking through the invisible barrier just as the voices from inside the house became crystal clear.

"That smell!"

"What is that?"

"That's disgusting."

"I see you've figured it out," Brady's deep bass grumbled as he appeared at the top of the stairs, a handkerchief held over his mouth and nose.

"Oh thank the heavens," Jones chimed in, dramatically taking his mask off and throwing it down onto the ground. "I saw my life flash before my eyes. I thought that was the end."

Alice picked up the two parts of the broken wooden disk, holding them out for Jones to place in an evidence bag. "A seclusion spell is designed for sound, not smell." It's probably why only the faintest scent could be recognised from the front path.

"How long can they last?" Brady asked as he stepped

onto the concrete, conscious not to disrupt the puddle of blood at the bottom right of the stairs.

"The seclusion spell? Depends on the quality of wood used," she shrugged. "But they're usually designed for short periods of time. Why?"

"Because Cohan McKee has been down here for well over a week, possibly two."

"You're saying that like it's unusual?"

"In a community with close and nosey neighbours it is. It's rare for a body to go unnoticed for so long, normally someone would have noted his absence, if not the odour."

"It's possible the amulet was close to its expiration date, which is why you could smell decay from the garden path."

"And that's what alerted a local dog walker to call us. He explained he walks past almost every morning and only just noticed something was off."

Alice looked towards the man, whose eyes were white in death. "It looks liked he fell down the stairs." Which might explain the large puddle of blood beneath his head.

"Possibly, or maybe pushed."

"What makes you think this isn't an accident?" she asked. "It's possible he had a breakdown and wrecked the place before falling down the stairs." There was a broken bottle of wine beside him, the glass shattered.

"Because of this," Jones said as he pulled up the blood soaked shirt of the man. It revealed a partially open abdomen, the skin crudely folded back over the incision marks.

"Ah yeah, I doubt he did that himself."

Alice carefully kneeled, noticing the tips of his fingers had begun to turn green while little pink buds pulled apart his fingernails.

"I can tell by visual and smell his bowel is perforated,"

Jones started. "Which is usually caused by blunt force trauma. Mainly in high velocity injuries, or if an intense weight is pressed against the abdomen." He held his hand over the body, simulating a pressing motion.

"Or, the initial fall down the stairs?"

"Unlikely. It could also be caused by a very poor surgeon with a very sharp knife."

"It needs to be checked," Brady added. "But we're pretty confident his heart is also missing."

"Well, it's not like he needs it," Jones said with an awkward smile.

"Hmmm," Brady grunted, not commenting on the poor taste in joke. "Which brings us to why we're here. Jones?"

"Ah, yes. I've been speaking to the lead Pathologist and she confirmed my suspicious that our first Vic, Rhys also had a perforated bowel... and a missing heart."

"Are you saying he had a missing heart, and we didn't notice?" You would think she would have detected a hole in his chest or something.

"His abdomen was stitched and bandaged a lot better than this guy," Jones nodded to Mr McKee. "His decay is easier to set a timeframe over a week, which, if we believe it's connected, would make McKee the first that we know of."

"So they're connected?" she asked.

"It would seem so," Brady said with a sparing glance to the dead. "Unless there are two people going around cutting people's hearts out."

"What about the girl?" Alice asked. "She doesn't fit."

"She's a conundrum," Jones shrugged. "She has the faint signature of magic, but other than her throat she had no other marks on her body. She also still had her heart."

Brady clapped, the noise loud enough it echoed against

the concrete walls. "We need some answers guys, and quick. I'll inform O'Neil about the situation and organise a team meeting for us to brainstorm." Brady mumbled a goodbye before heading back upstairs.

"Hey, Alice," Jones called from over the body. "Come check this out."

"Hey, have you seen Peyton?" she asked with a frown. "He never misses a crime scene."

"I think he's upstairs in the bedroom, but between you and me, he's been in a right mood the last week or so. Even more serious than normal."

Yeah, she had noticed that too.

"Hey," he nodded towards the body. "Why have his fingers gone green?"

"Looks like he's turning to earth, some earthy Fae like dryads do that." They would need a blood test to confirm his Breed, but she only knew of Fae that became the earth in death. She suspected as it was only his fingertips after two weeks that he wasn't a full Fae.

"That's so cool," he grinned.

"You're inappropriately happy around the dead, you know that right?"

"Yep!" he laughed.

The living room was empty when she entered, the team finalising the scene back in the basement while the crowd outside had been moved on. Upstairs she could hear movement, so she followed the noise until she found Peyton in the master bedroom, surrounded by books.

"Hey," she greeted, eyeing him suspiciously as he stared at the hardbacks. "What are you doing?"

Peyton frowned, his attention remaining on the books. "Being a detective."

"What exactly are you searching for?" The bedroom

was just as messy as the rest of the house. The sheets were a pile in the corner of the room, the mattress ripped to shreds and even more books were torn apart. The ones that survived were in a neat line on the patchy green carpet.

"He was a collector," Peyton whispered, transfixed. "Mr McKee, sixty-five, retired with no wife and kids but a collector of rare novels and first editions." He pointed to the furthest book to his left. "This was hidden in his mattress."

"That's a weird place to keep it," Alice mused. "You think someone wanted one from his collection?"

"I'm not sure, but something's wrong," he murmured quietly, almost to himself.

"You think? There's a dead body with a missing heart, I would say something is definitely wrong."

Peyton blinked, almost in a daze before he looked up. She had never seen him so... lost.

"Hey, are you okay?" she asked as his eyes widened.

"Your aura is cracked."

"My aura?" She immediately looked down at her arm, seeing only skin. "Can auras even crack?"

As a witch, she was able to open her third eye to see beyond ordinary perceptions. It gave her the ability to see others auras, but not her own. The closest she got was the faint shimmer of colour on her Aegis shield, which, she thought back, hadn't looked any different when she last used it. Had it?

Great, now she had anxiety with how her aura looked.

"What have you done?"

Shit. Shit. Shit. She hoped the guilt of her deal with Lucy wasn't painted across her face. She could already imagine Peyton's judgmental glare.

"Right now we should concentrate on this case," she

said, not wanting to acknowledge her aura. "Do we have any leads?"

Eyebrows creased Peyton handed over a scrap of paper with a messily written note. "I found this in the side table."

IATA, 354 Gardiners Lane, 3pm
East side
R. Longium – specialist.
Bring the book.

"This was dated a few days ago," she commented. "This must be one hell of a novel."

"Maybe, but looks like we have a specialist to visit."

CHAPTER 10

"Bloody weather," Alice murmured as she squinted through the windshield. She had lost Peyton a few minutes prior, the visibility poor as she parked the car and hoped he was close. The address for the specialist was just off the old shopping district, through one of the many overcast side roads. As it was restricted for pedestrians, cars couldn't go any further, which meant she had to brave the wind and the torrential rain.

As she opened the car door she saw a flash of white blonde. Peyton waved from the protection of the canopies, his crystal blue eyes watching her carefully as she made a dash for cover.

"You know where this place is?" she said, raising her voice above the roar of the wind.

"Just through there." He gestured to the road beside them.

Alice nodded, her wet hair sticking to her cheeks awkwardly.

With a little tinkle the door to the old antique shop

opened, the smell of old dust thick in the air. 'It's About Time Antiques' was tucked in a side road, an array of various sized cuckoo clocks on display in the front window.

Alice studied the dark oak shelves, covered in an array of random junk. Stained glass lamps, old beaten toys, silver tea sets as well as jewellery and folded vintage clothes all mixed together.

"Oh!" A slim man scrambled from behind the counter, his pale caramel skin flustered as he grinned wide. "Hello and welcome, how may I help..." The colour drained from his face, his fingers nervously adjusting the emerald ring on his right hand. "My Daeizan, I apologise I didn't realise. How are..."

"I'm Detective Peyton," Peyton interrupted, shoulders tight. "And this is Agent Skye. I was wondering if I can ask some questions regarding a customer who visited you a few days ago?"

"Oh, of course Daeizan. Anything I can do to help your investigation," the shopkeeper said before he bowed his head gently.

Alice looked towards Peyton, with what she assumed was a *what the fuck?* expression.

"A Mr McKee had an appointment with a specialist, I assume that would be you?" Alice asked.

"Ah yes, I own this establishment." The shopkeeper cleared his throat, a slight flush developing on his neck. "How can I help you exactly?"

"And your name is?" Alice pushed, interested in his nervous reaction.

"Oh, oh, I'm Rupert Longium. But please, call me Rupert. I specialise in many things, toys, jewellery, clocks..."

"Books?"

"Ah, yes. Books too, I suppose."

"Let's get back to Mr McKee, shall we Rupert?" Peyton asked, face straight.

"We know Mr McKee came to see you and he brought a book," Alice said.

"Did he?" he quickly answered, shaking his head.

Peyton huffed out a breath. "Let me re-phrase. Did Mr McKee come see you regarding a book?"

Rupert's cheeks puffed out.

"Answer the question. Did Mr McKee come see you regarding a book?"

"I would have to check my notes, but vaguely remember a gentlemen with a large book, yes."

"Can you tell us a bit more about this book?" Alice asked.

"I can."

Alice clenched her jaw. Sometimes it was hard work when speaking to the Fae.

"What did the book look like?"

"Ah, well it looked like a generic leather bound book with gold detailing down the spine. There was no title and no author. Unfortunately I couldn't help him."

"What about the inside?"

Rupert shrugged. "I barely glimpsed the inside. I explained it was probably a copy of some old faerie tales, possibly from before the Great War. It wasn't worth much so he took it back home. He seemed slightly annoyed because he only recently found it and thought it was of some interest."

"He found it?" Peyton began. "Do you know where?"

"I apologise Daeizan, but I didn't ask. Once I explained its worth he got hostile, so I asked him to leave."

A loud bang vibrated the ceiling, rattling the various knick-knacks hung high.

"Oh sorry about that, it's just my brother. He's a bit of a clutz so he stays upstairs. Bull in a china shop, you see."

"Okay I have just a few more questions and we will leave you in peace," Peyton said. "Do you keep records of everything that comes through? Specifically artefacts."

"I do." Rupert hesitated, rubbing the back of his neck. "But it's for my own records. There's no law stating I cannot resell anything I find unless it's been requested by Asherah."

"I know there's no law, I just wish out of interest to see what's been passing through."

Rupert shot Alice a sideways glance, a frown creasing his brow. "I will retrieve my little book, if you would excuse me." He bowed his head again before disappearing through the back.

"He seems nervous." Alice commented as soon as the man was out of earshot.

"Hmm," Peyton grunted. "You look threatening." He nodded towards the dagger displayed clearly on her thigh. "He may react better when there aren't two of us. Did you want to have a look around?"

"Is there anything specific I'm looking for?"

"Anything that looks Fae in origin," he said, voice low.

"What? Is there something..." she began, but he had already returned his attention to the shopkeeper.

She had no idea what she was looking for, her knowledge regarding the Fae pretty much zero. The Fae guarded their secrets to the point they were still a mystery, even though they had been on Earth Side since the beginning. They once hid amongst the humans just as everyone else did, then fought beside Breed through the Great War. They were as much part of the world as witches, shifters, vampires and druids, yet they were still very much other.

Alice frowned, wondering what Peyton was up to.

Every shelf seemed to be different, yet everything was the same drab colour scheme that made it all blend together. There was no specific section for any of the merchandise other than clocks, which were hung all along the side wall. They all ticked, not one in sync which added an annoying beat to the gramophone that squeaked out an old war song she was pretty sure was off key.

Alice picked up a cuddly teddy bear, the felt worn and an off white that looked dirty. One ear had been sewn back on poorly and the left eye was completely missing. Yet apparently it was worth over one-hundred pounds. As she put it back, it made a weird growling noise.

Beside it was a thin gold bangle bracelet with a small blue stone attached in the centre. The gold itself was tarnished, which meant it wasn't a very high carat and definitely not worth the obscene price tag attached. Alice picked up the bangle and placed it on her wrist so she could see it closer. She angled the stone to the light until she realised it wasn't stone or even a crystal, but a small glass bead with a weird blue liquid inside.

It was pretty, but still not worth the money. Not that she could casually afford it. With a sigh she pulled at the bangle, expecting it to pop off as easily as it went on. When it didn't, she frowned.

"Shit!" Alice spun the bangle around her wrist, confused as to how the gold was solid all the way round. There was no clasp, and no hole where she first slipped her wrist into.

"Hey, Agent Skye, you ready to go?" Peyton shouted from the front.

Fuck. Fuck. Fuck, she thought with a panic, trying and failing to remove it.

"Ah, yeah!" she called back. "Be right there!"

Alice pulled down her sleeve, hiding the bracelet and placing a twenty-pound note on the shelf. It wasn't even a tenth of its price, but that was all she had and he was over-charging anyway.

"So," she began when they were back outside, the clouds overcast but no longer pouring. "Are we going to discuss his very strange reaction to you?"

"I don't know what you're talking about," Peyton replied, voice flat.

Alice pursed her lips, deciding whether to pursue the argument or not.

"Were you searching for something specific in his little book?" She decided not. If he didn't want to talk about it, she wasn't going to push it.

Peyton turned to face her, his eyes hard. "Did you know he had a washing machine that created biscuits."

"Wait, what?" Alice jerked her head. "Did you say washing machine?"

"Yeah, it surprised me too."

Which was hard to believe from his expression.

"According to his notes the washing machine would spit out biscuits every time it was turned on."

"Stop trying to distract me." Although, she was really fascinated by the whole biscuit washing machine scenario. "You were searching for something. What is it?"

"Don't ask questions I cannot answer."

"You forget I do this for a living too." Annoyed, she tugged her hair from her face, the bracelet moving down her wrist. "The book Rupert was talking about wasn't at the scene, was it?"

Peyton looked away, jaw clenched.

"Which means it's missing, as well as the murder weapon from the first crime scene, a dagger."

"Alice..." he growled.

"You know something..."

"Alice..."

"They're artefacts, aren't they? The dagger and the book?" Which meant they were targeted murders.

"Alice," he growled another warning.

"What do they do?" She had heard of Fae artefacts, objects of Fae origin that sometimes held unusual abilities. In her life she had only seen a small handful, and they were either in museums or part of personal collections.

"That's enough," he snarled. "You have no idea what you're talking about."

"Peyton," she snapped back. "You're going to compromise the case. You need to..."

"You have no idea what's happening, what's at risk." He began to turn away, but she held onto his shoulder.

"Do you know what? I'm tired of the men in my life keeping important information from me! Tell me what's going on, let me do my job and help."

He shook his shoulder free. "This is down to me. Humans have no place in the world of Fae."

Alice fisted her hand. "Well, isn't it a good thing I'm not human."

CHAPTER 11

Alice's boots squelched loudly as she made her way down the familiar strip, the neon signs reflecting bursts of colour in the puddles. Along the long stretch were bars, tattoo parlours, pawn brokers, a few strip clubs and her destination, Club X. As seedy as the street looked from the outside, the inside of Club X was high-end. It was actually a strip bar, not a strip club like the name suggested, which meant the dancers were classed as artists. Just artists that danced with barely any clothes on and had legions of fans who threw money at them. Not the same at all, apparently. Not that she had much experience with the other type of dancers. Although, she had arrested a few of her targets in strip clubs, often with their trousers by their ankles while the dancers offered their 'extras.'

It was relatively quiet when she entered, the bouncer, one she had ncvcr met, growled as she passed the velvet rope into the main area, but didn't stop her. Considering she was clearly armed, the knife attached to the outside of her thigh, she wasn't impressed.

The room was purposely dark, the spotlight trained on the centre of the large stage where a beautiful woman danced in a skin tone leotard. It gave her the appearance of being naked, but the skin-tight fabric covered her from neck to ankles while diamantes shielded her important bits, which caught the light in a rainbow of colour.

"Hey, over here!" a voice excitedly called.

Startled by the enthusiasm, Alice swivelled to face the grinning man. "Roman?" she gasped as he dropped his tray on an empty table and crushed her into a bear hug. She instinctively embraced him back, even as other wait staff shot her aggravated scowls. "What are you doing here?"

Are you even old enough to work in a strip bar? she mentally added.

Roman released her, his warm hand stroking down her shoulders to grip her wrists. He looked healthier than she remembered, taller also, as if he had begun to fill into his promising shoulders. He had spent a lot of time in his wolf form, which reflected in the startling pale blue circle that shattered into his irises. The broken look would forever be a reminder of what he had suffered. But the way he smiled, the self-assured way he touched her, showed his recovery was going well.

She missed the company of his wolf, even though she knew if he'd stayed in his animal form too long he wouldn't have been able to come back.

"I work here," he said with a confidence that surprised her. "We've been having some power struggles with another pack, so all the businesses have taken on a few wolves," he shrugged as if it wasn't a big deal that other wolves wanted to take over their territory. Which it probably wasn't to a shifter. Regardless of their animal, shifter packs, prides or groups were generally autonomous, with Councilman Xavier only stepping in for extreme cases. Two Alpha wolves fighting it out for dominance was a normal occurrence, even if it was to the death.

"Ah, that would explain the angry stares." It hadn't just been the wait staff that seemed unimpressed with her arrival, it was the receptionist and the bouncer too. She had realised pretty quickly that White Dawn decided she was to blame for their former Alphas punishment.

"Ignore them," he said as he yanked her arm, encouraging her to take a seat in an empty booth by the back. "I see you've dressed for the occasion." His eyes lit up as he appraised her outfit.

Alice laughed, enjoying his mischievous smirk. "I suppose I have." She wore her usual work outfit of a dark T-shirt and jeans, however she had opted for the leather-synth which matched the unofficial dress code of leather and latex. Roman himself wore skin-tight leather trousers with a chain mesh shirt. It was slightly uncomfortable, Alice always thinking of him as a child although he probably wasn't much younger than her.

"So..." he began, his gaze not meeting hers. He looked at the table, his smile still in place. It wasn't because he thought the conversation was awkward, it was because he thought she had higher dominance.

Letting out a sigh she knocked her knuckles on the wood. "Roman, look at me."

He immediately lifted his head, but his eyes concentrated on her nose.

"I'm not a shifter, I hold no dominance over you." She had reminded him, as well as a few other wolves more than once, his wolf confused with the concept.

Roman's brows knitted, but he still wouldn't look up.

"Rex declared you an Alpha," he said as if that explained it.

"I'm not a shifter," she winced, wishing she had a drink to numb the conversation a little bit. "I'm not an Alpha."

Especially not Rex's.

"It doesn't work like that, and you know it." He caught her eye for a split second before a whimper escaped his throat. "My wolf thinks you're dominant."

Deciding to pick her battles, she changed subject. "How's Theo?" Romans older brother and Rex's twin was now the Alpha of White Dawn, which used to be one of the largest packs in Europe until Xavier culled the ones he believed had worked with The Master.

"He's doing what he can, but the pack's weak until he can fix it." He frowned for a moment, his mouth opening and closing as if considering his next words. "Look, I know what he did..."

She knew what he wanted to say, but she didn't want to hear about his other brother.

"Can you get Sam for me, please?" she interrupted. "I need to speak with him."

Roman shook his head, as if to clear it. "Of course," he said with a smile, but it didn't reach his eyes. "I'll bring over some drinks."

"No, it's okay. I..." He got up to leave when she grabbed his hand, curling her fingers through his. "I'm really happy for you, Roman."

He relaxed at her touch, his own hand squeezing back. "I know."

She watched him walk away, a heavy feeling in her gut before her attention drifted to the woman on the stage. She danced sexually, yet with an elegance that matched the slow, rhythmic beat of the drums. The place may be quiet, but she had every man and woman who sat in the front row mesmerised.

"What's up baby girl? Or should I say, wife?" Sam grinned when he sat down, his long, blonde hair loose around his shoulders. "Did we get married this year? Or last? Because I really need to update my harem."

"Nice choker," she commented on the thick latex necklace that covered his whole throat. "Maybe I wouldn't scare your lovers away if you gave me a little warning." She did not want a repeat of what she saw in that kitchen.

"But he was cute though," he said, eyes bright with amusement.

"You say that about all the people you bring back!" She dropped her head to the table, glad the wood had been freshly cleaned. "I didn't want to go home," she murmured into the grain.

"Aye, no shit. I thought you were over here looking for a career change or something." His fingers brushed her hair. "I have ten minutes, talk to me."

Alice released a heavy sigh, lifting her head. "Peyton's being an arse."

"He's always an arse," he said with a smirk. *But there's something else, isn't there?* He added with just a flick of the eyebrow.

Alice had no patience to reply the same way. "I think he's in danger, and I don't know what to do."

"What makes you say he's in danger?"

"I don't know," she shrugged. "A feeling?"

He was hiding something. She was sure of it.

"You sure you're not just pushing your anxieties out onto Peyton?"

Alice whipped her head back, the expression on his face serious. "Bloody hell, Sam." She hated when he became philosophical, because he was usually pretty accurate. "Hold back the blows, would you?"

"Your instincts have kept you alive, so you're probably right. But you have so much going on right now. You need a serious break from all this shit, and sitting here watching Lucinda shake her arse isn't going to help," he said with a half-smile.

"I've come to see you." *Not to dance, though,* she mentally added, much to his amusement. *Because that would be weird.*

She appreciated his animalistic beauty, and the grace in his movements when he danced. But she saw his bare arse on a regular basis, she didn't need to see it in a sexualised manner too.

"I love you, but, hard pass." She had always excused herself when he invited her to Club X and he was on stage.

Sam leant back in his chair, the plastic screeching at the movement before an impish grin creased his cheeks. "Ah, don't be jealous, you get to see it all while my fans only see it in glimpses."

"Ugh," she groaned. "Can we stop talking about your little pecker?"

Sam's dramatic gasp made her giggle. "Little?" He waved at someone behind her, his attention returning to her a moment later. "You're such a prude, you know that?"

"As you keep telling me."

Drinks landed on the table, an orange concoction for her, while he had a tall glass of water. The instant relief at his lack of alcohol was palpable. If he noticed, he didn't comment.

"Speaking of little peckers, you need to release your frustrations on someone. Release some of your energy."

"Why does it always come down to sex with you?" She

pushed the orange drink away, no longer interested. "I'm not lonely."

"I never said you were." His smile faltered. "But sometimes you need a connection with someone on a deeper level. You're an adult female, and if you were a shifter I would say you're purposely suffocating your animal."

"No, I'm not." Was she? "I'm not even sure what that means."

Sam growled low in his chest. "Stop punishing yourself for situations you can't control."

"You need to stop making sense, or I won't come back to you for advice."

He dismissed her moan with a wave of his hand. "You're moving through life, but you're not living."

"I work..."

"Work and hanging with me doesn't count. How many times have you been asked out on a date?"

The blush burned up her throat. "I don't date." It was inconvenient. How was she supposed to sit pretty at a dinner or movie while anxiously waiting for something to come and ruin it? Like a Daemon. Or an assassin.

"That's bullshit, baby girl. You need someone as strong as you, who understands the shit you're dealing with. Someone like *him*."

"It's complicated." The emotions she felt scared her, and she wasn't yet ready to explore it, even if it was Riley Storm. "Besides, I'm his ward."

"It's not as complicated as you think," he shrugged, creating a hole with his finger and thumb on one hand. "All you need is..."

Alice grabbed the other finger that was about to poke through. "Samion!"

"Just because your past is fucked up, doesn't mean your future has to be."

That's if I have a future, she thought, turning away so he couldn't read her expression.

"You need to communicate with each other, and I mean more than just in his bathtub."

Alice bit the inside of her cheek. "If you're going to keep throwing my secrets at me, I'm going to stop telling you the details."

"You both clearly have relationship issues." As she began to protest he held his hand up. "I know, I know. But have you, I don't know, talked about it?"

"What exactly am I supposed to say?"

"Oh, I don't know. *Riley –*" he mimicked her higher pitched voice, *"I love your big, beautiful cock. Shall we get married and have babies?"*

"There's something wrong with you, Sam." Alice said with a shake of her head.

"Oh, I'm more than aware of my own issues. But you deserve happiness, even though you don't believe it."

"Fuck sake, this was supposed to be a friendly cheer up. Not for you to psychoanalyse my life choices." She kept her head turned, unable to meet his gaze. "I don't know what I'm doing. I'm almost twenty-five and I can barely keep it together."

"You know what you want." Sam downed his water before he stepped out of the booth. "And he's over at The Spike."

"It's not..."

Sam blew her a kiss that caused a short, girly scream from the table over. "Treat yourself tonight, baby girl. Don't miss out on something that could be amazing, just because it could also be challenging. There might be more there than you're willing to see." With a smirk he turned to the girls, who almost fainted at the attention.

Alice was about to ask how he knew where Riley was when she realised he would own The Spike, the building named after the sharp glass design that pierced the sky. It was his father's main centre of operation, the name Storm illuminated down the side.

He had been asking her out, to more than just training and she had repeatedly made excuses.

"Shit." Riley confused her. She felt an almost animal magnetism when she was around him, one she didn't understand. But Sam was right, she had paused her life believing her future wasn't certain. Which was a crazy thought, considering the future was promised to no one.

CHAPTER 12

A heavy beat broke Alice out of thought, the loud techno music whipping through the air with a deep enough bass she could feel it vibrate her teeth. The place was busier, tables beginning to fill while a small crowd had formed directly in front of the stage. Bodies, half-naked and sweaty moved to pulsating lasers with excitement as the new dancers appeared on stage.

"You shouldn't be alone, you know." A masculine voice broke through the onslaught of drums. "You don't know what weirdos are about."

"I'm just leaving, actually," she said before a hand clamped hard onto her shoulder, forcing her back down onto the plastic cushion.

The stranger leant down until his lips touched her ear, his breath intimate against her cheek. "Sit down, or I'll take out the whole place."

With a shallow nod Alice waited, studying the man's harsh, pinched face and fiery red hair, which was shaved close to his head.

He held out his leather encased hand. "Bit rude, aren't you?" he said when she sat there, unmoving.

She watched his smile tighten as he flared his chi, a greeting, but also a test amongst witches to see who was more powerful. The feeling was a quick electric current across her skin, strong enough that it surprised her.

He was strong, strong enough to give her pause considering she would have felt empty in return, almost human. He had also given away his Breed, which would have been an advantage if she wasn't consciously aware of the many people that surrounded them. A witch generally didn't have excessive strength, not like shifters or vampires. They did, however have their magic, and right now, she had nothing to defend against it.

"Do I know you?" she asked, noticing the tell-tale bulge on his shoulder. He was packing, definitely a gun, but possibly knives under his long trench coat.

The security in this place was seriously lacking, she thought, her mind racing through options that didn't involve any casualties.

"No." He tilted his head, studying her with a frown. "I want to watch the life disappear from your eyes."

Alice sat there silent, her pulse loud inside her skull. When she caught his gaze, her chest tightened. A harsh, almost feral intelligence sharpened his green eyes, a colour very similar to her own.

"I don't understand why they're having such problems with you."

Alice remained silent, her heartbeat a chaotic mess. There was something about his eyes that bothered her, something that made her skin crawl and ice develop in her stomach.

"Their sole job was to destroy you. Yet here you still

are," he muttered, almost to himself. "I told them they should have sent me from the beginning. Especially once we realised that brother of yours," he chuckled, the sound hollow. "Now that's one interesting family tree. Actually, how is your brother? Last time I saw him he was at the end of my steel."

Alice clenched her teeth. "What do you want?" she asked, voice purposely soft. She needed to get him outside, away from everyone else where she could control the situation.

"Now what's the deal with the leopard? Are you mated or something? Or is he some kind of pet?"

"What do you want?" she repeated, finally feeling the slight burn of her anger. She hadn't felt her chi react in a while, the familiar red-hot sensation welcome. But it wasn't strong enough to defend against any attack, not yet.

He looked at her, confusion creasing his brow. "I want to win, of course. But the game has changed, *he* wants to meet you in person for some reason."

Alice licked her lips, the skin dry. "Who's he?"

"Oh, we both know I can't say that." He smiled, the emotion not reaching his lifeless eyes. "I don't have long, she will find me and we won't be able to play," he said, his voice holding an uncomfortable amount of innocence.

"Play?" *Shit. Shit. Shit.* "What would you like to play?"

His eyes widened as a smile stretched his cheeks. "You won't like my style of play."

No, she didn't doubt that.

"Now stand up," he barked. "We may have more time outside before she catches up to me." He nodded to himself, the movement overly enthusiastic before he curled his hand around her upper arm, yanking her towards him. "It must be a secret," he whispered against her hair. "You mustn't tell her what we've done, but don't worry, I'll only cut you up a little."

His hand tightened, hard enough she could feel a bruise developing as she sucked in a pained breath.

"Who is she?" she asked as he pulled her towards the green 'EXIT' sign. "Maybe I can help?" She kept her back straight, head high as she moved with him, trying not to draw attention to herself. She couldn't risk someone intervening.

His laughter vibrated against her back.

"Hey, Alice!"

Alice felt her stomach drop, her head turning automatically to the voice.

"I have something to discuss, you mind stepping into my office?" Mac stood by the exit, eyes narrowed on the hand gripping her upper arm. He was the owner of Club X, and a wolf.

"I'm just heading out," she said as she felt something sharp dig into her back. "Can it wait?"

"It's pretty urgent, actually."

The knife dug deeper, the tip piercing her skin.

Alice forced a smile. "I seriously can't right now." She waved her goodbye before rain touched her cheek, the drizzle making the alley behind the building even darker. The knife in her back moved away before an arm forced her to turn.

"This is better," he said, forcing her back against the wall. "We can talk uninterrupted before she ruins the fun." He held the knife in his hand, the tip a startling red.

"Yeah, but what If I ruin the fun?" Her hand shot out to his wrist, disarming the knife with a quick twist. With her momentum she rammed him with her shoulder, forcing a stumble before she turned to run.

Looked like she was listening to her training after all.

The night glowed as a ball of arcane evaporated the rain, the sudden steam burning across her skin. She dropped, hands on her head.

"ARMA!" She shouted, forgetting her chi was yet to refill when her circle appeared, then immediately dropped. "Oh, bloody hell!"

"Is that it?" The red-head grinned, his eyes alight. "All this fuss and you can't even make a circle?" He clicked his fingers, a wand appearing in his hand. "Disappointing."

"A wand? Really?" She jumped, scraping her knee as she rolled to miss whatever spell he had thrown at her. The stone sizzled on contact, which made her grateful it wasn't on her skin. "You know what they say about men with wands, don't you?" She glanced at the knife she had removed, noting the stylised sun on the steel.

He pointed the wand, the end glowing green. "Get up."

She climbed to her feet, the rain cold as it surrounded them.

"Give me my knife," he gestured to her hand. "And the one on your thigh."

She threw the first, hard enough they passed through his legs and clattered into the darkness.

"And the other."

She had to think. She couldn't use magic, not even to defend and the only weapon she had was her dagger. Alice eyed the wand, the instrument designed to concentrate arcane, resulting in stronger spells. He had already proven his ability with arcane just with his hand, she didn't really want to go up against a wand too.

"I bet you can't take me on without your magic," she goaded, hoping he took the bait.

He hesitated, almost eager before he shook his head. "I said throw it, or else." His arm was steady, the green tip pointed in threat.

Shit.

Alice unclipped her dagger, the thing weightier than she had trained with, but she didn't have many options. Without hesitation she threw, hoping the trajectory wasn't too off course due to the heavy rain. Her dagger soared, faster than he could have reacted and sliced deep into his thigh. She had been aiming for his chest, but never mind.

"What the?!" He pulled her dagger out, holding it in his other hand. "No one has ever hit me!"

Great, now she had just armed him with something sharp and pointy too.

"Well, there's a first time for everything."

Lightning lit up the alley in a flash, the light blinding as it was quickly followed by a deafening clap that made her flinch. It illuminated a set of eyes, hidden in the shadow.

Alice reached up as if she could stop the wolf, the beast jumping, teeth bared towards the wand before she could shout a warning.

"RURSUS VIRGAIOUS!" Arcane shot like a bullet out of the wand, hitting the wolf square in the chest. It crumpled to the ground, unmoving.

"No!" She went to reach for the wolf when she was yanked back.

"Face the wall," he said, voice uncomfortably calm. "Palms down."

Alice did as she was told, feeling him against her a second later. He yanked one arm back, holding it at a painful angle.

"I'm going to enjoy every second of torturing you. It's even worth the punishment I will receive."

Alice turned her face, the brick biting into her cheek. "Whatever turns you on," she hissed, the pain radiating up her shoulder as he clipped something onto her wrist.

He went to grab her other wrist when she spun, reaching down to grab his balls and yanking with all her strength. As he crumbled she brought her knee up, smashing his nose just as the wolf moaned.

Alice snapped the wand he dropped beneath her boot and clipped the dagger back onto her thigh, leaving him collapsed in a puddle.

"I thought you wanted to play?"

He smirked, spitting out blood as another crack of lighting pierced the sky. He climbed to his feet, a savage, almost excited look in his eyes.

"Chester?" a feminine voice seethed.

Red-head growled, blood covered teeth bared. "I just wanted a taste."

A tall, slim woman walked up to Chester, her palm on his chest, stroking. "You know you shouldn't run away like that." She turned her pout to Alice, her eyes a deep brown that matched the chestnut of her shoulder length hair. "Looks like you've already started," she sighed. "He isn't going to be happy with this."

"We should just bring her in now," Chester said, bending down to bury his face in her hair. "Play with her a little beforehand."

"That wasn't the order," she snapped at him, even as her hand continued to gently stroke his chest. "But I guess we have no choice now," she said, her voice softer.

Alice stepped back, just as the wolf wobblily climbed to its knees, a howl erupting from its throat a second later.

"You hear that?" Alice said just as another wolf returned the howl. "The pack is coming."

The woman flicked her eyes behind Alice, her smile tightening. "Then I guess we will have to wait. We will be seeing you very soon." With a click of her heels she walked away, pulling a reluctant Chester with her.

He sucked in a breath, a scream building before a hand covered his mouth. "Quiet," the shadow breathed directly into his ear, "or you'll meet the same fate as your father."

The shock turned quickly to anger. He clawed at the arm, kicking back with all his weight before he was thrown violently back into the living room. He hit the floor hard, hard enough to disorient him and cut his arms against the sharp glass shards. His head was pulled up by his hair, forced to face the sofa where his mother sat silently, still in her nightdress.

"Mum..." he tried to call before he was slapped. Her eyes were dazed, face calm as another stranger held a blade against her throat.

The man smirked, bringing up a single finger to his lips before his own mouth was covered, gagged.

He fought against the constriction, stopping as the blade pressed to his mother's skin produced a bright pearl of blood at the tip. So he froze, and watched in horror as his little sister, her teddy crushed to her chest walked past them hidden in the darkness, and into the kitchen where their father lay.

CHAPTER 13

The handcuffs rattled as Alice walked, the charms attached bouncing off one another. She had time to study them in the lift, the wooden star, shamrock and diamond well made enough she knew they were expensive. She could feel the slightest tingling when she touched them, but was unable to figure out what they were. Which was worrying, but, at least her hand hadn't fallen off or something equally as dramatic.

She walked through the offices, ignoring the curious stares from the few staff that remained so late at night. She knew what she looked like, having caught sight of herself in one of the reflective windows the whole of the building was covered in. She had attempted to fix the racoon eyes, but she was pretty confident she had made them much worse, and now she had a black smudge on her sleeve. At least she no longer squelched when she moved, her clothes drying a lot faster than her hair, which was starting to curl.

"I need those reports in by morning, and please

reschedule that call with New York." Riley said, his voice carrying through the open door.

"Yes, Mr Storm, anything else?"

"No Maggie, that's all, thank you."

Alice paused by the door, watching Riley talk to the assistant. She always forgot he was still one of the most influential business men in the city, only really seeing him as the warrior he was. His grey, tailored suit with a crisp white shirt suited him just as much as his skin-tight leathers.

He shot Alice a surprised smile before he returned his attention to the assistant, murmuring something quietly.

"What happened to selling this place?" Alice asked once they were alone. She had no idea how he managed to run his empire amongst everything else.

"It's bigger, more central compared to my other office." Riley said, stacking some papers together on his desk. "I'm in the middle of organising a management team to take over the day to day tasks. The Guardians are needing more of my attention, as well as... other things."

Alice knew exactly what the 'other things' were, but didn't comment. She had no idea the details of his businesses, other than owning the Blood Bar.

Riley crossed his arms, stretching the jacket across his shoulders. "While it's lovely to see you, why have you come? Other than training, you've been avoiding me."

Alice licked her dry lips, deliberating on an answer. She had been avoiding him, as he had avoided her, before when he was concentrating on his father. Their relationship was complicated, an almost animalistic sexual attraction that neither of them could explain. It's what made them cautious, at least, until they decided to act on it one evening.

"Well, sweetheart?" He raised an eyebrow, his stormy eyes watching her carefully.

The instant she locked his gaze, her heart skipped, the familiar electric warmth she felt near him making its usual appearance. The connection confused them both, even stronger since their night together, but she had also begun to crave it. It made her feel, whole.

Which scared her.

"I wanted to see you." Alice struggled with the words, not sure what to say. "I don't know what we're doing," she began, feeling exposed. "I..."

"I don't know what we're doing either." When she just stood there, he uncrossed his arms. "I can smell blood. Take a seat and I'll grab the first aid kit."

"I'm fine."

He just pulled out a chair, a challenge in his eyes.

With a sigh, Alice quietly sat behind his desk, studying the city of lights through the floor to ceiling glass wall. His office was freshly decorated a dark, hunters green, the scent of paint faint in the air. The shade, she knew, would complement the nature park on the street below, bringing the trees of the forest inside.

Dark oak bookshelves dominated one wall, mostly empty as he organised his books that were a neat pile beside it. In one of the gaps was a painting... her breath caught when she noticed the portrait of the beast, the artist catching the powerful, dangerous creature in a beautiful light. Riley had moved it, placed it in a place where it could only be seen from behind his desk.

"Why do you keep it?" she asked when he returned, a small bag in his hand. "The painting?"

"It's a reminder that power and beauty can be deceiving."

Alice frowned at the pain in his words. "You're not your father."

He looked away, unzipping the first aid kit. "So, you going to tell me why you're bleeding?"

"It's nothing." She lifted the back of her top, moving to sit on the chair sideways. "Barely a scratch."

"This scratch sure looks like a stab wound," he muttered. "It needs stitches. You going to tell me what happened?" His tone left no room for discussion.

"I had a small disagreement, which ended with that person now unable to have children," she said with a wince, the cream Riley applied stinging. "You know me, always making friends."

He frowned at the cuff, still hanging on her wrist. "You should have been more careful."

"Do you think I purposely look for trouble?" She leant further forward, giving him more access. His hands were gently on her skin, warm. "You sound like Xander."

Riley chuckled. "Where do you think he gets it from?" They remained silent as he applied a couple butterfly stitches, finishing it off with a bandage. He tugged down her top just as his nose touching her nape, followed by lips.

Alice tipped her head forward, craving the affection.

His hand brushed down her shoulder, down her arm until he touched the cuff locked around her wrist. "I want it noted that I could have made a very inappropriate joke, but didn't," he said, voice deeper than usual.

Alice couldn't help her smile, even as her stomach rolled with apprehension. She knew he wouldn't have approved of Lucy, The Guardians trained to take out beings like him. The Guardians of the Order, she had begun to realise, were more than just mercenaries. They were highly intelligent men who were trained in both magic combat as well as physical. Their abilities were beyond anything she could ever hope to achieve.

Which made them beyond deadly.

"Are you angry?" She could imagine Xander telling Riley all the dramatic, exaggerated details.

"Angry?" he asked, stepping back as she turned. "What should I be angry about? You getting stabbed? Or making a deal with a Daemon? Again." His right eyebrow arched, his grey eyes dark with impatience.

"Either, I suppose."

"What do you want me to say? I'm not exactly happy about it." Jaw clenched he rubbed his stubble. "To everyone else you seem reckless, reacting without thinking your plan through. I know you would do anything to save someone you love, even if that means sacrificing yourself."

Alice froze, listening intently.

"But I've come to appreciate that you do know exactly what you're doing, that you understand the risks. So no, I'm not angry. I would never judge your decision, even if I disagree with it greatly, because I trust you."

The statement left her speechless. She was tired with having to explain herself, explain her reasons and decisions to people who wouldn't understand, couldn't understand. The fact he did changed everything.

"I'm not your keeper, contrary to what you believe. I've never wanted to control you."

"You only do this because of The Council," she croaked, her emotions on edge. "All of this, is only because you were told to do it."

"You sure?" He reached forward, his palm touching her cheek. "You're strong. Powerful. You scare me Alice. I have this strong need to protect you, and you don't let me."

"I'm a big girl, I don't need protecting," she said, her voice humiliatingly hoarse as she stood, pushing into his touch. He watched her with an expectation that left her desiring more, needing more.

"Which makes wanting you, that much harder."

She closed the gap between their lips, savouring his moan when she lifted her hands to his neck. With a shock her chi became alight with sensation, the electric current sizzling across her flesh everywhere he touched. When his hands ran down her sides to grip the back of her thighs she jumped, allowing him to sit her on the edge of his desk, the neatly stacked paper falling to the floor.

"Yes," she moaned, stripping him of his jacket. She pulled her own one off, pulling at her top a second later before he caught her wrists, holding them both in one large hand. She began to protest, wanting skin on skin when he shut her complaint with his lips, her tongue battling for dominance she knew she couldn't win. And the hotly feminine part of her relished in that fact.

She wrapped her legs around his waist, forcing him closer until he added the friction they both wanted, both craved from one another. His hands went under her shirt, his rough, calloused hands moving up to brush the underside of one breast, and then the other.

"You make me fucking crazy," he groaned, pushing impossibly closer. She bit at his lip, enjoying the growl in return. Her breaths came in pants, her arousal at its peak as she pulled the rest of the shirt from his shoulders, feeling the soft skin over hard muscles. His tattoos glowed beneath her palm, following her touch as she moved to nip at his throat. With a curse he held still, allowing her to easily claim his skin as his hands carefully unfastened her leather-synth jeans, fingers slipping inside to find her ready for him.

At his first touch she moaned, already embarrassingly close as she rode his fingers in desperation. Her breaths came in pants, her muscles aching for something bigger before he flicked the bundle of nerves at the apex of her thighs. A cry erupted from her throat, the sounds caught between his lips as the strongest orgasm she had ever experienced overwhelmed her senses.

Her chi reacted, somehow back to full strength as it tingled every time Riley touched skin on skin, adding to the overpowering sensation. As she came down from the high Riley pulled her down, his breath close to her ear.

"The next time I take you," he growled. "I'm going to make sure there is no one around to interrupt." When he pulled back, his eyes were liquid silver.

CHAPTER 14

A lice sat cross-legged on the low brick wall, watching Jones carefully photograph the woman dead on the pavement. She had beaten both Peyton and Brady to the scene, which meant she was too early for once and had to wait for the forensic team to finish examining the evidence and properly cordon off the area.

She clutched her coffee, absorbing the warmth as the large floodlight buzzed beside her. It was early, early enough both the moon and sun were competing in a sky that was still dark.

"Did you know," Jones started when he stood up, his eyebrows creased in concentration. "That Brady may think he runs these things, but really it's me."

"Are you just saying that because Brady isn't here?" she laughed.

"Of course," he grinned, setting the camera down to grab an evidence bag. "No way would I say it to his face, that man is the size of a mountain. But it's still true. You guys actually can't do anything without my approval. I'm the one who organises the forensic aspect from start to finish." He kept working while talking, something she had learnt from their first couple of scenes that Jones loved nothing more than his own voice.

"I always knew you were the secret mastermind behind everything."

"And don't you forget it! Did you hear they've created their own specialised team up north?"

She had heard that, which meant they were doing something right.

"SPOOK SQUAD!" he barked, pumping his fist in the air. "We really need a theme tune or something, maybe even a cool van. Oooo, oooo, like the Mystery Van, but not one painted green, blue and orange."

"I'll just leave that all to you," she said, just as Peyton pulled up.

"What were you saying about a Mystery Van?" Peyton asked, taking a seat beside Alice.

"Jones wants us to have our own Spook Squad van," she smirked, hiding it behind her paper cup. "Because, you know, we fight crime and are clearly superheroes."

"I don't think it's in our budget," he commented with a straight face. "But I'll be sure to run it by O'Neil."

"Where's Brady?" Alice asked, turning to Peyton. "He's never the last to arrive." She was sure he took pleasure in pointing out she was always late, even when she wasn't.

"He mumbled something about pregnancy hormones, but he's setting up a meeting for us as soon as possible. Somebody has leaked the details of the missing hearts to the press so we have the pencil pushers on our arse to solve this."

"Well, we better get started then." Jones disposed of his plastic gloves before picking up a clipboard. "Jane Doe was found around three this morning. We are yet to find her purse, I.D. or mobile."

"Which is unusual considering she's dressed for a night out." Alice had already been warned by Jones that she couldn't get near until they were done, but from her vantage point on the wall she could clearly see the victims sparkly black dress, even if it was from her back. One heel was still on her foot, the knee bent at an awkward angle while the other was several feet away on its side.

"It looks like a robbery gone wrong," Peyton commented. "It's possible she stumbled out of a nearby club and was attacked on her way home for her bag."

"There's obviously more if he's called us in," Alice added.

"Clearly," Jones said as he carefully stepped over the body to shine a torch at the woman's chest. The floodlights had been pointed to her back and surrounding pavement, casting her front half in shadow. When the torch hit, it highlighted the open cavity between her breasts, the blood as dark as her dress.

"Erm, I'm going to assume a certain organ is missing."

"Shit," Peyton cursed. "Another one." He closed his eyes, neck corded as he let out an unsteady breath. "We need to get all the CCTV's from the clubs, bars and restaurants open late in a three mile radius. One of them must have picked something up."

"You think she was targeted?" Alice asked, watching Peyton closely.

"There's lots of women walking home alone at night," he replied, eyes flashing before he returned his attention to Jones. "This vic seems a lot messier than the others, her chest's still open."

"That's because the murderer was interrupted." The paper ruffled in his hand. "A Mr Richard Johnson found her after hearing a scream from his bedroom just a street over." Jones gestured to the building across the road. "A first respondent is sitting with him while we waited for you guys."

"Thanks, Jones."

The flat across the road was above a closed health food shop, the entrance blocked by a uniformed officer.

"How's Mr Johnson?" Alice asked as he opened the door for them.

"As good as anyone who witnessed something like that," the officer replied. "He asked to be alone, so I waited down here."

"Have you taken his statement?" Peyton asked.

"No Sir, he's in a bit of a state. He's in number 1A."

"Thank you, we'll take it from here," he said, waiting for the officer to return across the road and to the scene.

"Why her?" she asked, her voice quiet as they climbed the rickety wooden stairs. "What did she have that the murderer wanted?"

Peyton remained silent, shoulders tight as he knocked on the front door.

The door creaked open, a head appearing in the gap above the chain.

"Mr Johnson?" Alice started, her voice gentle. "I'm Agent Skye and this is Detective Peyton. Can we come inside and ask you some questions?"

Richard Johnson stared at them, his eyes puffy and red. Without a word he slammed the door shut.

"Hmmm." Peyton lifted his fist to knock again when the door opened once more.

The living room was surrounded in cardboard boxes,

the only furniture unpacked was the sofa and TV which was unplugged and leant against the wall.

"Ah, please excuse the place," Richard said, voice breaking as he wiped his tear streaked face. "I'm about to move into The Compound."

"It's not a problem," Peyton said.

"You're pack?" Alice asked, conscious of his sudden wariness of her. His dark eyes trained on the floor, only looking at Peyton when he spoke, never at Alice.

Richard replied with a tight nod, his hands fidgeting in front of him.

"This won't take long, Mr Johnson," Peyton said as Alice made herself as small and nonthreatening as possible. Which you wouldn't think was difficult considering she was the shortest in the room already, but she could still feel his uneasiness.

"Do you need me to leave?" she asked, much to Richard's distress.

"No, no, no. Please stay," he said, voice wobbling. "I feel... better when you're here."

"Okay," Alice said, ignoring Peyton's surprised expression. "Can you tell us what happened?"

"Start from when you first noticed something wrong," Peyton added.

Richard gripped his elbows, hugging his chest tight. Head bent his shoulder-length chestnut hair swept forward, partially covering his face. "I thought I heard a scream around two-thirty, but I wasn't sure." His fingers strained white as he dug into his skin. "I thought I imagined it, so just tried to go back to sleep. It wasn't until I scented..."

"It's okay, take your time," Alice said, her hand hesitantly reaching forward to touch his shoulder. As soon as she made contact he visibly relaxed.

"I scented blood," Richard said, lifting his head slightly. "I followed it and found this man, kneeling over the woman."

"Can you describe him?" Peyton asked. "It's important."

"Err..."

The front door swung open, hard enough it resonated off the wall with a bang. Peyton immediately drew his gun, pointing it at the two men.

"Hey, hey," the blonde said, lifting his arms up in surrender. "We're cool, we're cool."

"They're pack," Richard explained, wrapping his arms around Alice's waist before he rested his chin on her shoulder. "I called them earlier."

"Alice?" Peyton asked, his gun aimed at the floor. "You okay?"

She nodded in reply, gently stroking through Richard's hair. Having lived with a shifter for years, she understood the animals need for a physical connection.

"The name is Con," the blonde said, and this is..."

"Tyler," Alice interrupted, recognising the tall, dark man.

Tyler grunted, mouth pinched.

Wow, she thought, *he was just as vocal as she remembered.*

His hair was longer than last time, the sharp military style grown out enough to touch the top of his ears. Tyler's hazel eyes narrowed as she stared, but they wouldn't meet hers.

Oh shit. She really needed to look into the Alpha crap.

Con walked over to Richard, hand on his arm to pull him back before Richard cried low in his throat. "Hey Rich, you 'kay?"

"We need to finish questioning," Peyton said. "If you

two could stand outside."

"We don't leave pack," Tyler grumbled, the answer aimed at Alice.

"Can they stay? Please?" Richard begged, voice stronger as the pack bond helped. At Peyton's agreement he continued. "I found the man, kneeling over the woman. I already knew she was dead, but he just kept hacking at her chest, oblivious to his surroundings. I made a noise and he yanked something from her neck before he ran."

"What did he look like?"

"It was dark," he croaked, licking his lips. "All I could see was he was tall, over six foot easily, and heavy, big like he works out."

"I think that's enough for tonight," Con murmured, prying Richard's arms from Alice's waist.

"He will still need to attend the station for a written statement, but that can wait until later."

"Fine," Con said. "Now, if you could excuse us..."

Alice made her way towards the door, Peyton following quickly behind before Tyler stepped in front.

"You need to speak to him, the pack is weak because of you."

Alice tightened her smile. "It's not my problem."

His hand snapped out to grip her arm. When she turned to stare he immediately let go as if he had been burned. "He made it your problem. He's still Alpha until he kills his brother, which we both know he would never do."

Alice looked up, wanting him to meet his eyes. When he didn't she pushed past.

Screw Rex, she thought as she stepped back into the street. Even now, he was fucking with her.

The sky had begun to lighten, the darkness fading even as the temperature remained low.

"Do you have problems with the pack?" Peyton asked, brows pinched.

"No, but they have problems with me." And it had started to piss her off. "Now are we going to discuss the fact the murderer pulled something from her neck?"

Peyton looked away just as the clouds began to spit. "No."

"Three," she said through gritted teeth. "There's three victims so far. They're being targeted because of these artefacts and you withholding information is going ..."

His eyes were hard when he looked back at her. "This is more than just The Met, Alice."

"Then let me help."

"You don't understand," he said above the sudden roar of the wind. "You *can't* help. There are secrets amongst my kind, secrets that can ruin everything." He looked around, the street quiet as he moved closer. "You bring enough attention to yourself with your cracked aura, I can't risk you with the High Lords."

"My aura is fine." Probably.

Her aura actually felt great, her chi back to full strength much faster than she expected. The fact it seemed to boost itself from contact with Riley was interesting, and something she wasn't yet ready to explore.

"And don't change the subject," she said with a snap. "What have the High Lords got to do with this?"

"Don't ask questions I cannot answer."

"Then what can you answer? Because right now your silence is going to get someone else killed."

"Careful, Alice," he growled. "I cannot break my oath to my people."

"Then find a way, because right now we're fucked."

Peyton looked away, teeth grinding.

"What about a trade? I'll pay you for the knowledge?"

"You wouldn't be able to afford it."

"What? Last time it was only an earring!"

"This is different," Peyton argued before he shook his head. "Let me bind your tongue."

"Bind?"

"It's a spell used to bind secrets. Fae protect their secrets to the death, Alice. It's normal in both Seelie and Unseelie courts to do this to low caste fae who risk defecting."

Fuck. Shit. Bollocks.

She didn't have much of a choice if she had any chance of helping.

"Then do it."

"You need to understand what you're agreeing to…"

"I've already agreed, just do it," she said, hoping it didn't hurt.

"Let's hope this doesn't go wrong."

"Wait, what?"

As the rain picked up he held out his arm, wrist side up as he quietly mumbled beneath his breath. Before her eyes his skin separated, revealing a thin vertical line of red that immediately began to drip to the floor.

"Now you," he said, voice deeper before he returned to his whispers.

Alice immediately copied the action, using her knife to cut the identical line as her bracelet settled at her wrist, the bead a grey colour. As soon as the blade left her skin he grasped her elbow, pressing both cuts together. His voice amplified, the sound closer to a song than any language she had ever heard. A drum beat a steady rhythm in the background, one that complimented his words, but was nowhere to be seen as it overpowered the sounds of the rain.

Bom. Bom. Bom. Bom.

As she sucked in a breath the ocean tickled her nose, so strong she could have sworn she was at the sea-side and not a wet, and rainy high street.

Bom. Bom. Bom. Bom.

Peyton closed his eyes, his head rocking with the beat of the drum as the song tumbled from his throat.

Bom. Bom. Bom. Bom.

Magic prickled across her arm, winding its way up her shoulder and throat before it settled on her tongue.

Bom. Bom. Bom. Bom.

When Peyton opened his eyes they glowed, the blue of his iris bright enough to cast a light. With her stomach in knots she refused to look away, overwhelmed by the sudden power that flowed from him.

Fuck me. He has got to be strong enough to be a High Lord.

Well, wasn't that interesting.

"Whatever I say now must never be repeated," he said, voice dark. "Do you understand?"

Alice opened her mouth to reply, but her throat constricted, choking her vocal cords.

"Good, it's working," he said with a nod. "As you already figured out, I'm what you on Earth Side call a Fae."

No shit, the glowy eye thing really gave it away.

Alice hoped her face expressed her sarcasm.

"I willingly offer some of my kinds secrets, witch. You will honour my gift by keeping your silence in return."

There were a few rules she had been taught when dealing with the Fae.

One: Names have power, a high Fae would never give you their true Name

Two: Never thank the Fae, they took it as an admission for a debt owed.

Three: Neither high nor low caste Fae could lie, but they were able to twist the truth.

Four: Fae did not do anything for free.

Five: Be cautious of gifts given, Fae stuff had a mind of its own.

Six: Fae loved offerings, but be careful not to insult them.

Usually she wouldn't take much notice with Peyton, but that was when he was pretending to be human. So she nodded politely, making sure she didn't offend.

"Artefacts have leaked through the doorway between realms since the beginning, but some are far too dangerous for this world. Those artefacts are known as Objects of Power and I actively seek them out." He paused, checking to make sure they were still alone. "Of the four dead, I believe three were possessors of such artefacts."

"Hey, guys Brady just called," Jones said, skidding to a halt when he noticed their arms. "Oh, am I interrupting something?"

Peyton stepped back, separating their arms. "Just admiring her new bracelet," he said with a smirk.

With a snap, the magic unbound her tongue and throat.

"Bloody hell!" Alice coughed, hiding her arm, and the blood behind her back.

Jones stepped forward, hand on her shoulder as she bent at the waist. "You okay?"

"Sorry, think it's hay fever," she coughed again, the prickle of magic irritating her lungs before it dissipated. "You said Brady called?" Alice automatically stretched her chi, expecting to feel the electric sensation of Peyton. Instead she searched and found nothing but human.

"Yeah, he wants us to get to the station ASAP to discuss the case. I'm just cleaning up before heading over."

"Thanks, Jones. We'll meet you there," Peyton said as he turned towards his car.

Alice quickly followed.

"Peyton," she whispered. "That was... I have never experienced..."

"Wild magic. It's a lot rawer than you're used to and I don't like to use it. It's... unpredictable at times." He stopped by his car, his eyes sweeping the surrounding area.

"Are you telling me you still did that spell knowing your magic is unpredictable? What happened if you turned me into a frog or something?"

"Why would it turn you into a frog?"

"I don't know!" A frog was the first thing that popped into her head.

"Well it didn't, so it does it matter." Peyton looked at her wrist, a frown creasing his brow as he reached forward to touch the glass bead with his fingertip. "So looks like you found something interesting at the antique shop then."

Alice hid the bracelet back beneath her sleeve, as if that would protect her. "I paid for it." Just not the full price.

"You should have mentioned it." He shot her a dark look. "It's full of residual magic, but I can't tell you what it does. It's definitely Fae, possibly a level two artefact, but as you're not dead already, you're probably okay."

"Well, that's comforting."

"I'm sure it will come off easily enough, when it's ready."

Alice crossed her arms, feeling the bracelet dig into her skin. "We need to come up with a game plan, today."

"Right now we need to head to the station. After that, I'll tell you everything I know."

CHAPTER 15

B rady sat at the head of the table, ignoring both Peyton and Alice as he scribbled on the paperwork in front of him. He had removed his jacket, and his sleeves were rolled past his elbows, revealing thick forearms with a sprinkling of dark hair. It was the most flesh she had ever seen from him, as he always wore a full suit including tie, even when they weren't working.

Peyton, on the other hand, was still dressed in his full suit and coat as if he was outside and not in a small, stuffy room with the heating on full blast. With his white blonde hair and blue eyes, they looked polar opposites. One dark, the other light.

Alice had been sitting at the table nibbling a cinnamon sugar covered doughnut for over an hour, sat in silence listening only to Brady muttering to himself every now and then. Impatience ate away at her as she kept finding herself staring at Peyton, much to his annoyance. She was eager to know more about the Objects of Power, the only lead they had to the four murders, and something only he knew.

"Sorry for the wait," O'Neil said as he opened the door, followed by a casually dressed Jones.

"It's my fault," Jones explained, "the clean-up took longer than expected to organise, considering the rain." He frowned, taking the seat beside Alice. "Vital DNA evidence could have been washed away."

O'Neil stood beside the board, his usual cigarette tucked beneath his left ear. "Let's get this started, I have another meeting with both Commissioners in an hour and I need an update of where we're at."

"S.I?" Alice asked, curious. She had spoken to both Rose and Bee, Paladins who still worked for the Supernatural Intelligence Bureau, but neither had mentioned whether the slime ball Mickey was still acting Commissioner. "What do they want?"

"We're deliberating contracting help for this case, especially considering details we would rather have kept from the public are about to hit headline news tomorrow." O'Neil stroked his dark goatee, the hair slowly turning to grey. "I would rather go into that meeting with positive news rather than negative, so if you would please." He gestured for Brady to begin.

Brady shuffled his paperwork as O'Neil took his seat. "So we have four confirmed victims, three of whom have had their hearts removed. Let's start with Macey Little, twenty three, and Rhys Kellen, thirty, who were found inside Mr Kellen's flat."

"The Pathologist has confirmed the C.O.D for Mr Kellen was blunt force trauma to the abdomen while Miss Little was a stab wound consistent with an eight inch knife," Jones added, looking at his own notes. "Miss Little also is the one victim who still retains her heart, but is decaying at an alarming rate."

"Where's the knife?" O'Neil asked, turning his head to look at the photographs pinned to the grey felt board at the back of the room.

"Never recovered."

"And the reason behind the decay?"

"Unknown as of yet."

"Now the second victim," Brady squinted down at the paper. "A Mr Cohan McKee was found at the bottom of his basement stairs, C.O.D. was also blunt force trauma, but to his head."

"So he died when he fell down the stairs?" Alice asked.

"Initial impact killed him, yes. His time of death has been noted twelve days before both Mr Kellen and Miss Little, making him the first known victim. His heart was also removed. The last victim has yet to be identified. She was attacked early this morning but was interrupted, so her heart was only partially removed."

"So there's a witness?" O'Neil asked.

Peyton sat straighter in his chair. "We interviewed the man who witnessed the attack this morning, but he was incredibly traumatised. The only description he could give was that It was a man."

"Which doesn't mean shit when glamour charms are becoming more affordable," O'Neil grunted. "Make sure we get that written statement. He might give us more details once he's calmed down. Something we could have missed."

"It may take a while for him to calm down, he's a submissive in White Dawn." She was sure of it.

Alice hadn't met many of the pack, only a handful and they were all dominants. It was her first experience with a sub, their general aura much different, calmer.

"Even if he wanted to, the pack wouldn't put him in a distressing situation."

The pack worked with hierarchy, with the Alpha at the top, descending levels of dominants before finally those that were submissive. It didn't mean they were weak, but they weren't influenced by their wolf as easily. According to Sam, when she asked once, a submissive made the packs stronger, as it gave the dominant wolves a reason to protect.

"I'll make sure we get it," Brady said.

Jones flinched as something beeped.

"Shit, sorry." He fumbled for his phone, eyes widening as he scanned the message. "Our latest Vic has just been I.D'd as a Miss Rachael Cart. Her handbag was recovered a couple streets over, purse, money and phone still inside."

"So it was stolen to make it look like a robbery?"

"Actually, I think it was a robbery." Jones shuffled through his files until he found two photographs of dark marks around Rachael's throat. "I would need to check, but the bruising is consistent of something being yanked."

"If he threw away her money and phone, and kept her necklace it suggests she was targeted." O'Neil tapped the end of his cigarette against the table. "What connection do we have between the victims?"

"Nothing obvious," Brady muttered. "Different ages, genders, financial situations."

"They're all Fae," Jones added.

"A large chunk of the population have some percentage of Fae in them," Alice said. "That doesn't necessary mean that's the connection."

"Both Mr Kellen and Mr McKee have strong markers that one parent was one-hundred per cent Fae. We haven't checked Miss Cart yet."

"What about Miss Little?"

"It keeps coming up inconclusive, but as she doesn't

match anything else it's a strong possibility she was just at the wrong place at the wrong time."

"That's the understatement of the year," Alice muttered. "To my knowledge half-Fae generally inherit some traits of their Fae parent."

O'Neil faced her with a frown. "Does that mean anything?"

Alice shook her head. "The possibilities are too extensive, the DNA test wouldn't even be able to tell us what type of Fae they were."

"What was their other half?" Peyton asked, eyes focused.

Jones checked his notes. "Human."

"Shit," he exhaled. "Drenics."

"Drenics?" Brady asked. "I haven't heard that term."

"Because Drenics, who are human and Fae mix are treated as abominations and aren't accepted. Fae believe they are the superior race, and breeding with a human is severely frowned upon. While the Seelie and Unseelie court would recognise them as Fae heritage, they're not allowed to be classified as one."

"That's a bit draconic, don't you think?" Jones said.

"Prejudice is in every Breed, even one that believe themselves above everyone else."

"Okay, so excusing Miss Little for the moment, we have a connection of the three remaining victims being half-Fae, or Drenics." O'Neil said, leaning back in his chair. "I need more than that."

"We have found DNA evidence, not from our victims at both the first and second crime scenes. It's already run through the system, but nothing was found. It flagged as ninety-eight per cent match to Fae."

O'Neil touched his cigarette. "So we need the lab

results on any evidence found at the latest scene, and the witness statement. Is there anything else anyone wants to add?"

"An old colleague of mine sent me details on a homicide dated six months ago," Brady said as she pulled out his phone. "Two dead, both with their hearts missing."

"You would think that would make the news or something," Alice murmured as Brady handed over his phone to O'Neil.

"We need someone down there to look into this further, it may be the same person." O'Neil handed back the phone. "Peyton, I want you to head down ASAP."

"I need to speak to my Fae contact first, see if he knows anything," Peyton added with a nod.

O'Neil sucked in his cheeks. "Take Agent Skye with you, the Fae are notoriously tight lipped, they might feel better with someone that's Breed. In fact, take her with you down to Kings Garden, she may pick up some magic residue or something. Now, is there anything else?" When everyone remained silent he pinched his nose. "Fine, I'll be in contact once a decision has been made with the Commissioners. Meeting dismissed."

Alice followed Peyton out, not speaking until they were alone by their cars.

"Is there a reason our visit to the antique shop wasn't mentioned?"

Peyton turned, jaw clenched.

"Did you even submit the note to evidence?" When he just stared, she cursed. "Fuck sake, Peyton. That's tampering with evidence and can get this whole case thrown out of court!"

"I know what it is, Alice," he growled. "But this is

beyond human law enforcement. The person behind this isn't going to see inside a court."

"You don't get to decide that!"

"Actually, I do," he said, blue eyes glowing slightly. "We need to meet my contact before we head out. Are you coming or not?"

CHAPTER 16

A lice stared at the red brick. "It's a wall," she frowned, turning to Peyton. "Why are we at a wall?"

A wall on one of the busiest areas in London too. A crowd of people surrounded them, a buzz of noise that seemed to be oblivious to them standing there. Then she spotted the cleverly disguised charm carved into a small circular disk imbedded into the pavement.

"This is The Three Headed Dog." Peyton replied, slightly impatient. "It's a pub."

No it's not, it's a bloody wall, she thought.

"A pub? Why are we at a pub?" Alice touched the brick hesitantly, the wall hard beneath her fingertips, the brick crumbling. "Yep, feels like a wall."

He pointed to the two black lanterns, both lit. "Two lanterns mean it's busy, one lantern means it's quiet."

"What about no lanterns?"

Peyton moved to stand beside her, arm linking hers.

"They're closed." With a smirk he stepped forward, the wall shimmering around his leg before he pulled her through.

Alice sucked in a breath as an intense cold overwhelmed her, the sensation only lasting for a second, however, the yelp she made loud enough to gain the attention of an annoyed pixie.

"Hey, keep the screeching down, would ya?" It yelled at her with a surprisingly deep tone, considering he was the size of her forearm. "Bloody humans!"

"Holy shit, it really is a pub!" The noise of the busy street had been replaced with the sound of punters laughing. Glasses clinked, drinks sloshed and a creature Alice had never seen before stood on stage blowing into what looked like a bagpipe, but it had six eyes and three legs that he yanked at intervals. Unfortunately, it sounded similar to an actual bagpipe.

"This is the one place in the city Fae can be themselves. Glamour breaks when you pass through the door." Peyton said, voice quiet even as two tables closest spun to gape at him. Alice turned too, interested in other than a slight glow to his iris', he looked exactly the same. Except... she looked closer, his hair was silver, not white blonde.

"I prefer your hair like this," she murmured. It was a weird decision for him just to change the slight tint to his hair. He rocked the silver, grey look.

Peyton ignored the attention as he moved through the busy pub, finding a table against the back wall by the stage. When Alice took her seat beside him, almost everyone had turned to stare, their gazes a mixture of curiosity, excitement and anger. She decided she was going to stay the hell away from the tall blue guy sitting two tables down, his stare was hungry. And she wasn't sure which type.

It was just pure luck the bagpipe dude had just finished

his set, for which Alice was grateful. As soon as he stepped off the stage, it turned into three more tables which were immediately taken up.

With arms crossed Peyton closed his eyes, leaning his head back against the wall. Alice sat there, uncomfortable as the hostile stares turned to spiteful murmurs. Annoyed, Alice locked gaze with the woman on the table beside her, unclipped her dagger and placed it loudly on the table. She was grey, everything from her skin, to her hair and eyes. It was all the same shade until she noticed the dagger, then she paled and quickly looked away.

"Stop scaring the punters," Peyton said, eyes still closed but a smile curled his lips.

"I don't think it's me they're worried about," she replied. "What's the grey woman?"

"That's a rude question."

"Shit, sorry." It probably was rude, but that didn't stop Alice wanting to know.

Peyton turned to look before he returned to his position, head back and eyes closed. "She's a banshee in her corporeal form."

"Seriously?" She had never seen a banshee, never mind a corporeal one. They were usually found in the Irish countryside, not a built up city. She was a type of faerie, usually found in her ethereal form who, notoriously, would screech before an imminent death. So it was a surprise to see one sitting casually with a leprechaun drinking the pinkest cocktail Alice had ever seen.

She bit her lip, wanting to know more when something dropped onto her hand.

"Oh, sorry!" a voice squeaked as a blur of glitter twinkled down. A tiny girl, the size of Alice's palm landed beside the miniature teddy bear. She picked up her toy, hugging it to her chest before spinning to stare at Alice.

"Er, hello."

"Hi!" she giggled, her round cheeks reddening before she hid her face into the felt of her bear. She wore a dress of periwinkle with a white, crisp apron. "You're not like me."

"No," Alice said. "I'm a witch." She whispered the last part, as if it were a secret between them.

The little pixie girl grinned, rubbing her wings together to make a high pitched squeak. She had six wings in total, four at the top that overlapped each other and two on the bottom, all with jagged edges. The membrane was thin, opaque with a slight sheen that was iridescent if the light hit it at the right angle. Similar to a dragonfly, but even more delicate.

"Nyra?" a voice called.

"Oh, my mama is calling!" With a burst of speed she shot up, leaving a trail of glitter in her wake. Alice tracked her all the way up to the little house on a shelf high up the wall. On that one shelf there were six houses, all painted various pastel shades that clashed with the dark green ivy that draped down the side. Little Nyra hugged the taller pixie before running off to sit with two others, their legs dangling off the side of the shelf to rain glitter down on the tables below.

"Pixies are a rarity Earth Side," Peyton murmured, his eyes still closed. "They find it difficult to get a job. They're great at security, fast and as strong as a small human, but are rarely given the chance due to their size."

It was only the second or third time Alice had ever met, or even seen a pixie.

"Who are we waiting for?" she asked, unable to take her eyes off the creatures with wings of rainbow. She found more houses along another shelf, this one almost as high as the ceiling which was three stories tall.

"He knows we're here." Was all he replied.

The ceiling was alive with colour, a reflection of the aurora borealis before it turned to a starry night, the full moon moving slowly across the room. As the scene changed again the light in the room adapted, around one hundred floating candles changed their intensity to match whatever was pictured on the ceiling. As a witch, she could easily make a candle float, but she would have to concentrate. Here, they just floated. It was magic, but magic like she had never experienced before.

"Witches can manipulate arcane and the elements," Peyton said, his eyes narrowed, but watching her when she returned her attention to him. "Something learnt. But Fae *are* magic. We don't need incantations or wands, we live and breathe it because magic is part of what makes us."

"Why have I never heard of this place before?"

"Because you're a witch. Only Fae are allowed here."

"That's right," something snarled behind her, its breath hot and stale. "Only Fae are allowed here."

Alice stood, the chair scraping against the floor. As she turned to calm the situation she froze, her words dying in her throat.

Bloody hell!

"Your kind aren't welcome here," the creature growled, spitting saliva through the two tusks each side of its large, red mouth. Hair covered both arms, shoulders and knees but everywhere else was bare, the skin a dirty purple. With a slightly elongated nose, and its small eyes on the side of its face, it looked like a mixture of a werewolf with mange and a mole.

It was not an attractive combination.

"Buggane," Peyton said, tone hard. "Aren't you supposed to stay on the island?"

"Is there a problem here?" A man walked over, towering over the table in a black suit that was just as dark as his shoulder length hair. His hand landed on the buggane's thick shoulder, the fingers, as well as the arm elongated.

"Yes, Ilzake," the buggane snarled. "This man has brought a witch amongst us Fae folk. I believe a forfeit would be a suitable punishment."

"Ah, my friend," Ilzake said, eyelashes low as his nails grew longer, digging into the purple flesh. "You clearly don't recognise the elf or you wouldn't be suggesting a punishment."

Alice glanced towards Peyton, his own attention focused on mole man.

"Elf?" The buggane laughed, saliva dripping from its mouth as the tusks grew. "Chaos and destruction is all an elf is good for. Tricksters who don't deserve their prestige back in Asherah. What court do you belong to? Which royal did you fuck to get your status?"

"That's enough." Ilzake dug his fingernails, breaking skin. He slowly moved his face closer, his cheek brushing against the purple skin of the bruggane's before his lips touched the creature's ear.

The buggane paled, and when Ilzake released his palm it stepped away, moving a lot faster than Alice though it could on hooves.

"I apologise about that," Ilzake turned to Alice, his head cocked to one side. He lifted his lashes to reveal completely black eyes, no white. "Buggane is a distant cousin of the troll, and his intelligence is only marginally better."

Alice stared into those eyes, unable to look away even as she felt like she was falling.

"Hmmm," Ilzake purred. "Now your depravities would taste delicious."

"Sin-eater." Peyton blocked her sight with his arm, breaking the eye contact. "It would be wise not to harm my colleague."

"No harm meant, my Daeizan," the man grinned, showing off three sets of sharp teeth. "But I am interested in the reason you have brought a witch into my establishment."

"Business."

"I had heard whispers you walked amongst us. But alas, we're neutral, there's no courts here." Ilzake folded his long legs, too long to fit beneath the table so he lent them against the vacant seat. His arms stretched the length of the table, and then some.

"What's a Sin-eater?" Alice asked.

Ilzake darted his attention to her, but she wouldn't meet his eyes. "I am just one of the many variety of faerie."

"He absorbs people's memories and sins, whether they want him to or not," Peyton commented. "Which is why I have some questions."

"I will not speak to a witch," Ilzake sneered, nails scraping the wood of the table. "Even if her memories are dark and full of pain."

"She's bound."

"Is she?" Ilzake faced Alice once more, his eyes no longer sucking her in, but instead glittered with a dark curiosity. Slowly his cheekbones shifted, protruding beneath the paleness of his skin to angle his already long face. Quick as a whip he lunged across the table, his lips touching hers with the slightest of pressure.

On instinct Alice stood up, chair crashing to the floor as

she unsheathed her blade. As soon as she palmed the hilt blue flames cracked along the steel.

Laughter erupted from Ilzake's throat, like thunder that echoed around the large room. With a flick of his hand the twenty pixies with swords pointed at Alice flew away, cursing amongst themselves.

"How... interesting. I have never met a witch with her tongue bound, but my lips tingled at your touch. For this fascination I will hear you out."

"I want to know what you've heard about any Objects of Power sightings throughout the city recently."

Ilzake relaxed back, a slight smirk curling his lip. "And what exactly do I get in return?"

"What would you like?"

Ilzake sucked in his cheeks, thinking it through. "I would like a memory, but we both know you may be lacking those," he chuckled. "So I will settle for a favour."

Peyton remained calm but for the slightest tightening of his shoulders. "That can be arranged."

The Sin-eater grinned. "I've heard *Her* box was spotted at auction six months ago."

"Her?" Alice asked, but was ignored.

"Who bought it?"

Ilzake licked his lips, his dark grey tongue forked. "You know a favour isn't worth that information." He tilted his head, his straight, shoulder length hair partially blocking his face. "I could lose my other clients."

"Do you know if Her box is complete?"

Ilzake paused, his head rocking to the other side. "No I believe not, they say she's not yet whole. But that may have changed recently, before I received this memory."

"What about the other pieces? Have you heard where they are?"

"Isn't it your job to keep track?" Ilzake crossed his arms, the limbs so long his hands brushed the floor. "I heard Soulrise was used recently, which means the Book of Shadow and the Grave Stone can't be far. You know how those artefacts actively seek their paramour."

"What is the box?" Alice asked. "And what has it got to do with the missing artefacts?"

"I'll leave you two to business." Ilzake uncurled from his seat, stretching to his full height. As he turned to leave he paused, a frown pinching his features. "There was a time once when I would have welcomed and encouraged someone such as Her to wreak havoc and misfortune on this world. But it seems I have settled here, along with many of us who now call Earth Side home. This realm is beautiful, but fragile. The natives easily manipulated into wars and terror. If she were to be opened, she would be the end of it all." With a snap of his long fingers a tray floated towards them, held by a male pixie. The two drinks sloshed as they were placed on the table, the pixie staring, hand on the hilt of the needle on his hip before he flew off, taking the tray and Ilzake with him.

Alice picked up her glass, staring at the deep pearlescent amber liquid before Peyton placed his hand over the top.

"I wouldn't advise you drink or eat anything from Beyond the Veil. You may suffer some... ill effects."

With a sigh she set the glass back down, pushing it across to Peyton instead. "I'm thinking there's a bigger threat than you want to admit."

"It would seem so." Peyton looked into his glass, lips pursed. "Elves are one of the most powerful Fae," he began, a frown creasing his brow, "but also the most feared because of it." He looked up, eyes glowing from within.

"There was once this sorceress, an elf whose name has since been removed from our memories. She was an Unseelie Princess, beautiful but manipulative. She got whatever she desired, and she desired the crown, and would have destroyed either Court to get it. The Dark King heard of her plans and destroyed her, removing her very essence and trapping it into a small wooden box, made from chasomin trees, and tordeem stones only found in the heart of his kingdom."

"She's still in there, isn't she?"

"The Light Queen broke the box, removing the three stones and casting them through the door between realms. Over time the stones changed, became their own artefacts but they still long for Her."

"Soulrise?"

"A dagger that can force the soul to remain in the body once it's dead. The flesh would rot around them, but they would be forced to endure an eternity stuck, unable to entirely die even when they turned to dust. The stone is in the hilt."

"Wait... does that mean..."

"Macey Little was stabbed with Soulrise."

Fuck!

"The Book of Shadow, a leather-bound grimoire with blank pages. The stone is on the front cover. It has the ability to control souls, so whoever writes a name in blood on one of the pages can control that person. It's also the only way to release Macey from her endless torment."

"Why are Fae artefacts so creepy?"

"They're not all like that." Peyton shrugged, sipping the amber drink.

"And what about Grave Stone?"

"If put on a corpse it can animate the dead, indefinitely.

They would no longer rot, and can regrow flesh by eating the living."

"What were you saying about them not being creepy?" Alice leant back in the chair, her eyes tracing her dagger that she had left on the table. She was aware of the other patrons, their uneasiness hard to ignore. So she sheathed the blade, placing it back on her thigh. "What will happen if she's opened?"

He tapped his knuckles on the table. "I don't know, but I believe it's wise we don't find out."

"Peyton, what do you actually do? Except being a Detective."

He paused before he pushed his glass across the table. "I look for Objects of Power, and some other Fae artefacts."

"What, to keep them safe?"

"No." He shook his head. "I keep the world safe from them."

A chair scraped, the noise loud as everyone else in the pub had gone quiet. She had noticed the angry stares and aggressive murmurs, decidedly ignoring them. But it was only a matter of time before another one struck up the courage to confront them.

"I think it's time to go," she said, her own chair scraping.

"Hmmm." As Peyton stood, he glared at each Fae that had also gotten to their feet. Very slowly they sat back down, so they left without incident, even as she felt their curiosity and hostility prickle across her skin.

"I don't think I'm welcome back," Alice murmured as she stepped through the wall, back into the reasonably bust street. "I doubt you're welcome either. What did you do to piss them off?"

Peyton scanned the street, his iris' back to their usual blue. "Let's keep moving." He walked her towards the

Beetle, cautious before a glint of light appeared in front of them.

"Daeizan, I have been asked to give you this." A female pixie handed over a piece of paper, that even folded was still half her size. As soon as Peyton took the note she floated up, moving too fast for their eyes to track.

Without looking Peyton placed it in his breast pocket. "We'll leave tonight for Kings Garden and start investigating fresh in the morning."

"What was in the note?"

"Probably details about the favour."

Alice opened the car door, hesitating at the frame. "Why are they calling..."

"What the fuck is that?" Peyton interrupted, peeking through the window. "Is that a garden gnome?"

"Oh." Alice noticed Jordan in the back seat. "Yeah, he seems to enjoy sitting in the car recently." It has gotten to the point she had started not to notice him anymore.

"That explains why your aura is broken."

"What?" She glanced back at Jordan smiling on her backseat, the spank paddle still glued to his fist.

"He's feeding off you, probably others too." Peyton looked closer, opening the back door to touch Jordan's face. "You noticed anyone becoming unwell?"

"No..." *Oh please don't be related to the neighbours dying,* she mentally added. She couldn't deal with that on her conscience. "Xander told me he was haunted."

"Well, he's not technically wrong. But your gnome isn't haunted by a generic ghost." He touched the cracks along Jordan's face before he snapped his hand back with a hiss. "This needs to be dealt with, but right now we need to concentrate on Her."

"Great," she muttered. "Not only do we have a homicidal box to find, I have a dangerous garden gnome with a sex paddle glued to his fist."

"Well," Peyton said as he stepped away, turning to his own car. "You can't say it isn't boring. Meet at yours in an hour."

CHAPTER 17

Alice clutched her coffee as if it were a lifeline. They had stayed in a local bed and breakfast above a pub, the beds cheap and uncomfortable. Which meant she spent most of the night tossing and turning, all while she heard strange growling noises from the room next door.

"How can you be so happy in the morning?" she said with a yawn.

Peyton studied the road signs as he drove down a windy road, eyes bright and awake. "Who says I'm happy?"

Alice smirked. "Point taken."

He lifted an eyebrow, eyeing her coffee until she handed it over with a dramatic frown.

"How is this even coffee?" He grimaced at the flavour.

Alice snatched the paper cup back. "I like it sugary, okay?" She sipped the caramel latte, savouring the taste. "So, where are we going?"

"I called Brady's contact last night after we arrived.

He's meeting us at the station in about ten. Seems like a cheerful chap."

"Translation, he seems like an arsehole."

Peyton smiled, the emotion only lasting a second before he pulled into a side road, the station tucked between two large trees. Kings Garden was a small town in the south west part of England, only a mile from the River Tamar and around two-hundred and fifty from London. Two-hundred and fifty or so miles of Peyton's passive-aggressive road rage.

They pulled up in one of the free parking spaces, a short man in a dark coat waiting outside with a frown.

"Detective Tallack?" Peyton greeted with a surprising friendliness. "I'm..."

"I know who you are," Tallack said with a snarl. "I told Brady I don't appreciate no city folk coming down 'ere to tell me how to do my job." His eyes flickered to Alice, the snarl depending. "'Specially with no witch." He spat the last word.

"How did you know I was a witch?"

"Just do. Now shall we get this over with? Some of us have proper jobs to get back to." Without a backwards glance he walked into the station, expecting them to follow.

"Wow, he's friendly," Alice murmured as she took a step beside Peyton.

"Told you he's a cheerful chap," Peyton grunted, his fake smile disappearing along with his overenthusiasm.

"Just through here." Tallack sat at his desk, impatiently waiting for them to sit across from him. "Come on, I don't have all day." His office was a small square space consisting of a desk, three chairs, a filing cabinet and a sad looking plant.

"We appreciate you taking the time to see us this morning, Detective," Alice began, studying his broad brow and receding hairline. "I..."

"Yeah, yeah," Tallack snapped. "Here's the files you wanted." He slapped down a thick folder, the paper loose inside. "This is a closed case."

Peyton flipped over the file, studying the photographs while Alice checked out the autopsy report to the first victim.

Report of examination

Decedent: ███████████████████

Case Number: RF 65626-963002

Cause of death: Asphyxiation

Identified by: *Teeth were used to check medical records. Maternal Grandmother confirmed deceased on*

████████████████████

Age: *21 years*

Sex: *Male*   **Race:** *Caucasian*

Date of death: ████████████████

....

Date of Examination:

████████████████████████████

Examination and summary analysis performed by: *Dr Lucas Sheffiel*

Cause of death: *Asphyxiation (Process of being deprived of oxygen. Suffocation)*

....

Findings

1. Neck abrasions around throat.

2. ████████████████████

3. *Damage to both hands, including marks and scratches. Suggests a struggle.*

4. *Unknown DNA found* ▮▮▮▮▮▮▮▮▮▮▮▮▮▮▮▮▮▮

5. *Toxicology report clear.*

6. *Surgical marks around abdomen.*

7. *Heart removed through chest cavity.*

8. *Swollen tongue and oropharynx.*

....

Conclusion:

The surgical marks along the incision on the chest have been confirmed to have been caused by a medical grade scalpel. ▮▮▮▮▮▮▮▮▮▮▮▮▮▮▮▮▮▮▮▮▮▮▮▮ *damage to the surrounding tissue, including the lungs which were found beside the subject. These were removed after the subject was already deceased.*

The abrasions patterned around the throat match the collapsed trachea. ▮▮▮▮▮▮▮▮▮▮▮▮▮▮▮▮▮▮ *verification, but consistent with medium sized hands.*

The subject was deprived of oxygen for an extended period of time, resulting in suffocation.

"Why have some details been redacted?" Alice asked as she scanned the second report, annoyed that it was also heavily edited.

"Sensitive information. It's all I could get approved on such short notice without a court order to re-open the case."

Peyton handed over the photographs. "Do you know what Breed they were?"

"Both registered as Human." Tallack narrowed his eyes. "Why?"

"So no Fae ancestry?"

"I can't confidently say no. The families wanted to bury

their dead as soon as they could, so bloods weren't run to determine their full Breed. It didn't seem relevant at the time considering their C.O.D. Does them having faerie blood mean anything?"

Peyton pursed his lips. "We're not sure yet. But I'm sure Detective Brady has let you know about the victims we've found in London under similar circumstances."

"He did." Tallack sat back, his leather seat squeaking beneath his weight. "There was also a hitchhiker that registered a complaint with Brickly-heathe, which is a few hours' drive from 'ere. He claimed a man gave him a ride but got spooked when he noticed a coppery smell from inside the glove compartment. Apparently, according to the report, a dark liquid oozed out. He jumped out at the next set of traffic lights."

"Was this investigated further?"

"No, put down as a coincidence. Unfortunately the hitchhiker was intoxicated at the time so wasn't taken too seriously."

"What about leads from the crime scenes?" Alice asked, carefully tucking the paperwork back into the folder. The photographs showed two young men, their chests cut, and left open for the world to see.

"Crime *scene*. They were both found together. There were no fingerprints, marks or DNA that we could identify. No witnesses. The families hired a separate investigation which concluded it was a ghoul attack. It's not unknown that they harvest organs."

"Did you confirm this with the local vampire clan?" Alice asked, noting how Tallack's lip curled at 'vampire.' "They would have been able..."

"Those filthy bloodsuckers denied everything, which wasn't surprising. If it was a ghoul, as the independent investigation determined, it would have been from out of town. None of our cemeteries were disturbed." His eyes flickered to the file, then back up again. "Something like this doesn't happen very often down 'ere, it upset the whole town. I will not allow you to re-open it unless I confirm with your superiors of your competence."

"Actually, you don't get to decide that." Peyton stood, clutching the file to his chest. "We appreciate your time Detective Tallack. We will see ourselves out."

Alice followed Peyton's long strides, waiting until they were inside his car before she spoke. "Well, that's a whole new level of incompetence."

"Indeed." Peyton placed the file onto his back seat.

"Do you think they're connected? Or is that a stupid question?"

"It sure is an interesting coincidence, is it not?" He tapped the steering wheel. "After all that time in the box, she would probably be weak."

"So we think she's what? Absorbing hearts to regain power?" Alice grimaced. "Wow, how original."

Peyton chuckled. "I would put money on it. I also bet there are other victims."

"I wouldn't, we both know how shit you are at poker." Alice rolled down the window, allowing the ocean breeze to tangle in her hair. "I think you're right. I doubt she absorbed two hearts, then had a six month break."

"Shit!" Peyton pulled out his phone, clicking on the map. "Ilzake said Her box was spotted at auction six months ago."

"You think this is where she was found?"

He placed the car into gear. "It's worth a look."

The only auction house in a fifty-mile radius was situated down a short pier, surrounded by white sands. It was low tide, leaving wet slush that a few families were hunting for shells in. Two old men sat at the end of the pier with home-made crab rods, the ends dipped into the shallow rock pool below while they looked silently into the distance.

"It's not open," Alice commented at the sign plastered on the front door.

Peyton knocked loudly three times. When there was no answer, he knocked three more times.

"Hey, can't you read a sign?" A teenager, no older than seventeen unlocked the glass door, face tight with annoyance. "We don't open until five-thirty. You'll have to come back then."

Peyton flashed his badge, too fast for the young man to really study it. Unfortunately, Detective Tallack was right, they didn't have authority unless they re-opened the case. But the assistant didn't know that. "This is official police business. We need to ask questions regarding an ongoing case, Mr..."

"It's Brandon, call me Brandon," he flustered, opening the door further. "What's this about?"

"We need to know whether you keep records of all the items that come through here?" Alice asked, stepping inside the dark atrium.

"Err, I'll have to get the manager. If you would excuse me." He locked the door behind them, disappearing through an archway just as the above lights flickered on.

They were only left for a few seconds before an older man walked back through, followed by the lookalike teenager.

"Hello, the name is Mr Hudgins and I own this establishment. May I ask who you both are?" he asked with a slight sneer.

"I'm Detective Peyton, and this is my colleague Agent Skye," Peyton introduced them. "We're here because we had a tip that something you sold around six months ago is involved with an ongoing homicide case. Do you keep records of all the sales?"

"We follow the Data Protection Act, which means we keep the relevant data for up to a year. However only those paid by credit card are recorded."

"What about cash?" Alice asked, gaining Mr Hudgins attention.

"Some of our clients like to remain anonymous."

"We're interested in a box, wooden. Is that something you could help with?" Peyton said with a bored expression. His professional voice that of complete monotone.

"If you follow me."

Hudgins walked them to a computer in the corner, the screen dark until he moved the mouse. "Six months ago, did you say?" He input some data before a screen filled with various styles of boxes. Cigar boxes, makeup, vintage wine and jewellery. He carefully scrolled through them until Peyton pointed to the bottom right.

"Can you enlarge that one please?"

With a click the wooden box was enlarged. It was small, smaller than she expected with unusual designs carved along the side as well as the top, surrounding three round indents. There seemed to be no seam, no obvious way to open it.

There was no information other than the reference number, and that it was paid for with a credit card.

"Do you have the details of who bought this?" Peyton asked, eyes alight.

Hudgins sniffed, closing down the screen. "I'm sorry, can I see your badges?"

Peyton pulled his out, allowing Hudgins to study it with a frown.

"London? You city guys always think you can come and take over." With a tut he handed the badge back. "But I know I don't have to hand you any confidential information without a warrant. I will not risk the integrity of my business."

"So what you're saying..." Alice began. "Is that you don't care that this box could be an integral part to solving a homicide. Actually, more than one homicide, two in your home county, as well as several in London."

Hudgin's grit his teeth. "I'm going to have to ask you to leave."

"Don't worry Mr Hudgin's," Peyton grunted. "We will get that warrant."

CHAPTER 18

For a 'boutique' pub, it wasn't very boutique. To Alice, it looked like a generic pub with ugly patterned carpets, sticky wooden tables and a pool table with holes in the felt. Even the bar, where she sat and ate her chips, was a generic as they came.

"Hey, what's with the antlers?" Alice asked the barmaid as she gestured to the monstrosity that was the wall decoration. A set of antlers was pinned above the seating area, almost the span of the whole place.

The barmaid smirked, flicking the tea towel over his shoulder. "According to the owner, the guy on the wall attacked his herd. So he put them up as a warning to all other shifters."

"Wow. How... passive aggressive." Surely it was illegal to have body parts of shifters on the wall? "Reminds me of Vlad and his spikes."

"I think he would like being compared to Vlad the Impaler," she smirked, placing a glass back on the shelf. "You in town long?"

"Who says I'm visiting?" Alice asked as she munched on a chip.

"The fact you're staying in one of our rooms?"

Alice hesitated, another chip halfway to her mouth.

The door slammed, the glass rattling as it made contact with the wall behind. Peyton stormed inside, his usual frown deeper than usual. With his face flushed he took the stool beside her, and stole a chip.

"Hey!" She attempted to pull them away, but Peyton grabbed two more. "Order your own bloody food."

Peyton faced the barmaid. "One plate of chips and a glass of whatever is on tap please."

"Coming up." The barmaid walked off.

"What's up with you?" Alice asked, curving her arm protectively around her plate.

"I've just received an update from Detective Prick."

"Ah, we're so good at making friends," Alice chuckled. "What's happened?"

"After some convincing he's going to push for the warrant, but it's going to take a couple days."

"Why are you so pissed? That's good news?"

"With such a high-profile case it should have been within the hour." Peyton smacked his hand on the bar, drawing attention. "We can't hang around here for days, we need to be back before tomorrow."

"So is he going to forward us the information?"

"Yeah, he has my contact details." He sat for a moment, brows creased. "We're so close to having a name, any delay could mean the box being opened."

"One thing has bothered me though," Alice said as she pushed her plate away. "Don't you think it's strange Her box was bought with a trackable card? And not cash?"

Peyton's eyes widened. "It's possible it wasn't planned, even an impulse buy."

"Like he just happened to come across a dangerous sorceress trapped in a box? Now that's a coincidence."

"Hmmm." A plate of chips and a beer was placed on the bar. Peyton murmured a thanks as he left the cash, grabbing his plate and glass. "I need to do something, I'll come get you when I'm ready to go."

"Oh, you're really going to leave me alone?" Alice asked as Peyton turned towards the corridor that lead up to the rooms.

"Yep."

"Arsehole," she muttered.

"You never answered the question," the barmaid asked, wiping down the wood. "You staying long? Your room hasn't got an end date on it."

"Oh, not long."

"You come for a sexy weekend or something?"

Alice smirked. "What, with two rooms?"

"Yeah, I thought that was weird," she snorted. "Thought maybe he snored. Although, through these walls it wouldn't matter if you were beside him or next door."

"No, we're here down on business."

"You a cop or something?" she asked, tilting her head. "Now he definitely looked like a cop."

"Or something."

A chi flared, strong enough Alice turned to see who it was. A man had walked into the pub, a large leather coat draped over his shoulders, poorly hiding the serrated dagger strapped to his hip. His dark eyes scanned the room, settling on her before he moved onto the barmaid. Alice concealed her chi as she turned back, feeling the hairs on her arms stand on edge as he took a seat beside her.

He flared again, a greeting amongst witches that was responded to by the barmaid. It washed over her like water, sparkling that bubbled against her aura.

"Please don't make a scene," the barmaid said, voice quiet as all the colour drained from her face.

"I can do what the fuck I want," he growled, his hand snapping out to fist in her shirt, pulling her forward until her stomach smashed against the side of the bar.

"Please, baby..."

He yanked her harder, forcing her over the bar and onto his lap.

With a click Alice had unclipped her own knife and held it against his throat. "I need you to let her go," she said as calmly as she could, even as rage simmered through her blood. "Nice and slowly."

The barmaid squeaked as he quickly released his fist and she scrambled off his lap and out the room. The remaining patrons remained quiet at the tables, some even shrinking in their seats.

"You're making a huge fucking mistake," he growled, her blade precariously close to his bobbing Adams apple. "You have no idea what you're dealing with."

"And you have no idea who you're dealing with. Now I think you should leave." She pulled her knife away as he stood up, muscles tense.

He jumped off the stool, shrugging his coat from his shoulders. He wasn't much taller than she was, which made him rather short for a man. But what he lacked in height, he made up with muscle to the point she doubted he could cross his arms.

When he dropped his coat it clanged, like the pockets were full of metal. The knife on his hip came into display, as if the sight of it alone was enough to intimidate her. She barely gave it a glance, her eyes settling on the large sun tattoo on his bicep.

Oh, fuck.

"PATRICK, GET THE FUCK OUT OF MY PUB!" A gun cocked, the barrel pointing at the mans head. "I warned you last time."

Patrick grinned, keeping his eyes settled on Alice. "Do I know you?"

"Last warning," the voice snarled behind her. "Get out."

Slowly Patrick reached for his coat, the smile tightening before he glanced behind her. "See you real soon, Jess." He blew a kiss as he walked out the door.

"Fucking prick," the man with the gun growled, his reddish-brown eyes large in his face. "One day I would love to pin him on my wall." He turned to the barmaid, her face tear stained. She had wiped away at her cheeks with a tissue, smudging her makeup enough that it showed light bruises beneath. "Jess you okay?"

"Ye...yes," she hiccupped. "Thanks Markus."

"I thought you were done with that guy?"

"I am!" she sniffled. "Sort of." She looked up through her wet lashes at Alice. "Thank you, but you really shouldn't have done that."

Alice shrugged, putting away her knife. "Was he your boyfriend?"

She hesitated, her eyes flashing to Markus then back again. With a tight nod she looked down at her feet. "Please be careful, he isn't a nice guy."

"I can tell by your face." When she flinched, Alice felt her stomach drop. "What's with the tattoo? The one of the sun?"

Jess's eyes grew large. "It's nothing," she answered too quickly. "Just some stupid tattoo."

"It's important."

"Jess, you sure you're okay?" Markus asked, his hand itching to point his gun again.

She looked at her boss, biting her lip. "Yeah, I'm all good now, thanks."

"Hmmm, okay. Holla if you need me." He shot Alice a warning look. "You got a license for that knife?"

"We both know there's no license," Alice replied. "Do you have a license for the gun?"

Markus' top lip curved as he left.

Jess sat on a stool, gesturing for Alice to join her. "He was never like this, you know. He was kind. Thoughtful." She began to rip a tissue, her hands shaking. "Then he joined this group, and got the tattoo."

"What's the group?"

"It's a secret," she whispered. "He wasn't even supposed to tell me. It's something about serving the true King. They wear the emblem of the sun to show their loyalty."

"King?"

"Yeah, you know, King Arthur."

"What do they do, exactly?"

"I'm sorry, I don't know." She stood, stepping back behind the bar. "I'm sorry you had to see all that. He's not supposed to bother me at work."

The stool scraped behind Alice. "Thank you, but I think we're going to be checking out as soon as possible."

"Oh, okay." Jess blinked, shaking herself as she reached beneath the bar. "I'll get that sorted for you."

Alice paused, her hand fisting. "It's not your fault, you know. Ignore what he says, you deserve to be treated with the respect. Don't settle for an arsehole like him." Without a backwards glance she headed towards the rooms.

Alice hitched her overnight bag higher on her shoulder as she knocked on Peyton's door.

"Answer the bloody door," she groaned, knocking again but getting no reply. "Shit." She tried the handle, the room locked from the inside.

"Please don't be naked," she mumbled as she jimmied her credit card in the latch, pressing her weight against the door gradually until it clicked open.

Thank the goddess for cheap locks, she thought as she quietly slipped inside, closing the door behind her.

"Peyton?" she called out. The curtains were drawn, giving an orange hue to the small room that consisted of a double bed, a set of drawers, two bedside cabinets and a threadbare rug. The exact same as her room, except her bed wasn't made.

Keys, wallet and an empty plate was placed on the nightstand, his jacket draped over a chair.

"Peyton?" The bathroom was just as empty, the light off.

A high-pitched whine drew her attention to the bed.

An ornate frame was placed in the centre, the glass humming. Lines swirled, glowing bright enough to illuminate the gloomy room as Alice approached. The patterns cracked, separating as light burst through.

"Alice, what the fuck are you doing in my room?" Peyton growled.

"Ow." Alice rubbed at her eyes, blinking to clear them. "I was calling you!" Peyton stood on the bed. "Where did you come from?"

Peyton jumped off, reaching back for the frame. The

glass was no longer broken, but slightly mirrored with a mercury effect.

"What do you want, Alice?"

Questions around the frame landed on her tongue, but they didn't have time. "We need to leave." She picked up his bag, settling it on the bed. "Like now."

His eyes narrowed. "Why?"

"It's a long story..."

CHAPTER 19

A lice opened her front door to the delicious scent of garlic and cheese. "Please say that's Giovanni's!" she called through the front door, placing Jordan down on the sofa facing the TV. She had found him sitting in her locked car. At least inside she could keep an eye on his behaviour, or lock him in the cupboard until she could exorcise him. Or whatever it was called when removing an unknown entity from a garden gnome.

"Come through baby girl!" Sam shouted back, "It's only just arrived."

Sam had just started plating the food when Alice walked through into the kitchen, pausing at the man who sat quietly at the table.

"Hello," he greeted, his cheeks burning a bright red. "It's nice to meet you again."

"It's nice to see you fully clothed," she smirked, turning to Sam. "What, are we getting divorced now?"

"Shut up!" he threw a tea towel, the one stating 'rock

out with your crock out' with a picture of a large pot. "This is Ash, be nice," he warned, his amber eyes flashing.

"Okay, okay," she laughed, bringing her arms up in defence. "It's nice to meet you Ash."

Ash smiled shyly in return, ducking his head to cover his ever increasing blush. Now she wasn't distracted with his larger than life appendage, she took her time to take in his flawless caramel skin and honey brown hair.

"I didn't think you were back until tomorrow?" Sam asked, eyebrows raised. "Your trip go okay?"

Alice felt her smile tighten. "Uh huh."

Sam's eyes flashed. *What happened?*

Later, she shook her head. "So, where did you guys meet?" she asked out loud as she took a seat, salivating at the chicken pesto pizza.

"At work," Sam answered, taking his own seat after plating a mountain of garlic bread and a bowl of pasta. "Ash is a paramedic."

"Why would an ambulance be called..." Then she remembered the seven deadly sins themed sex rooms at the back. "Actually, I don't want to know."

"Yeah, that would be wise," Ash laughed, his nervousness dissipating as he tucked into some pasta. "Sam told me you're dating Riley Storm? I've seen him in those gossip magazines."

"Yeah, I wouldn't say we were dating, more..."

"Sharing each other's bath water?" Sam added.

"SAM!" Alice bit down hard on the pizza, her jaw working overtime as she glared at her hysterically laughing roommate. "Bloody hell, I'm never telling you anything again!"

"You know you will," he grinned.

"Where's Poe? Have you fed him?"

"Oh, your cat is sleeping on my feet," Ash shrugged.

"And yes Alice, I've fed your pussy..." he paused, an impish grin creasing his cheeks. "Someone has to."

Ash began to choke on his pasta as he laughed.

"That's it boys, laugh it up. I'll get my own back, don't you worry," she warned with a grin. When she reached across to grab a slice of bread Sam gestured to her bracelet, the bead a deep violet before it swirled into a green.

"Cute, looks like one of those novelty mood stones." Sam pressed his finger against the glass, waiting until the heat changed the colour, when it didn't, he frowned. "Maybe it's broken?"

"Hmm," Alice mumbled, pulling her arm back before he noticed there was no clasp.

"Mood rings are cute," Ash said with a quiet smile. "My old boyfriend bought me one when he was unhappy with my mood swings. We discovered that when I was in a good mood, it was green. When I was in a bad mood it left a big red mark on his forehead."

"Well, maybe he should have bought you a diamond?" Sam snorted, opening the bottle of red wine and pouring three glasses, his own only half full. "A toast!" He held up his glass. "To new friends." He nodded towards Ash. "And to water aerobics with sexy as sin men." His eyes glittered at Alice.

Ash grinned. "Do you have plans to meet him again?"

Alice smiled into her glass. "He invited me to a dinner this Saturday, the restaurant that's at the Lunar Wharf."

"Does that mean you took my advice and went to see him the other day? Did something sexy happen?"

"Sam..." she said, her voice a warning as she hid her smile.

"Wait! This Saturday?" Sam choked on his wine. "As in

169

the celebratory dinner for the new Arch Druid?"

"Ah yeah, that's the one."

"You do realise it's one of the biggest events this year?" Sam rubbed his hands together in anticipation. "As in, will be blasted over every magazine available. Think of all those pictures. Do you know what that means...?"

"Wait..."

"That means we get to go shopping for a gown!"

"Wait, hold on. I don't need a gown."

Fuck! Do I?

"Of course you need a gown," Sam tutted.

"I thought it was just a dinner?" Alice sipped her wine as her stomach rolled, nausea coating her throat. She hated the idea of being in magazines, especially as the date as one of the most eligible bachelors in the city. She had no interest in being tabloid gossip, not when she had everything else to deal with. "Maybe I should just cancel."

"What? No you have to go! It is a dinner, it just has the whole Council in attendance as well as a few other people. You'll enjoy it."

Ash slowly reached over, gripping her hand in his. "You'll be fine."

Will I?

Ash released her hand with a last squeeze, his phone buzzing beside him. "I'm sorry guys, I've been called into work."

Sam paused, a slice of garlic bread halfway to his mouth. "I'll walk you to the door."

Alice nibbled the pizza as Poe curled himself around her feet, a warm lump that purred. "Do I really need a new gown?" she moaned loud enough for Sam to hear. "Can't I wear something I already have?" It was only a dinner.

"Alice," A deep voice said from the doorway.

Her head snapped up. "Dread?"

His dark, obsidian eyes shone when she came over, his arms automatically crushing her when she raised her own. She wasn't used to affection from him, but the hug was welcome.

"Where have you been?" She hadn't heard from him in weeks. "Leaving a voicemail stating you'll be gone for a while and not to worry, doesn't make me not worry!"

"You should have called," Sam stated, his usual smile gone as he sat back down to dinner.

"I'm sorry," Dread said, releasing her to take a seat. "I've been back in Paris." He opened the red wine, pouring himself a glass. His face was composed, hiding his emotions but the creases, which he received before the turn, seemed deeper than usual. As if he had aged, which was something vampires didn't do. His hair, usually cut close to his scalp had grown out an inch, the colour the same dark shade as his bushy eyebrows that dominated his otherwise hair-free face.

"Why did you go back to Paris?" Sam asked as he not-so-subtly pushed the plate of garlic bread closer to Dread, who raised an eyebrow and ate one piece.

Alice smiled at the exchange, reminding her of the last time she saw Dread eat, which at her seventh birthday party when Sam challenged him to eat cake. Vampires usually didn't eat physical food, their nourishment coming solely from blood. So it was a great memory watching a vampire, who terrified the other kids and parents eat the pinkest cake with sprinkles. He even had frosting on his nose for the rest of the party, something neither Sam or Alice pointed out, but he later told her he was aware, deciding to leave it there for her amusement.

Dread was one of the scariest men she had ever met, his

demeanour cold, hard and strict, someone who once organised some of the strongest men and women under the Supernatural Intelligence Bureau. Yet he left bright pink frosting on his nose because it made a young child smile on her first birthday without her parents.

"I didn't go back by choice," he said, voice the softest she had ever heard it. "Never by choice would I leave you in such a tense time. I was trying to convince Valentina to forfeit the trial."

"What do you mean the trial?" *Shit. Shit. Shit.* "What exactly did you offer in return?"

Dread sipped his wine, taking his time before he answered. "It doesn't matter, because she didn't accept. But it confirmed my suspicion that she has an ulterior motive, as do the others, I'm sure."

"Dread, what trial?"

"The Council have decided to test your abilities in a trial to determine how dangerous you are."

"Alice is hardly dangerous," Sam said around a mouthful of pasta. "Look at her!"

"The Council believe she could be a threat." Poe attempted to jump onto Dread's lap, his daisy cone hitting the side of the table before he crashed ungracefully to the floor. "A cat?" Dread stared down as Poe stared back, a loud yowl begging for attention.

"Yep, she's a real witch now," Sam commented, but didn't smile.

"Dread, what did you find out about the trial?" Alice pushed her plate away, her appetite vanishing at Dread's defeated look. "Is it bad?"

"There have been two previous trials brought forward by The Magicka, but never by The Council. Both the participants failed."

"What happened when they failed?"

Dread hesitated, his attention on Poe who had started to purr by his feet. "You need to run."

"What?"

"What?" Both Alice and Sam said in unison. "You can't be serious."

When Dread remained silent she let out a frustrated growl. "I'm not running, not from The Magicka, not from The Council, not from anyone."

"I thought you would say that." Dread gave her a weak smile.

"I thought the whole point of training with Riley was to prepare her?" Sam pushed his own plate away. "Is this what he was preparing her for? The trial?"

"We never knew what the training was for exactly, except to help her control. But, the training may not be enough." Dread stood, his hand automatically adjusting his waistcoat. "Frederick is going to trick you into failing, of that I'm sure. He's always wished for more power, and here you are, a pretty little witch he can manipulate and control."

"Who says he can manipulate and control me?"

"I'm sorry, I must leave in case they believe I'm giving you an advantage." Dread moved towards the front of the house, Alice and Sam running after him. "You have some more time, not much, but enough to prepare."

"Wait, you can't leave! Prepare what?"

Dread paused, the cool air flirting through the open door. "Don't underestimate Frederick, Alice. Don't underestimate any of The Council, they may be a collective, but they all have their own intentions when it comes to power. And even untrained, you are a power none of them has ever experienced."

CHAPTER 20

The grimoire growled beneath her fingertips, the pages rustling as it tried to close before she had even finished reading the spell. She had caught Jordan in her neighbours garden again, just facing into their house like an eerily happy peeping Tom. Which was worse was she had actually locked him in the cupboard, and he had somehow broken the lock and escaped. So not only did she have a gnome sucking peoples auras, she had a broken cupboard to match the ones Xander had melted. Which was just perfect considering they had painted the kitchen only a few weeks ago.

Okay, Sam had painted. She had just watched and cheered him on while eating ice cream.

"Stop it!" she scolded the book as a page moved and cut her. A single drop of blood fell, the paper absorbing it instantly. "Bloody thing!"

She wouldn't be looking in her mother's dark grimoire if she could find a suitable spell in any of her others. Unfortunately, a sort-of-haunted gnome wasn't that common according to the internet, so that hadn't really been a help either unless she went on some questionable websites.

With a tut she checked her phone, hoping Peyton had replied to her text for help.

Nothing. She couldn't even get hold of Alistair, the man who owned Jordan before he decided he liked her more.

Poe hissed in the corner, ears flat and back arched as it faced Jordan who had his back to the room.

"You're not helping!" she said to her cat, as if he could understand her. "Hissing isn't going to work now, is it? We need to remove whatever thing is haunting him and put it in this bottle." Alice held up the glass bottle, shaking it so it caught Poe's attention.

Poe just hissed again.

Alice rolled her eyes, a smile curving her lip at the sight of the small black cat trying to look as threatening as possible, with its head surrounded in a bright yellow daisy.

Sentient Spell

Can be used to remove someone's thoughts, ideas, consciousness and, or soul and trap it.

Alice reached for a pen, carefully removing the word soul before she continued. She hoped the spell would be able to trap Jordan, at least temporarily so he would stop eating her neighbours until she was able to figure out what to do with him. She had thought about smashing him, but was unsure if that wouldn't make the situation one-hundred times worse.

WHAT YOU WILL NEED:
10 Rowan Bark shavings

50 grams Mandrake
~~One~~ Two flower heads Datura
One flower head Henbane
One flower head Belladonna
250ml of boiling water
~~Salt pentagram~~
Salt concentric circle (around 30cm in diameter) with
internal pentagram
~~Metal~~ Copper pot
Glass bottle
DNA from focus
Five incantation candles
Medium sacrifice

Alice bit her lip, nervous at the 'medium sacrifice.' Even in her mother's cursive handwriting, it looked dreadful.

"What even is a medium sacrifice?" she asked Poe, who barely acknowledged her. "What classes as medium?" She poked at the dead mouse her cat had gifted her that morning. She hated the idea of ever using a sacrifice, but surely using one that was already dead wasn't too bad? Black and earth magic had a rigid dichotomy, black being malicious compared to the benevolent earth. Yet her mum created spells that seemed to be in shades of grey. At least, that was the way she had decided to see it.

"I would say this is a medium mouse, wouldn't you?"

"Meow."

METHOD:

Draw two concentric circles, filling in the gap with the appropriate runes of protection. Inside, create the usual pentagram making sure the points touch the inner circle.

Alice carefully drew the exact design her mother marked on the corner of the page. The chalk scraped against the tiled floor before she finished off by adding a layer of salt onto the lines, strengthening the connection. The kitchen was the only room she was able to create a decent circle, the earth solid beneath her feet to help the elements anchor.

Poe growled, his butt still in the air as he perched himself on one of the chairs she had pushed against the wall, continuing to stare at Jordan in the corner.

Set the five candles on the elemental points of the pentagram, lighting them in sequence to close both the circles. Light them in order starting with the anchor points, Earth, then fire. Next light air, and then water as the magic flows through the space. Finish with spirit to close.

Alice followed the basic instructions, quickening each flame with a drop of her blood. A pop, the tiles around the salt cracking as the circle glowed.

"Shit. Shit. Shit!" Alice shuffled back, the grimoire balanced on her knees as she watched the circle permanently scar itself into the tiles. "Sam is going to kill me!"

He had been working so hard to make the house that still held nightmares a home for them both, a haven. And she had just created a spiderweb of cracks in the centre of their kitchen.

Alice closed her eyes, taking a deep breath. *'And even untrained, you are a power none of them has ever experienced.'* Dread's statement floated through her mind.

"Yeah... untrained." She had always called herself an earth witch, preferring to experiment with charms, amulets and potions rather than arcane even though she had never studied above high school. Her fire was different, it came

177

naturally to her ever since she was a child. It was arcane, in a sense. But stronger. Unique.

She wasn't really an earth witch like her mother, was she?

Alice glanced back down at her mother's handwriting, staring at her own scribble as 'soul' peeked through the hard lines. Maybe her mother wasn't simply just an earth witch either.

Burn the Rowan bark until there is nothing but ash, adding this into the boiling water. With the copper pot placed in the centre of the pentagram, add the flora before pouring the ash/water mixture over the top. Add the sacrifice and place the glass bottle, lid removed at the top of the pentagram.

Break the DNA sample into five pieces, adding it into the mixture piece by piece while repeating the incantation.

Anima mea inu speculsium

Once the final piece has touched the water quickly close the lid of the bottle, trapping the soul inside.

Alice followed the instructions before she picked up the chunk of painted terracotta Sam had forgotten to glue back on, breaking it into five chunks. Scanning the instructions one more time, she gently dropped the first piece into the boiled water.

"*Anima mea inu speculsium.*"

An ear-splitting scrape, like nails along a chalkboard. Jordan had moved towards her, almost as if he was pulled by an invisible hand.

Alice added the second piece.

"Anima mea inu speculsium."

Another screech as he moved forward.

A cupboard door slammed open, a single plate falling and smashing to the floor.

Third piece.

"Anima mea inu speculsium." Jordan moved closer, but turned so he was side on.

Fourth piece.

Anima mea inu speculsium." Jordan turned once again, barely an inch away as his smiling face stared at Alice.

Final piece.

"Anima mea inu speculsium."

Every cupboard opened as a roar of wind shot through the room. Poe screeched, scrambling against the tiles as he tried to run away. Alice reached forward, scooping him up and into her arms as a black cloud surrounded the gnome.

"Lid! Lid! Lid!" Alice crawled to the lid, screwing on the top just as the entire contents of her shelves fell to the floor.

Alice stared, open mouthed at the shattered remains of every plate and mug she owned. The glass bottle remained unscathed, the dark cloud trapped inside. It crashed itself against the glass, creating little cracks.

"Shit. Shit. Shit." It wasn't going to hold, but would have to do for the moment.

"Meow!"

"Yeah..." she began, an hysterical laugh tickling her throat. "This looks like something we're going to have to deny later."

CHAPTER 21

S am stroked the store front window, eyes bright with excitement. "What about this one?"

Alice huffed, arms crossed as she observed the bright red dress with train. "I want to blend in, not stand out." She hated shopping, especially when it was for her. Sam, on the other hand, loved it. "Besides, it's way too much!"

"Let's just take a look in here anyway," he said, pulling her inside as she groaned. They had been looking for a dress for over an hour, every single one either not her style or out of her budget. Which wasn't much to begin with.

Why can't I just wear something that's in my wardrobe again?"she grumbled, tired and bored. "I can't afford it anyway." She needed to replace the entire contents of her kitchen.

She was better off than she was working for S.I, but that didn't mean she had money spare to spend on a dress she would never wear again.

"I wouldn't have agreed to this bloody dinner if I had to

wear something like that..." she gestured to a glittery monstrosity that took pride of place in the front window.

"Stop moaning, you need to look beautiful." Sam beamed at the sales assistant, her own smile glowing at the attention. "Besides, we both know how boring your wardrobe is. There are other colours than black and grey, you know. Now get into that dressing room and strip, I'll find a dress you'll love. Trust me."

"Ugh, fine." She stormed behind the single dressing room curtain, muttering to herself along the way. "This is the last shop!" She was sure a skirt and a nice top would suffice.

"Hey, what about this one?" Sam said as he held out a baby pink dress.

Alice poked her head through the curtain with a scowl. "I would get more coverage wearing your Gran's net curtain!"

"We both know I haven't seen my Nana since I was a wee lad. Besides, you're being dramatic. It clearly has strategically placed flowers," he teased with a grin. "It's sexy slutty, it's exactly what will get you in the papers as worst dressed."

Alice glared, waiting patiently for him to hand her one that was appropriate. She had no interest in being in the papers. The whole idea of being photographed brought her out in hives.

"Fine," he rolled his eyes at her less-than-impressed expression. "Try this, and it's even in your favourite colour."

"Black, like my soul," she smiled as she carefully stepped into the lace dress, the fabric soft. The lace was delicate, hinting at her skin beneath while still remaining elegant with thin spaghetti straps, a deep, yet not overly exposing neckline and a tulle skirt that came out gently at her hips. Beads decorated the bodice, ones that glittered underneath the lights and slowly blended into the layered skirt.

"Hey, I think you're on to something Sam!" she said, admiring her reflection.

"Did you ever doubt me?"

Alice pulled back the curtain, stepping out before her jaw hit the ground and laughter exploded from her throat.

"Don't I look fabulous?" Sam posed in the silver glittery monstrosity she had pointed out when they had first walked into the store. She had no idea how he had fit into the tiny thing, the fabric stretched across his wide chest while the tassels barely covered his important bits.

"What can I say..." she said through laughter. "It suits you, especially with the t-shirt underneath and the princess style puffed sleeves." With his trousers stuck by his ankles, Sam hadn't gotten all the way undressed.

He grinned, eyebrows wiggling. "And that, baby girl, is the dress you're wearing tomorrow night." He tilted his head, examining the fabric at her hips. "It's fitted in the right places, yet loose enough to strap your knives beneath the layers."

"You know me so well." Alice turned in the mirror beside him, checking out the back. He was right, it would easily conceal two knives strapped to her thighs. The only problem was she would have to flash the world to unclip them, which in all honesty, she had done before anyway. She doubted that if the situation arose and she needed the weapons anybody would take offence at a quick flash of knicker.

Alice cringed at the idea. *I'll just have to wear nice knickers.*

"Go take it off while I sort the price," Sam mumbled,

distracted as a tall brunette walked over, fluttering her eyelashes.

Only Sam could attract a date while he was both dressed in an ugly sequined dress, and undressed at the same time.

With a sigh Alice let the dress drop from her shoulders. She knew if the shop didn't display their prices, she couldn't afford it.

"Sam, you ready to go? I need to try and contact Kyle again." She had to tell him about the sun tattoo down in Kings Garden, but he wasn't answering her scry.

Alice carefully placed the dress on the counter.

"Sam?" He wasn't on the shop floor.

"Aye, I'm ready," he said when he appeared from a back room, a lipstick smear on his neck while the tall brunette followed behind with a quiet smile. Without a word she carefully folded the dress and put it into a box. With a pen she wrote down a number on top before handing it over to Sam.

"Hope to do business again soon, sir," she all but purred.

Sam winked as he ushered Alice out the door and back into the high street, the box tucked neatly under his arm.

"What was that?"

"What was what?" He rubbed at his neck, removing the lipstick. When he noticed her scowl he laughed. "Don't worry, I already paid for the dress. I was just checking out the... extras."

"Sam, I can't afford something like that. How much did it cost?"

"Oh, only one of my kidneys and half a lung," he smiled as he nudged her with his arm. "Don't worry about it, it wasn't as expensive as it looked and I've been making some great tips lately."

"I'll pay you back. Just add it to everything else."

"Not going to happen, baby girl. Besides, I already said we don't need mugs or plates. Plastic is the future... or maybe paper? More sustainable that way." He chuckled, opening the car door and placing the box neatly on the back seat. "I doubt you could destroy paper. Besides, it's my gift to you. You deserve a treat with all this shit going on." He patted the roof, both ignoring the rust as it fluttered to the floor.

She loved her car, one of the first things she had ever bought with her own money. But the car clearly didn't love her back. She had attempted to save the Beetle by painting a safety ward onto the back bumper she had found on the internet, beside the scraped off bad luck spell. It hadn't worked though because it was only the next day when the brake light fixture fell off and cracked. She had to reattach it with duct tape.

"I..." she began, before she was interrupted by her phone. "Shit, it's Brady." With a click of a button she answered. "Tell me there hasn't been another homicide?"

"Agent Skye, have you heard from Detective Peyton in the last twenty four hours?"

"Not since he dropped me home the other night." She frowned, remembering he never texted her back, which was unusual for him. "Is there something wrong?"

"We're not sure, he's gone AWOL. He was supposed to report in two hours ago but we can't seem to get hold of him. We've just found his car parked under the motorway leading out of the city towards Waycastle."

"Was there a sign of a struggle?"

"The car's been torched."

"Shit. Can you triangulate his phone?"

"It pinged three hours ago within a mile radius of the Breed District. Nothing since."

Alice looked towards Sam, who through his leopard heard every word. "Okay, I'm going to check somewhere out, I'll let you know if I find anything."

———

Alice hit the brick wall with her hand. "Fuck," she cursed, hitting it again.

She had left Sam by the car, parked several streets over while she had ran the rest of the way to the Three Headed Dog. But, what she hadn't anticipated was the two lanterns not to be lit.

"Fuck sake, it's only just after five, surely you bloody faeries like to party harder than that?"

"Who you calling a faerie?"

Alice froze, slowly turning to find the voice.

"Up here short arse!" the voice chuckled.

On the left lantern a pixie sat, legs swinging.

"Did you really just call *me* short?"

The pixie rustled his wings, the sharp sound accompanied by a cloud of glitter. "What are you doing here witch? You weren't exactly welcomed with open arms last time."

"I need to speak to Ilzake, it's an emergency."

"What do I look like? An errand boy?" He tugged at his bright blue jacket, the lapels stitched in a contrasting motif.

"Please..."

"You called." A man stepped through the wall, even though it remained solid beneath her palm. "Witch, what has made you bang at my door?" The man was tall, with a square jawline, sharp cheekbones, and eyes that made her hesitate.

185

"Ilzake?" she asked. His gaze was dark, the iris' almost black.

The man grinned, showing off blunt, human teeth. "Trevan," he barked, looking up towards the pixie. "Why are the lanterns off?"

"I didn't think you wanted the witch inside, boss."

Ilzake dismissed him with a flick of his hand. "Get back to work, Trevan, before you cost me more money."

"On it, boss!" Trevan lit both lanterns before flying through the brick.

"Now," Ilzake purred, turning towards Alice as if he were a predator looking at prey. "What can I do you for?"

"I need to know where Peyton is, and I'm hoping you've heard of something."

"What makes you think I know?"

"Surely you've heard something?" she asked, standing her ground as he stepped closer. She made herself rigid, even as he leant down to sniff her neck.

Oh, please let him know where Peyton is, she thought as she slowly palmed a knife.

"What's in it for me?" he asked, his breaths coming out in puffs against her throat.

"Me making sure he returns your favour."

Ilzake's sudden laughter startled her. "You have no idea who he is, do you?" he mused, stepping back. "A recent recollection tells me where he is, little witch. But in return I want a memory, a painful one." His hand shot forward to grab her hand, his fingertip brushing down the crescent scar on her palm. "This memory."

Alice licked her lips. "What do you do with the memory?"

"Whatever I want, it will become my memory. Maybe sell it on, or keep it for my own amusement." His finger continued to stroke the length of the scar. "You keep the memory yourself, only it's slightly muted. You would no longer feel the emotions remembered, no pain, or sadness."

Shit.

"Do it."

As soon as the confirmation left her tongue his hand glowed red, the memory of how she received the scar flashing through her head.

He grabbed Alice's left wrist, holding it immobile in his large hand.

"The blood of your mother was corrupted by that druid, useless." A long nail cut across the delicate flesh at the crease of her wrist, blood pooling along the wound. "But with your life force, we will Become. The blood of the dragon, the blood of war." His head hovered over her wound, an intimate bloody kiss.

Her flesh tore as she pulled her arm free from his teeth.

A slow smile, his canines covered in red.

A scream built up, Alice only just preventing the noise from escaping as Ilzake let go.

"It'll pass in a moment," he said, tilting his head to look at the blue ball of flame that popped into existence beside her.

Alice tried to calm her pulse as adrenaline shot through her body, causing her to shake. Her scar unpleasantly tingled, but didn't ache as she expected it to.

"If you ever want to sell more of those, you know where to find me," Ilzake grinned, his teeth covered in blood, before she blinked the memory away. "I'll offer you a great exchange rate."

"Where's Peyton?" she asked, her voice raw as if she had actually screamed.

"What has arms but cannot feel?"

Alice paused. "A clock?" she answered, even as realisation hit her. "Oh fuck!"

"**M**ummy?" His sister called gently, voice wet as she struggled with the kitchen door. "Daddy?"

His heart was a rabbit in his chest, almost painful as he tried to control his panic. The man who hurt his mother stepped back, an unpleasant smile curling his lips as he stalked after his sister.

"Come here little girl," the man snarled, followed by her scream.

He couldn't wait any longer, couldn't risk his sister coming to harm.

He smacked his head back, knocking his captive hard enough to release him. He called to the closest ley line, felt its power course through his body without an anchor as he tried to summon arcane. A splitting pain hit his head, forcing him to his knees as the untrained power seeped away.

His mother continued to stare blankly, eyes weeping, yet held no recognition.

"Stay quiet, or else," his captive threatened, his features dark, mostly hidden in shadow.

"Amon, she's escaped into the garden," the man who followed his sister scowled.

"Well go fucking get her then, Cali."

Cali huffed, but left as Amon the shadow moved towards his mother, slapping her with the back of his hand. She gave a bones-chilling scream that rattled his already sore head. He tried to get up, a foot kicking him back down just as he had climbed to his feet.

"Hmmm," Amon smirked. "Go outside and call your sister. If you bring her inside, I won't slit your mothers throat." He emphasised his words by cutting a thin line

189

across her skin. His mother whimpered, but didn't flinch as her eyes remained vacant.

"Mum..." he began before Amon cut deeper. "What's wrong with her?"

His voice seemed to rouse her, her face creasing into a frown as her shaking hand hesitantly touched the blood seeping down her neck.

"Go," Amon snarled. "Or else."

CHAPTER 22

The car door slammed, echoing loudly across the vacant street as Alice ran through the puddles and down the side road. It was getting late, the lampposts attracting various flying insects while the dark sky threatened more rain.

"I told you to wait by the car!" she snarled at Sam, who had kept up with her quick strides with little effort.

"You have no weapon and no backup," he argued, his amber eyes glowing as he channelled his leopard.

"Back up is on the way." She had called Brady as soon as she could, but he was on the other side of the city, and it was rush hour. "I also have a knife." It had gotten to the point she wouldn't leave the house unarmed, which just showed her life had taken a pretty sad turn.

Sam shot her a dark look, his canines on full display.

"Don't you dare go all dominant on me, Samion Murphy!"

The door to 'It's About Time Antiques' was locked, the lights inside shut off just like the rest of the shops down the street. Alice patted down her jacket, panic setting in when she realised she didn't have her lock picking kit.

"Fuck." She hadn't had time to return home to retrieve her blade or the kit, not when Peyton hadn't been heard from in over three hours and there was a crazy person going around cutting out people's hearts.

Alice started to look around, hoping to find something, anything she could use to open the door.

With a crash Sam kicked forward, the wood crashing off its hinges with a loud bang.

"That's one way to do it." She held out her arm, keeping him from stepping inside. "Stay here, I can't go in there and worry about you too."

With a reluctant growl, Sam agreed.

The antiques were just as bland as before, the colours even more muted in the dark as the continuous ticking of the clocks set her on edge. Light penetrated through from a door in the back, a thin sliver that illuminated the faces of several porcelain dolls, their blank eyes following her progress across the floor. A turntable played a few seconds of an old song, before it skipped and started again, repeating the process.

Alice gently pushed the door, finding rickety old stairs that squeaked at every step. By the time she had made it to the top a voice filtered through, one she recognised.

"STOP! Agent Skye of the Metropolitan Police." Alice held her knife with both hands, a circle of blue flame surrounding the tip. She had stepped into what looked like a large storage room, with floor to ceiling cardboard boxes pushed against the walls. Across the room was Peyton, bare chested and strapped haphazardly to a table. His chest was a flash of red, blood dripping to the floor in a regular pattern.

Large red blobs surrounded him. The missing hearts, more than what she was expecting.

"Peyton?" she called out.

He didn't react, his hand limp as it hung off the side.

"Peyton?"

Fuck. Fuck. Fuck.

"No!" The shopkeeper squealed, holding his hands in the air, a bloodied knife held in his right. "She's mine, I must make her whole again. She told me to!"

"Rupert," she said calmly as he began to shake, sweat drenching his brow. "I need you to put the weapon down."

"No, I can't until I'm finished," he cried, gripping the knife harder. "Not until I'm finished."

Rupert, darling, just a little more...

Alice heard the feminine voice float through her head, the accent unusual, yet reminding her of Peyton. Her eyes immediately settling on the beautifully hand carved box behind Rupert, the wood covered in dry blood.

Oh shit, that can't be good. If Alice could hear her, she was regaining her power, absorbing the life force from the hearts.

"Hey, hey, look at me," Alice said as he turned towards the table behind, using the bloodied knife to carefully remove a large stone from the front of a leather-bound book.

"The blood of a Rìoghail is needed," he mumbled to himself, but he turned to face her, the stone in his palm. A song tumbled out of his throat, the words alien as she felt pressure in her head.

"Hey, stop!" she shouted, taking a step forward as he dipped the stone into Peyton's bloody chest. He carefully dropped it into the first indent on the box, the stone glowing as soon as it settled.

With a wheeze one of the hearts beside Peyton shrivelled before turning black.

Only a little more, Rupert. Then we can be together, the husky voice said.

Rupert grinned just as blood began to drip from his nose.

Alice jumped forward, knocking the knife from his hand with little effort. Rupert crumpled to the ground, his arms shielding his face.

"Please don't hurt me!"

"Stay down!"

Peyton still hadn't moved, his chest cut to pieces with chunks of muscle exposed to the air. With a quick flick she cut along his bindings, releasing his arms and legs before she carefully felt for a pulse, her own beating loudly. His hair was back to his natural silver, the colour washing him out even more.

"Please, please, please," she whispered as Rupert sobbed by her feet, rocking back and forth.

Peyton's pulse was there, but weak.

"Rupert, go stand by the wall."

He ignored her, his sobs wracking his body violently.

He's almost gone, darling, the woman's voice sang. *Not long now.* A chuckle.

Alice turned the table, the box beside an intricately designed dagger with a large stone decorating its hilt, and a gold necklace. The Book of Shadows lay forgotten on the other side, its stone already removed leaving a dark hole in the leather. Using her own knife she tried to remove the glowing stone from the box.

With a flash of light she was thrown across the room, her knife burning the flesh of her palm as she crashed into a pile of boxes, losing her grip on the blade. As she climbed back up Rupert stared, his face puffy and tear stained.

"You can't stop her from coming," he said, an almost sad twist to his lips. "She will come eventually."

Rupert, darling...

"Rupert, don't listen to her, think about what you're doing," Alice said calmly, her boot carefully searching for her blade.

But Rupert, the voice purred, *think of all those people you've killed already. For me...*

"I can't go to jail." Rupert panicked, his eyes wide as he reached into a box and pulled out a rope. "I just can't." With a flick he threw it.

As she caught it automatically, the rope coiled around her arm, tightening like a python. She desperately tried to pull it off, but it only got tighter as it slowly slithered across her chest.

"No, no jail." Rupert reached for the Book of Shadows, opening to show a name scrawled across the entire page. "STUART!" he called, touching the faded name with his fingertip.

Alice struggled with the rope. "Please don't do this."

With a click of his fingers a quill appeared in his palm, the tip sharp as he dipped it in Peyton's blood before retracing the name on the page. "STUART!"

"Shit," Alice gasped, breathing laboured as her chest tightened. *"ADOLEBITQUE!"*

The rope snapped from the heat, dropping to the floor charred as heavy footsteps vibrated behind. The temperature from the rope scorched the wooden floor, embers sparking before she recalled the fire. The majority of the street's buildings were old wooden Tudor, if she let the fire get out of control, the whole place would go up in flames, including Peyton.

Alice spun just as a wall of muscle appeared at the door, eyes vacant.

"She's trying to stop us," Rupert squeaked. "Remove her."

Stuart reached forward, clamping his large palms on her upper arms and lifting her as if she weighed nothing. Alice fought, kicking out as he slowly walked her across the room. With a thrust her back shattered the window, showering shards of glass across them both.

She scrambled on the ledge, her toes barely touching the thin slice of wood.

"Stuart?" She felt her chi ignite, flames sparking at her fingertips as she struggled in his grip. "I don't want to hurt you." Cold air whipped at her hair.

He can't hear you...

His name was in the book, his body and soul out of his control.

"ARDENTI TURRIS!" A spiral of fire uncurled from her fingertips, seeking the book. But it was out of eyesight, the magic not understanding where she wanted it to go. "Shit."

She wiggled, his hands clamping down harder as he lifted her higher.

"Ventilabis!" A wall of heat and fire erupted from her core, eating away at Stuart's flesh at impact. His skin bubbled, raising in lumps before bursting open and turning black. Yet, he held her as if he felt nothing, his features relaxed and eyes empty. It was hard to believe he was still alive.

"Let go!" Bone appeared through his skin, tendons snapped and flesh melting as if it were wax.

A flash of blonde as Stuart was tackled like a rugby player, hard enough his hands were wretched free and Alice dropped like a stone. She gripped the window frame, trusting her reflexes as her feet climbed on the ledge. She swung herself inside, ignoring the pins and needles as blood rushed back to her upper arms.

"STUART! GET THEM!" Rupert screeched, the second stone in his hand.

I'm almost there...

Rupert placed the stone, blood dripping from his ears when he turned, eyes wide. "Stuart?" He reached for the book.

Another wheeze, another heart shrivelling.

A snarl as Sam was thrown across the room, his features sharp as his leopard threatened to shift. With a twist in the air he landed on his feet, his claws scratching indents into the floor to help slow his momentum. Stuart emerged slowly from beneath the pile of collapsed boxes, his neck broken at an impossible angle.

"I'll deal with him," Sam growled, his teeth sharpening.

Alice hesitated, her heart in her throat but she didn't have time to argue, not when she could hear Rupert panicking as he struggled to remove the last stone from its artefact. Sam wasn't trained, his shifter speed and strength only getting him so far.

"GO!" he snarled, jaw dripping saliva.

Alice ducked out the way, barely missing a meaty fist before Sam pulled at the arm, the limb dislocating with a strong tug.

"Shit!"

That's it, one more... Her voice whispered.

"I'm going as fast as I can," Rupert said, his hands shaking. "It won't come out."

Then break it.

Alice lunged forward, grabbing hold of Rupert just as the stone dislodged from Soulraise. With a twist he swung the dagger, the blade barely scraping her stomach as she jumped back.

She couldn't let it cut her, not even a scratch.

Fuck sake, she thought, looking around for something to block with. *Where's my bloody sword when I need it?!*

A sword you say darling? The box purred, her voice deep and sensual. *I think it's a bit late for that, don't you think?*

Alice snarled. *GET OUT OF MY HEAD!*

Rupert lifted the dagger, his grip tight.

"I'm a specialist in blades too," he said, his voice strained even as his nose and ears continued to bleed, red stripes that patterned his white shirt.

In his other hand he held the stone, the last one that would open the box. He relaxed his legs, spreading his stance as he took a deep breath. His arm steadied, eyes hard as he stabbed forward.

At the last moment Alice pulled at the loose restraints on Peyton, tangling Rupert's arm before twisting it behind his back. Her knee slammed into his legs, forcing him to collapse.

He hissed, the dagger still tight in his fist but the stone had slipped, clattering across the floor.

She looked up, searching for Sam to find him across the room, his mouth bloodied but otherwise unharmed. Stuart's head was barely attached to his neck, the skin stretched and raw. With a loud roar Sam sliced forward, forcing Stuart out the window with a sickening splat.

Rupert rocked forward, cutting the restraints from his arms as well as his skin. Words tumbled from his mouth, making her head pulsate before a burst of white light sent her skidding across the floor. She covered her head with her arms, eyes burning before she blinked to clear her vision.

Sam helped her up, just as she saw Rupert with his quill, the end dipped in blood. With a quick swish he wrote something on a blank page.

CHAPTER 23

"Dark Daeizan Raeron, I command you to destroy the witch and shifter."

Oh shit.

Peyton slowly sat up, his back facing them as blood trickled off the table.

"So, what's the plan?" Sam asked, his voice deeper, huskier when the leopard was in control.

Peyton turned, his chest seeping as the wounds gaped open, the cuts sliced in a clearly specific pattern. His eyes were vacant, expression empty as he bounced onto his feet as elegantly as any cat. A shrivelled heart fell beside him, his foot crushing it as he stepped forward.

Shit. Shit. Shit.

Sirens blared in the distance, loud enough she only needed to distract him for a short period of time.

"It's the book." Her eyes quickly fell on the artefact that had been placed on the table, open. "He's being controlled by the book."

Peyton tilted his head, his pale hair tainted pink as he began to sing.

"What's he doing?" Sam asked before he shrieked.

"SAM!"

Fur ripped through his skin, bones breaking and shifting as he transformed before her eyes in a matter of seconds.

"SAM?!" Peyton had forced his shift, something that was supposed to take a few minutes, not seconds. "Hey, hey?"

He hissed a growl, his bones clicking into place as he rolled his shoulders. His legs shook, unable to bear his weight before he collapsed to the ground, panting violently. With a groan he began to shift back.

Peyton approached, his words alien as they pulsated through her head. Pressure built with a dull pain, one matching the thumping of a drum beat. Wild magic flowed over her like water, poking and prodding, searching for a weakness.

Alice stepped over Sam. *"ARMA!"*

She threw out her hand, concentrating as her Aegis shield popped into existence around them. The molecule thin barrier strained against the roof, unable to anchor itself. It needed solid ground, but there was something beneath the floor that was blocking it.

Shit, it's not going to last, she thought, carefully checking Sam, his skin drenched in sweat. He was in mid shift, the grotesque transformation his most vulnerable as Peyton calmly stood on the outside, staring.

He reached up, pushing his hand against the shield, her aura shaping itself around his fingers rather than instantly repelling him.

In the background Rupert scrambled, searching for the stone.

Fuck sake! Alice cursed.

"This is going to hurt." Alice launched herself through the Aegis, her aura rebounding back as soon as she touched the shield. With all her weight she tumbled onto Peyton, bringing him down hard enough his head cracked against the floor.

The pressure continued to build inside her mind, all while the drums intensified and warmth began to drip from her ear. Peyton lifted his arms, moving it faster than her eyes could track to dislodge her with an ease that hinted at combat training. He was stronger than she thought, his movements fast and hard and difficult to block without hurting him. She couldn't risk any more damage, not when his chest continued to bleed, the colour turning to black at the deepest points.

FINISH THIS! The voice cried.

Alice made a run for the stone, Peyton's hand snapping out to grab her ankle and yank her off her feet. She stretched her right hand out, her left holding Peyton at bay as she searched for something to help. She touched a box, pulling it onto its side just as Peyton caught her with a right hook.

A blur passed, knocking the box closer.

Her hand gripped something cool to the touch.

"Sorry!" She smashed it against him, the expensive looking vase shattering on impact.

Tyres screeched through the broken window, the sirens deafening.

"ALICE!" Sam, fully naked with red skin that glowed with pain threw the book into the air before he immediately jumped out the way as Rupert swung Soulraise.

"ARDENTI TURRIS!" Her eyes settled on the book,

her flames concentrated as she felt the power leave her fingertips with a burst of heat. The fire crackled as it shot out, curling into a spiral that Peyton ignored as he swiped at her with a vase shard. "Fuck!" She purposely crowded him, barely dodging the sharp edge.

Her flames found the book, the pages disintegrating on contact.

As soon as his name was erased, Peyton collapsed, along with the pressure in her head.

"COME OUT WITH YOUR HANDS UP!"

Rupert squeaked at the guns pointed to him, his hand hovering above the box with the stone.

"PUT DOWN THE WEAPON!"

"Agent Skye?" Brady asked as he edged inside the room, his eyes never leaving Rupert even though she knew he was concerned for his partner. She had never been so glad to see his grumpy face.

Alice carefully settled Peyton's dead weight onto the floor before she moved forward, her hands raised in a nonthreatening way. "Rupert, I need you to give me the stone."

Sweat dripped from his forehead, his eyes wide as he brandished the dagger. "I can't," he croaked.

I'm almost here, Rupert...

"What the fuck was that?" an officer asked, looking around for the owner of the voice. "Did anybody hear that?"

Rupert swung the dagger.

A gunshot rung out.

Alice gasped at the sudden temperature drop, the intense cold chocking, constricting her throat. A cool wind surrounded her, lifting her hair and sending needles down her spine.

She blinked, trying to clear her vision, but it didn't change. She was in the same room, boxes stacked and piled with a shattered window, the glass glittering on the floor. But, everything was in shades of grey, cold, heartless.

She was alone. There was no Sam, who had just been by her side, or Brady or any of the other officers. Peyton was gone, only a puddle of black left where he had lain.

Alice tried to call out, her voice refusing to work as she breathed out a fine mist.

"Now what do we have here?"

Alice's eyes settled on the box, the last stone glowing in its position. Slowly, a black figure climbed out, tall and slim with a slight curve to her hips and breast. She reached down, grabbing a shrivelled heart and squeezing it with one hand until grey liquid dripped from beneath her fingers.

"Beautiful, isn't it? Such a simple life force."

Alice tried to step back as the feminine figure approached, but she couldn't move, her muscles frozen even though her body trembled. The black figure reached forward to touch her, causing her skin to crawl. Up close it had no features, no shadows or definitive shape to its face.

"I've been trapped in that forsaken creation for eons, unable to touch another living being." The sensual voice was soft as she brushed her fingertips across Alice's jaw, then her lips and cheek. "Oh how I've missed it," she said with a laugh.

Alice tried to speak again, her lips barely opening as her tongue froze inside her mouth.

"But I could hear, and I could sometimes talk to those of mine blood."

She cupped Alice's jaw, bringing her shadow face closer as she began to change. The tall figure made herself shorter, adding width to her hips.

Alice, with all her strength called her power, but she couldn't feel it, her chi empty. Gone.

"I don't remember my original name, it long forgotten by my own people." A nose started to appear, followed by the outline of her lips and eyes, the lashes dramatically long. "I have been named many things over time, from different civilisations and societies, but not once did someone succeed in freeing me. But one was whispered to me once..."

Alice tried her magic again, hoping for the comfort of her flame. But there was nothing.

She felt nothing.

"Pandora." The name sounded exotic with her curious accent. "Named after a beautiful woman who opened a box to release evil and plague across the earth. Fitting, don't you think?"

She paused, tilting her head.

"Do you want to know why I was put in that forsaken box?" She touched her lips to Alice's jaw, moving along her skin until she whispered into her ear. "Because I wanted something, and when I want something, I take it, destroying everything in my way."

Alice felt her hand stick into her chest, phantom fingers pushing beneath her flesh.

"And I need a body, darling. And it looks like yours is the only one..." Her fingers pressed forward, curling around Alice's heart.

Alice blinked, the colours bright as noise overwhelmed her

senses. Sam appeared in her face, his skin ashen and covered in sweat.

"Hey, hey? You back?"

"Back?" Alice gasped, clutching her neck as she struggled to suck in a breath. Sam helped her to the ground, her head dropping between her knees as her heart beat heavy against her chest.

"Take a deep breath, that's it, in and out."

Her arms trembled as she closed her eyes, taking Sam's advice and concentrating on her breathing. When her chest didn't feel as tight she looked up, finding Brady applying CPR to Peyton. "What happened?" she croaked.

"Rupert dropped the stone and it landed on the box," Sam replied, rubbing her back in circular motions. "You went weird, cold to the touch and unresponsive."

"And Peyton?"

"He woke up, said something strange then started to convulse." Alice wanted to check Rupert, but she couldn't tear her eyes away from Peyton, who remained lifeless on the floor.

"WHERE'S THE FUCKING PARAMEDICS?" Brady shouted, his face creased with worry, but he didn't miss a compression.

"Brady, his chest." Alice crawled, her limbs weak.

"His heart isn't beating." He continued his rhythmic movements.

Peyton was grey, his lips open slightly while his eyes remained closed. His chest was a mess, even worse with Brady pressing repeatedly and reopening each individual cut.

Before she even registered the movement her hand reached out, seeking Peyton's skin. As soon as her fingertip came into contact she felt heat burn from within, a searing force that leaked from her pores.

"Alice?" Sam gripped her shoulder before he stepped back with a hiss.

Her skin glowed, a golden shine that began to trickle on to Peyton. She felt a connection, the wild magic inside him dwindling.

'Witches can manipulate arcane and the elements. Something learnt. But Fae are magic.'

His words flared in memory. 'Fae *are* magic,' and his was fading.

"Brady I need you to stop."

"I can't..."

"You need to trust me." She looked him in the eye, hoping he would allow her to help his partner. "He's not human."

The realisation caused Brady's pupils to flare, his deep imbedded prejudice peeking through. Yet, he wouldn't stop the compressions. "I can't let him die."

"I won't let him." Her fingertips pulsed, the wild magic weakening with every second. "Brady, please, he's fading!"

With a final compression he growled. "Do it." Brady lifted away.

As soon as she had space she forced her aura into him, hoping it had more of an idea what to do than she did. She channelled the energy, her chi colliding with his wild magic with such force she envisioned thunder and lightning cracking inside his body. They were two different types of magic, hers powered by arcane and the elements, while his was an unpredictable storm older than anything she had ever felt before. It was raw, and powerful.

The bloody drums beat in her head as wild magic trickled through his fingertips, tangling with her own chi, curious. It wasn't *his* magic, it was something else, something almost sentient as it began to entangle itself back into Peyton's skin.

The wild magic snapped at her just as he took a deep breath.

CHAPTER 24

B eep. Beep. Beep. If Alice wasn't confident the machine was keeping Peyton alive, she would have happily shoved it out of the window.

Beep. Beep. Beep.

She had sat at Peyton's beside for over an hour, unable to look at him covered in wires and tubes. Instead she had plonked herself, cross legged in the most uncomfortable chair the hospital had to offer, with a plastic straight back and cracked seat that dug into her arse. But she couldn't complain, not really. So she instead had stared at her mood bracelet, the liquid inside the glass bead flickering from black to blue, then back again. She had no idea what any of the colours meant, if anything. It wasn't as if it came with an instructional manual.

Alice tapped it, wondering if it was broken.

To be fair, at that point, she was sure it was just fucking with her.

Beep. Beep. Beep.

Peyton sucked in a wet breath, causing another machine

to start making more repetitive noises that made her anxious. She had no idea how the doctors could decipher which beep meant what. They all sounded the same to her, like a tone deaf orchestra.

She recognised some monitors, ones she's been attached to regularly herself when she was being tested like a lab rat. Luckily for her, she hadn't turned up to an appointment for two months, essentially telling them where to shove their research. The Council had already made the decision scientific tests weren't enough. They wanted to know more, it was just unfortunate Alice had no idea what that 'more' was.

Another machine went off, but not as loud or alarming. Considering a nurse or doctor hadn't come rushing in, it must be okay. She hoped at least. It would really suck if after all that drama Peyton died because of some ridiculous error, and she had just sat there like an idiot glaring at a weird glass bead that taunted her with its colour changing ways.

A warmth grew in her chest just as Peyton turned his head, face tired before his eyes grew alarmed.

"Alice," he croaked, his voice hoarse. "What have you done?"

She could feel him, inside her like a slow burning furnace.

"Oh shit." She had never felt anything like it, but she was pretty sure what had happened. "I'm so sorry." She loudly scraped her chair closer to the bed. "I didn't mean to, I promise."

"Why can I feel you?" Peyton tried to sit up, his face pained as he struggled. Alice reached over to help when his power snapped out, an electric grey light that curled up her arm.

"I didn't know that it would happen!" She adjusted his bed before she sat back down, trying to shake off the wild magic in a slight panic. "I don't even know how it's done!"

"I'm your familiar, aren't I?" Peyton slowly reached out, his breath coming in pants as he absorbed his magic back.

Fae couldn't receive normal painkillers, their bodies unable to process them. Add that to the fact Peyton was an Elf, a Fae so rare the doctors had flustered when trying to type his blood. The general consensus was they had no bloody clue as it wasn't charted. But it also meant the doctors couldn't give him willow bark ash, which could only be administered through a blood bag.

"Can you reverse it?"

"I don't even know how it happened in the first place." The heat was comforting, but she could also feel the untouched power that was just as curious as she was. It was strange to think of Peyton and his magic as two different entities. "You were dying, your wild magic was fading so I panicked and pushed my aura through you."

Peyton stared at her, jaw clenched. "I can block it until we figure out how to fix it."

Alice let out a cry, the warmth she felt gone, leaving a cold, empty hole. "I'm sorry, I really didn't mean it."

"I know. I didn't even know it was possible. Our magic is too different." With a sigh, he relaxed back into his pillow. "I see you're not possessed." He closed his eyes, a frown creasing his brow before he looked up at the ceiling. "Where's her box?"

"Er..." She wasn't actually sure, her attention on Peyton as the paramedics had strapped him into the ambulance. "Probably in evidence by now. Rupert didn't make it."

"That's not surprising, she wouldn't have allowed him

to survive." He turned back to face her, his eyes sharp. "It will disappear soon, even if she's not in it."

"Is she out there then?" Alice remembered the feeling of phantom fingers around her heart, squeezing.

"She can be destroyed, just as she tried to destroy me."

"What are..." The room began to pulse, the anti-violence enchantment written high on the walls blurring as it activated.

Alice was up, plastic chair in hand before a man appeared with a pop, a weirdly curved sword held in front of him.

"Daeizan Raeron." The stranger bowed his head, his hair the same pale silver as Peyton's natural shade, his ears sharply pointed. He relaxed his arm, the sword dropping to his side as the writing relaxed.

Alice held the chair tighter. "Erm, hello?" She wasn't surprised the room thought of him as a threat, not with the wavy blade, the metal looking almost warped in the light and the dark blue scaled armour. It even had little horns down the arms.

The stranger shot her a disgusted look, his upper lip lifting to reveal short sharp canines. "You are dismissed," he replied with a heavy accent before turning to Peyton, speaking in an unfamiliar language.

"Dismissed my arse." She wanted to hit him over the head with the chair anyway, just on principle. But the agonising headache from the enchantment wasn't worth it. Probably. "Who are you?"

He ignored her, instead moving to remove the various equipment from Peyton.

"Hey!"

The man turned with a hiss. "Stand back from the Dark Prince."

Alice immediately stepped away, her jaw dropping. "Did you just say Dark Prince?"

Surely she hadn't heard that right?

The rumours were the Far Side, beyond the veil was ruled by the Dark King, who controlled half of the lands, and the Light Queen who controlled the other half. Within the courts there were two princesses and two princes for each faction. It wasn't known whether they were born into their roles, or chosen. But, according to the same rumour, royalty didn't leave their realm.

However, in typical Fae fashion, they never confirmed the rumour, nor denied it.

Peyton spoke softly, but his tone was harsh as he replied to the man in the same musical language. An argument ensued, one the stranger lost when he snarled, looking at Alice with an accusation.

"You have ten minutes," he said in a ostentatiously pompous tone. "Then we're going." He stormed out the room.

"So..." Alice couldn't help her awkward smile. "He seems nice. He a friend?"

"Elduin is my commander."

"Oh, so you're not only a Dark Prince, but you also have your own army?" Alice sat back into her seat, the plastic straining beneath her weight.

"You going to judge me for being Unseelie now?"

"No, I judged you way before that," she sniggered. "But I don't understand why you hide who you are."

Peyton shifted his head until his ear peeked through his hair, the top only gently pointed. "Glamour isn't always reliable, as you can see." He touched the silver strands, the colour almost metallic. "But it's easier to blend in, in my job, rather than stand out."

213

Alice pulled up her legs, resting her chin on her knees. "So you pretend to be human?"

"I've never pretended to be human, I just never said I wasn't."

A knock at the door, Brady's face peeking through the window.

"Looks like I'm getting replaced." She stood up, pushing the chair back against the wall. "Don't die, you still owe me from our last poker match."

A small smirk lifted his lips.

Alice stepped into the corridor, closing the door behind her. "Hey, did you get hold of Michelle?" His wife was getting close to her due date.

"Yeah she's fine. How is he?" Brady nodded at the door, arms crossed as his jacket strained against his shoulders. His gun was attached to his hip, on full display.

"He'll be fine, just a bit beaten up."

"The docs said they haven't treated an..."

"Elf."

"An elf before." Brady pinched the bridge of his nose. "I didn't even know elves existed. What sort of partner am I if I didn't even know his Breed existed?"

"They're not common." She hadn't known either, but wasn't going to admit it. It wasn't like she was some encyclopaedia on Fae, even though she was expected to be.

Brady dropped his hand, but clenched it into a fist. "How's Samion?"

"Sam's resting at home, whatever happened to him has left him exhausted." She had wanted him to get checked over at the hospital, but due to his fear he refused. "I'm heading home now to check on him."

Brady stared through the window into the hospital room.

"Detective?" Alice briefly touched his arm.

"Oh, sorry. Tell Sam I wish him well." He continued to stare through the window.

"He's the same person you know. He was just born different."

"I know," he smiled, the look almost alien on his permanently scowled face. "We've been on the force together for ten years, both in uniform together before I got promoted. The first official thing I did was ask him to be on Spook Squad." He turned to face her. "Thank you for saving my partner."

"Of course, we're a team." Alice squeezed his arm before she left, spotting a pissed off looking elf trying to figure out a vending machine. From his aggravated tone she guessed the vending machine was winning. "Oh. And Brady..."

He paused with his hand on the door handle. "Yeah?"

"Enjoy Elduin, he seems like a right character."

Brady frowned. "Who's Elduin?"

CHAPTER 25

Alice had been hyperconscious of Riley the whole car journey across London, every movement, every breath. They had sat beside each other, not touching, yet his chi caressed hers.

"Stop it," she whispered, her voice embarrassingly husky. "We're almost there." She had already debated whether she wanted to go to the bloody event, and Riley making her all hot and bothered beforehand wasn't helping.

The idea of being photographed for newspapers and magazines gave her heart palpitations. She had been to several events before, but she was always background noise, staff. She was never a pretty bauble attached to Riley Storm, one of the most sought after bachelors in the city. Luckily he was a private person, so never gave interviews or photoshoots unless he wanted to. But he was still photographed outside his office, or walking in the park, the dentist or something equally as mundane. The thought of losing her privacy was hard, especially with her history.

"Stop what?" he replied, giving her a deliciously slow smile.

The limousine pulled smoothly outside the Luna Wharf, lights flashing across the tinted glass almost immediately, spiking her anxiety. She fidgeted with her cosmetic ring, the charm concealing the beautiful bruise that had darkened her cheek. Peyton's right fist really left its mark, but she was grateful that the swelling had gone down, because that was a lot harder to hide.

"The last time I was on the news, I was almost sacrificed to a Daemon." Her crescent scar was a constant reminder.

"That can still happen," Riley chuckled, the door to the limousine opening. "I can make a call."

Alice wanted to scowl, but she couldn't help her smirk. "For our next date, I want greasy fast food and a bad movie." No paparazzi.

Riley hesitated, half out the door before he turned with a grin. "As long as you understand that there will be a second date." He stepped onto the cobbled street, his hand held out as she followed.

The lights were blinding, almost disorientating as Riley guided her towards the entrance. Photographers shouted, waved and begged for an exclusive.

"Who's the date?"

"What designer are you wearing?"

"Mr Storm! Mr Storm!"

Riley stopped to lean down, his breath against her ear. "You look beautiful tonight."

Alice felt her cheeks immediately curve. "Sam chose the dress," she whispered back, tugging him quickly through the archway and onto the wharf, out of the lens of the photographers.

"I know."

Alice looked at him expectantly.

"If it was left to you to decide, you would have worn a pair of jeans, boots and a T-shirt with something like, 'I'm sorry I'm late. I didn't want to come' printed on." He leant closer. "Your weapons would be on full display, with your sword strapped right here..." He stroked a finger down her spine. "And those daggers you so love..."

Alice laughed, the sound loud enough to get her an amused look from another guest. "Who says I'm not armed?"

Riley's eyes swirled, teasing liquid silver as his hands gripped her hips, pulling her closer. "Yeah?" Those hands started to search further down.

"Am I interrupting?" A cough.

"Yes," Riley said without turning. "You are."

"Speak to me with the respect I deserve," came the sharp reply. "Now where are The Guardians? I must introduce them." Bartholomew Edwards stood with a sneer, his mouth twisted in repugnance, stretching the scar on his chin. String light cast him with a yellow glow, making him look ill.

"*My* Guardians have decided not to attend this evening."

"What do you mean?" Councillor Edwards jerked his head, face flushed. "They were *told* to attend. Call them. Now!"

Riley stepped forward, almost a head taller. "Told? They're not puppies that sit and bark on your command."

"They are, and they will do as I say." Edwards smirked. "You know exactly what I can take away." His gaze slipped to Alice, the smile turning dark. "Remember that."

Alice calmly placed her hand on Riley's arm, the muscle tensed. "Congratulations on the new position,

Councillor. But acting like a big dick won't actually make yours bigger," she said, flicking her eyes down to emphasise her point. "I hope you'll do better than your predecessor."

Edwards began to choke on his own spit, his eyes bloodshot. "How dare you!" He tried to step closer, his path blocked by Riley. "Be careful, little witch. I've heard many interesting things about you, I wouldn't want my opinion to be biased when you have so much to lose." With a tut he spun, stomping inside just as the string quartet began to play.

"He seems nice," Alice mused as she watched him bark commands at an attendant. His angry snap carrying across the distance. "So this evening is to welcome him into The Council? Why couldn't it be private? Why all this fuss?"

"Because they want you to see them, know they're there and watching. They're the pendulum hanging over everyone's heads, just waiting to drop."

Alice felt eyes on her, her skin prickling at the attention. Xavier stood in the corner, head tilted as he stared unapologetically. His dark, tailored suit failed to hide his barbarian nature. His eyes were just too wild, too savage. When he settled on Riley his lip lifted in a silent snarl.

"Hey." She tugged on Riley's arm, uncomfortable with the attention. "Why would he want to introduce the Guardians?"

"We were created to be the monster of all monsters," he replied, jaw clenched. "Why wouldn't he want to show off his new power?" Riley bent down, his lips brushing her cheek in a gentle caress. "I have to deal with something, I'll be back in a moment."

"Okay."

The wind was cool against her bare skin, spring showers threatening in the sky above. The moon glittered off the

Thames, adding to the hundreds of string lights reflected in the calm water. They were draped across the wharf, blending into the stars while adding soft lighting to the otherwise hard decking.

She could hear the snaps of the paparazzi in the far distance, the yells and calls as other guests arrived while inside sounded like they were almost ready.

"How the bloody hell did you get an invite?" a slightly nasally voice whined. "Seems they let just anyone attend these days."

Alice had no need to turn to identify her old colleague, but did so anyway. "Hello to you too, Mickey."

"Erm, It's *Commissioner* Brooks," he muttered, tugging on his suit, two sizes too large. It was strange, but a familiar face was what she needed. Even if it was his.

"How's The Tower?" She still saw Rose, Bee and a few others, but their conflicting work schedules made it difficult.

He leant against the wall, a smirk curling his lips. "That's privy information. You're the competitor now."

"We do the same job, I'm just private." *And cheaper,* she wanted to add. "We both hunt down contracts."

"We shall see, I'm already in final talks with The Met to sort out a *real* Paladin for your Spook Squad. Then where will you be?" he laughed, the sound ending in a snort.

"What's so funny?"

Both Alice and Mickey spun as one, having not heard Valentina walk up. The vampire was barely five foot, but she still oozed a dangerous aura that Alice was cautious of.

"Oh," Valentina frowned, the expression making her look closer to a child despite the sharp suit she wore, the V of the neckline deep. She wore nothing beneath, the small curves of her breasts barely contained. "You're not wearing the necklace I gifted you."

Alice clutched her lapis lazuli pendant, wrapped tightly around her throat.

"Wait, you know each other?" The colour drained from Mickey's face.

Valentina turned her dark eyes to Mickey. "Tell me, what was so amusant that I heard your obnoxious noise from across the room."

Mickey gulped. "Oh, well..."

"It couldn't possibly be because you see Alice as competition? Non? Because surely the Commissioner wouldn't see a single woman as a threat?"

"No, no." Mickey flustered.

"Leave us," she dismissed him with a wave of her hand. "Now, Alice..."

"Councilman," Alice politely greeted, dipping her head.

"Ces manières," Valentina smiled, enough that her fangs appeared against the painted red of her lips. "I do look forward to seeing everything you can do."

"It would help if I knew what was expected of me." Alice was careful with how she phrased her words, not wanting to offend, but also needing answers.

"You will find out soon enough." She carefully reached forward, a single finger touching Alice's cheek. The skin ice cold. "If your heritage is true, then you'll be even more extraordinary than originally thought." Her fingernail sliced into skin.

"Alice?" Riley appeared beside them, his arm knocking Valentina with a burst of speed.

"It's just a scratch," her smile tightened. "An accident." She raised the fingernail to her lips, a pearl of blood on the end.

Riley pulled Alice against his chest, a snarl building in his throat. "Councilman."

"Well, isn't this interesting," she mused. "Your father would be most displeased."

"My father is dead," Riley replied, not caring about offending.

"Yes, such an unfortunate... accident," she smirked, a knowing glint in her eye. "But I'm sure Councilman Edwards will suffice at the trial."

"What is the trial?" Alice asked even as Riley squeezed her shoulder. "At least let me know that."

Valentina sucked in a heavy breath, highlighting the fact she hadn't breathed the whole time she was standing there. "Hmm, it's such a shame about Monsieur Grayson."

"Dread?"

"Alice," Riley whispered against her ear. "I think we should..."

"Yes, he was always loyal," Valentina interrupted with a slow smile. "It's such a terrible thing to be charged with treason."

CHAPTER 26

N ausea teased her throat as the sense of urgency grew.

"It's going to be fine," Riley repeated for the hundredth time as the limousine shot through London at a speed she thought was impossible for such a long car.

"Treason," she croaked. "Treason, Riley!" Dread was her father in everything but blood, the man who took in his best friend's daughter, and taught her to be strong. She couldn't lose him. "What did he even do?"

Riley squeezed her hand. "Alice..."

"Don't say it." The look on his face was tragic, something she refused to acknowledge.

With a tight nod they elapsed into silence, and remained that way until she recognised the street. Before the limo could even park she shot out, and ran to Dread's end of terrace townhouse, the front door hanging off its hinges.

"Dread?" she called into the dark interior. "Dread?"

Shoes crunched behind her. "Careful," Riley growled. "We're not alone."

"Put your hands up!" Two men stepped onto the drive, both with wands pointed.

"State your business." Riley turned his body so she was behind him. Usually she would have gotten annoyed at the macho shit, but then she wouldn't have been able to pull up her skirt to retrieve her dagger. At least without getting some strange looks. Or shot at.

As soon as the steel hit her palm she relaxed.

"Alice Skye?" Another voice, this time from behind, inside the house.

A hand grabbed her wrist before she could turn, trying to knock the dagger from her grip before she thrust her other fist into his throat. As he gasped for breath she hit him again, this time breaking his nose.

"PUT YOUR HANDS UP!"

Alice raised her hands in front of her chest, the dagger on full display. "Where's Dread Grayson?" Her adrenaline pumped, her chi responding in a burst of heat that she welcomed.

"Alice Skye, you have been charged with conspiracy to murder Frederick Gallagher. You will be held by The Magicka until a date can be set for your prosecution."

"This is bullshit," Riley growled. "This is just being used to disadvantage Alice at the upcoming trial."

"Sir, I'm going to need you to step away." The man to the left held his wand tighter, the end a bright red.

"Or what?" A threat.

"*Celeritatius imperium!*" A shot of arcane glowed from the tip of the wand, as quick as a bullet.

Riley deflected it with little effort, his tattoos flaring up beneath his clothes at the movement.

"Sir, step away or we will be forced to remove you."

"Shit," Alice cursed as she stepped forward.

Another two men appeared from her right, surrounding them.

"Was all this really necessary?" Seemed like bit of an overkill to have five Officers from the Department of Magic & Mystery.

"Miss Skye, hand yourself in now or we will use force."

Alice clenched her teeth. "Riley, what do we do?" They didn't exactly have many options.

"Edwards mentioned the trial is set for within the week, there's no reason for them to take you now. They're up to something."

"Yeah, no shit."

The man in the doorway seemed to cough up a lung, his nose crooked. That was the problem with the Magicka in general, they believed magic was superior to physical force when in reality some people just really needed a fist to the face.

"I have to go with them."

"No." His tone was absolute.

"Riley..."

"LAST WARNING! SIR IF YOU DO NOT STEP AWAY WE WILL TREAT YOU AS A THREAT."

"You know as well as I do The Councils influence. If I don't go they will use it against me Monday anyway."

"I don't think you understand," Riley growled. "I *can't* let you go."

"What did Edwards say exactly?" *Shit. Shit. Shit.* "I'm not supposed to pass this trial, am I?"

He hesitated long enough for her stomach to sink.

"Pelliturious somnum!"

Alice flung her arm out, but Riley turned so his back

caught the brunt of the spell. With a screech they were flung apart, her back hitting the brick with a crack. With a howl Riley transformed in a burst of colour, the beast snarling as it turned towards the closest officers.

"What the fuck is that?"

"What do we do?"

"We'll have to kill it."

Alice heard the chanting of a death curse. "NO!" She reached for the white fur, tugging on it. The black patterns that matched the tattoos of the man pulsed, power leaking from them as the beast tensed. "PLEASE STOP!"

Her shout got everyone's attention.

The beast turned his head, eyes pure silver, so clear they reflected her own image back at her. His tail separated, turning into several distinctive whips that gently curled around her waist, tugging her closer.

"He needs to calm down," she said with a deliberately soft voice, her fingers threading through his heavy fur, the sensation like silk. "You need to step back."

The closest officer hesitated, looking at the others. "Miss Skye, you need to come with us," he said in a tone matching hers. "We have orders."

"I know." She gently untangled herself from the tails.

A phone vibrated, the noise making everyone on edge flinch. Riley's clothes had disintegrated, but his phone had fallen onto the drive, along with his wallet. She went to answer when they threatened her with their wands.

Riley opened his jaws, showing off his large, sharp teeth.

She bent for the phone, relieved at the name. With a click, she answered.

"I don't have long to explain..." Alice began.

"Alice? What the fuck have you done?" Xander growled. "Why is he the beast?"

Alice rattled off Dread's address. "You don't have long to get here..."

"I swear, if you've hurt him..."

Alice hung up.

"Someone's coming to help." Alice carefully set down her dagger, kicking it towards the closest officer with the broken nose. He gave her a dark look, his face red and flushed.

"You've called backup."

"You either wait, or be eaten," she warned, continuing to stroke her fingers through the fur. Her left hand burst into flames, ready to use if they tried a death curse again. Something that was black magic, forbidden by The Magicka themselves. Yet the officers knew the spell.

Xander took ten minutes, shadowed by Sythe and Jax.

"What the fuck?" Xander asked as they all stared curiously at her hand in the beasts pelt.

"I'm being arrested by the Magicka."

The beast snarled.

She patted him. "He's not taking it well."

"Arrested, huh." Jax turned his attention to the men. When the officers took a wary step back she wasn't surprised, with his perpetual scowl and long scar across his face he looked the most volatile out of the Guardians. "Are these the only witnesses?"

The wands hummed as power was pushed into them, their ends shining a piercing light.

"I have to go." It wasn't like she had a choice. "But I need you to distract him."

Xander pulled off his wrap around glasses, his eyes pinched. "No."

"You think I would do this if I didn't have an option?" She cautiously flickered her eyes to the officers who had made themselves into an impenetrable line. They were becoming impatient. "Don't do this for me, do this for Riley who will be arrested if he obstructs an active Magic & Mystery officer." Or five.

Xander carefully turned his attention to the wands, his mouth set in a thin line. "I'm going to regret this." In a burst of colour he transformed, his own beast darker, but almost identical. Riley growled a warning.

In a burst of speed Xander launched himself, his long serrated claws barely missing her as he tackled Riley.

Both Jax and Sythe drew their weapons, cautious.

"What do we tell him?" one of them asked. She wasn't sure which one.

A wand pressed into her back, the end hot. "No sudden movements," the officer stated.

Alice lifted her wrists for the handcuffs, the metal cold against her skin. "Tell him I'm sorry."

CHAPTER 27

A lice didn't want to open her eyes. Not when she knew she would see the same four stone walls, the same locked door. They had even put bars on the ceiling, as if out of all the options for escape, she chose the place she couldn't even reach while standing on the bed.

What did they expect her to do? Dig upwards?

She tried to melt the door, spending hours concentrating on one point until the man guarding called her a very decorative name. It would have worked, probably. Except they had refused to remove the heavy manacles, ones that covered her wrist and majority of her forearm. Manacles fit for He-Man, or maybe The Hulk. Charms hung from the adjoining chain, various magically infused wooden shapes that stripped away her magic. Essentially making her human.

It could have been worse, they could have put her in the dungeon, which was the go-to threat by the doctors when she refused to co-operate. As she was being kept inside a castle, she had decided giving two Docs black eyes and one an interesting bite mark would be enough. It was cold inside the room, the single paned window barely keeping any heat inside. She couldn't even imagine how cold a dungeon would be.

Her throat burned, forcing her to get up off the mattress. They had stripped the room of all fabrics and decorations, keeping only the most basic furniture. The light above was artificially bright, blinding that stayed on regardless of the time. She had tried to sleep in the attached bathroom, but as soon as she had drifted off she was moved back into the bedroom and back beneath the torturous light.

She had smashed the room in retaliation, which pissed off the guards even more, but made her feel a whole lot better.

Movement beneath the door.

Alice braced herself across the room, ready for a fight. She had never felt weak. Yet her arms were covered in finger shaped bruises and pinpricks from the various blood tests. Her wrists were cut red-raw beneath the manacles and a large graze was on the inside of her thigh from when a guard had become a bit handsy. When she pushed away he split her lip, and she broke his arm in return.

The door clicked open, the sound making her flinch.

Frederick stepped inside with a smirk, his long velvet coat billowing around him dramatically. With his tight leather trousers and white ruffled shirt – open to his navel, he looked like he stepped out off a period romance novel. He flared his chi, a greeting.

She ignored it.

"I hope the accommodation is to your standard," he muttered, taking in the vacant room in one sweep. "Not all criminals get this type of luxury."

"Well, I wouldn't check out your star rating," she said

back, her voice hoarse. They had restricted her food and water, only allowing small rations.

"You look a state."

She wouldn't know, she had broken the mirror within five minutes of being thrown in the room. She could feel her hair was a wavy mess. She still wore the same dress, the hem shredded and she did not want to know what her face looked like.

"How nice of you to visit me," she said, dripping in sarcasm. It was the first time she had seen anyone other than the guards and doctors. "I feel honoured."

"As you should be," he said with a nod, his expression stern.

"How long have I been here?" The days seemed to blend together, especially with the constant light.

"Four days, your trial is set for tomorrow."

"Fabulous, I can't wait." Her voice croaked.

Frederick mumbled something as he produced a glass of water. He held it out, waiting for her to take it.

"Cute trick, do you do kids parties too?" It was actually impressive, but she wasn't going to admit it. Frederick was the strongest witch according to the tiered system. It was why he was the head of The Magicka, as well as a councilman.

When she didn't he set it on the stone windowsill, staring out onto the green.

"You're amazing, do you know that?"

Alice remained silent.

"Witches' magic is limited, once they use up their chi reserve they must wait until it refills. Some take a day, other, weaker witches can take up to a week." He turned, the dying sunlight highlighting a dark bruise in his hairline. "Our Breed have diluted their magic throughout history.

You, however are the closest to our ancestors than I have ever seen. Your power is unlimited, as if you had over a thousand familiars. If only you knew how to wield it."

"What's your point?" She found herself staring at the water.

Frederick took a sip, showing her it was safe before he handed it over. "I need you lucid before I state my offer."

Alice savoured the cold water.

"I gained my position by being strategic. Which is why I offer this to you now. You won't survive the trial, it's specifically designed to break you. You would either be killed, or if you do survive, you would be sentenced to death," he said matter of factly. "However, if you do survive, I would, as a Councilman, offer you a position within The Magicka."

"What position?" Alice asked warily.

He stepped away from the window, closing the gap between them. "I offer you a partnership. With my position and your power we would become the strongest power couple in the world."

"Partnership?" Her stomach dropped.

Humans marry, vampires claim one another, shifters mate and those that are magic based, such as druids, witches and Fae, bond.

"Yes, a soul-bond."

"You want us to soul-bond?" It was a joining of chi's, a permanent marriage between two magic bearers. "This is a joke right?"

"Why? I'm sure you haven't had a better offer. You would be in a position to really make a difference to your own kind."

"But I'd have to bond with you?" Alice pulled at her manacles, the metal digging further into her skin.

"I'm not looking for anything intimate," he said,

shooting her a disgusted look. "I have enough women throwing themselves at me. This will be solely professional."

"Was this why Dread was arrested? To trick me into a lifetime with you?"

Fredericks face turned into a feral snarl. "Dread Grayson will meet his fate because he tried to murder a councilman." He subconsciously touched his bruise. "The fool is old, and has been behind his desk too long."

Alice couldn't believe what she was hearing.

"So, what do you say?"

She didn't even need to think about it. "Go fuck yourself."

He grinned. "Great, option three it is then." The door slammed open and two guards rushed in to pin her arms. Frederick slowly walked forward, his hand holding her jaw in a tight grip. "When you lose, and you *will* lose, I will command that you be given into my care. You're too dangerous on your own, too unpredictable."

Alice tried to move, but he just held her tighter.

"And when I get what I want, I'll syphon you until you're nothing but a snivelling shell. I will break you into pieces until you beg for death. And when that happens..." He moved his face closer. "I'll make you my familiar and expand my own chi."

"You would break your own laws?"

He tilted her head, his breath against her ear. "Who said the laws apply to me?"

He jumped to his feet, the pain in his head nauseating as he moved into the kitchen. He could see through the window that it was pitch black, the moon and stars barely illuminating the garden. Without risking a glance towards his father he grabbed a torch before he stepped into the cool night air.

"Have you found her?" he asked, trying to keep his voice from shaking.

Cali tilted his head, his eyes scanning the darkness before he started to check the bushes and flowerbeds that surrounded the entirety of the garden.

"Alice," he called. "Alice. It's me. It's Kyle. Come out from where you are hiding."

"She's not here," Cali growled. "I was promised the girl."

"Shut up," he whispered back, his torch sweeping the garden as he desperately thought of a plan. He knew where she hid, where she always hid. But he couldn't reveal her yet, not until he knew what to do.

"Alice." He raised his voice. "You know how Mum doesn't like you playing out here in the dark." The torch began to shake in his hand. "Alice," he called once again, his voice scared.

"Fuck this," Cali stormed into the kitchen, returning moments later with his mother screaming, dragged her by her hair as she flailed wildly.

He stood terrified as his mum reacted.

"Mummy!" A tiny squeal, the noise automatically pulling his attention.

"What are you doing?" he shouted as Cali grabbed their

mother's hair, wrapping it around his fist as she fought the bonds holding her.

"Please. Please," she begged. "Why?"

"NO, STOP!" He dropped the torch to grab the man's arm.

"I knew this was a mistake." Cali pushed him back effortlessly, turning to lift him by the throat with one arm. "Fucking kid." He flung him away as if he weighed nothing.

He landed back in the kitchen, his head cracking against the floor. His sister's sobs echoed as he scrambled in the wet blood to get on his feet, his efforts failing as he fell back down. His head was heavy as he watched his sister dart to their mother while Cali snarled in the background, his clawed hand covering his face. He had to blink several times to concentrate, not understanding as Cali's eyes glowed red, horns piercing through his hair before he disappeared into thin air.

Someone grabbed him around the back of his throat, lifting him onto his toes.

He struggled for air, his consciousness weakening.

Sirens in the distance, traveling fast.

"You'll just have to do," Amon said as he tightened his fist, both disappearing into the night.

CHAPTER 28

Alice stared into the new mirror, jaw clenched as she tried to pull down the crop top two sizes too small. Frederick had taken great delight in handing her the clothing, stating he wanted her to have a fighting chance. The crop top left the majority of her arms bare, as well as her whole midriff. She was pretty sure if she lifted her arms the spectators were going to see a lot more than they bargained for. Even with her arms down, there was a slight under boob problem.

"I need a bra!" she shouted through the door. *And my weapons,* she mentally added. Unfortunately her daggers were removed pretty quickly, and were yet to be returned.

"Doesn't seem like my problem princess." Came the swift reply. "Hurry up, we need to be down in a few minutes."

Great, she thought to herself. *Looks like the girls are going free.*

The leather trousers, on the other hand, were a size too big. The only good thing were the knee high boots, which thankfully fit decently considering they looked like they were stolen from a pirate.

She had no idea what she expected to walk into as she was escorted through the castle and out into the surrounding green. The London skyline was in the far distance, the lights a glare against the quickly darkening sky. They had removed her manacles when she was handed the clothes, warning her that they had permission to kill.

"Come on, it's just over here," a guard gruffed, his hand clenched on his wand while his female partner walked behind.

Torches surrounded a large circle on the green, a pentagram cut into the grass with five oversized thrones facing it. Her eyes quickly settled on Dread, who was held to his own chair just to the side by Danton. They had muzzled him like an animal, a metallic band that covered his whole mouth and nose. Metal manacles hung on his wrist, thicker than hers was, and reinforced by chains that looped around his neck.

"Dread!" she called, her legs moving towards him.

"Ventilabis pedesium!"

Alice felt the blast to her side, throwing her off her feet and onto the slightly damp ground.

"Get up," the male guard growled, forcing her back onto her feet.

Without thought she grabbed his wand, breaking it with her knee and throwing the pieces in opposite directions. "Touch me again, I dare you." She was beyond rational.

"Alice, please enter the circle," Valentina said in her high, girly voice.

With a straight back Alice stepped into the centre, facing the five thrones, carefully making eye contact with each member of The Council. The twins were first, both their petite figures sitting on an arm each, their matching silver boots rested on the seat. Dreads voice floated through her mind.

'Listen Alice, this is important. There are two that speak for the Fae, twins Quention and Liliannia. Faeries, both exceedingly powerful in their own right. One chose Seelie, the other Unseelie which made them the ideal choice for the seat.'

Alice stared, fascinated with their identical appearances until she figured out who was who. They returned her gaze with interest, with matching pale eyes that seemed just as curious.

"How nice to see you again," Edwards smirked, eyes lingering on her chest. "Interesting clothing choice." He sat beside the twins, expression slightly bored. "Is it cold tonight?"

She didn't need to look down to understand what he meant.

"Her body is covered in bruises, and I can smell faint blood from here." Xavier added, who sat to the furthest left, beside Frederick. He turned to the witch, his orange eyes flashing. "You seem to take great care of your people." He laughed, the noise loud but short. "What do you think?" He asked the person who stood to his side.

It automatically brought her eyes down, meeting another pair, this time blue.

Breath caught in her throat as Rex observed her coolly, his face empty of emotion. He stood to Xavier's right, leaning against the throne with his arms crossed.

Great. Just fucking great.

Frederick tipped his chin. "Be careful Xavier, slander is dangerous in certain circumstances."

"She doesn't look particularly –"

"– threatening," the Fae twins chimed in. "Almost a disappointment."

Alice kept her reply to herself.

An old woman sat silently a few feet away, her long white hair covering her eyes as she bent over two knitting needles.

"Alice Skye, it has come to my attention that Frederick has charged you with conspiracy in his murder." Alice met Valentina's gaze last, the dark depths glittering with something she couldn't decipher.

"That will be dealt with after this," Frederick said.

'Non, they will not. Those charges will be dismissed immediately."

Frederick burst to his feet. "She is under my authority."

"Then you should be pleased to know that while under *your* authority, Monsieur Grayson has admitted sole responsibility of the attack on your life." She elegantly rolled her wrist, her hand pointed towards the vampire in question. "I thought it would be appropriée for Monsieur Grayson to witness, non?"

Alice flicked her gaze to Dread, but his obsidian eyes were unnaturally relaxed for the situation. His eyes were something he often used to scare people, the creepiness of them enough to make anyone hesitate, but she had always been able to read them. Yet he projected fake calm, closing himself off until she read nothing.

Which meant he was a lot more worried than he wanted her to see.

They were fucked.

"Interesting," Frederick smirked, calmly adjusting his velvet coat before taking his seat once more. "Then I will allow the charges to drop, but that does not mean Alice is not under my authority."

"How noble of you," Valentina said with an arch of her eyebrow.

"Let's get this over with," Alice said with as much strength as she could muster.

"Straight to the point, I like that." Valentina smiled, her fangs bright against her black painted lips. The shade made her face look porcelain, her eyes hollow as if she were a living doll. Her legs swung freely on the throne, too short to touch the ground. "Frederick, if you wouldn't mind."

With a dramatic flair Frederick stepped down, turning to face the others. "My fellow councilman, we have decided to call this trial because we believe Miss Alice Skye is a direct descendant of the original Elementals, and therefore a threat."

Alice sniggered. "Only a threat to you." She was alone, there was no one to fight in her corner.

"This isn't a normal trial," one of the twins said. Alice wasn't sure which one. "You don't get to speak."

This is bullshit, she thought, but kept her lips sealed.

"She isn't wrong," Valentina added, facing the witch. "It was you, was it not, who was insistent that Alice was a threat to us all."

Frederick continued as if he hadn't been interrupted, his smile tightening. "She already shows the signs of a true Draco, a direct descendent to the most powerful of our Breed. The prophecy states if she were to embrace her power, she would become War."

"This just sounds like you're scared of her," Xavier said with a slow smile, his posture relaxed as he watched everyone with predator eyes. "You're talking about the apocalypse, a canonical event."

"The Four Horsemen have been depicted in many religions and mythologies, all throughout history. It is said they would have the power to create a rift between the multiple realms, colliding our worlds and releasing the Shadow-Veyn."

"The Shadow-Veyn were imprisoned –"

"– a millennium ago," Quention finished for his sister. "They cannot pass onto Earth Side, or Far Side."

Frederick tugged on his lapels. "Then why have there been multiple sightings of Shadow-Veyn in the last year alone?"

"He speaks true," Edwards said with a tip of his head. "We've dealt with a few, but there's been a noticeable increase. A fallen angel has also been spotted."

"Let us not forget who imprisoned the Shadow-Veyn in the lower planes in the first place," Xavier chuckled, staring at the twins. "I'm sure they shared their magical knowledge of Far Side with the druid traitors down in The Nether."

"Never call them druids," Edwards snarled. "They are not worthy of our name."

"They are thousands of miles –"

"– beneath the earth's crust."

"What are Shadow-Veyn?" Alice asked as they began to bicker.

All eyes turned to her, and they all pointily ignored her question.

Edwards returned his attention to Frederick. "Do you believe Alice's power surge is in relation to the increased activity?"

Frederick hesitated. "It's a possibility the Daemons are aggravating the situation."

"Well," Xavier said with a smirk, "they are forced to live in Hell."

"Then what has this got to do with her?" Liliannia asked, her lilac eyes sharp. She tilted her head, watching as if Alice were a bug she could crush with her palm.

"Because, according to the scripts, it's the first sign that a Horseman is ascending."

This is ridiculous, Alice thought as her eyes wandered to the old woman. She was still sat on a stool, her hands slowly repeating the same movements as she continued to knit.

"Then what do you propose?" Edwards asked, mouth pursed.

Frederick straightened his spine. "I suggest if Alice is deemed too dangerous that she should be handed over to The Magicka, where she can be contained until such time she can control herself."

"So you want her all to yourself?" Xavier said. "It's almost as if you had this planned all along. Would it not make more sense to eliminate the threat?"

Frederick shot him a baleful look, his neck becoming flushed in irritation. "We're not barbarians, why kill her when she could be an asset to us in the future?"

"You mean an asset to you."

Valentina tapped her long nails against the arm of her throne. "This trial is to show us the power you believe Alice to have. Get on with it."

Frederick clenched his jaw. "As we all must remain impartial, I have decided to invite an outside witch to assist with the trials."

"Wait, trials? Plural?" Alice took a threatening step forward. "You're testing me because of some stupid poem!"

Hands pressed against her shoulder, forcing her to her knees.

"The poem is just one of the representations," Frederick said as he approached. He crouched, his hand holding her chin as he leaned in to whisper, his voice too low for the others to overhear. "I'm going to enjoy watching you fight for your life, and then I'm going to enjoy draining you dry."

Alice felt her chi snap out as a blue flame curled around his hand. With a yelp he jumped back, patting his sleeve to stop it from burning. Xavier laughed in the background, the sound loud and exaggerated.

Alice shrugged her shoulders, dislodging the two guards.

"Be gone," a husky voice shouted in a thick Russian accent. The old lady stood painfully, her knees creaking loudly enough to carry across the small distance. She set down her needles before she began to hobble over, her weight resting on a thick staff.

She murmured something beneath her breath before she looked up, and Alice froze.

Her eyes were cloudy white, just a pale shadow where her iris and pupil were supposed to be. Yet Alice felt her gaze, like something creeping across her skin.

"Be gone," the old woman hissed, tapping her staff against the earth.

The guards exchanged meaningful glances before they stepped back, leaving Alice kneeling in the grass.

"I would like to introduce Baba Yaga," Frederick presented with a flare of his arm. "Renowned for her talents in both earth and necromancy. She will be testing Alice in three separate trials to determine her power and control."

"What exactly is the point?" Xavier said as he crouched on his throne. "The strong survive, the weak die. It's how it's always been."

"For you animals, maybe," Frederick shot back. "But

with magic, the consequences of someone unable to control their chi can be catastrophic."

"He's right," Quention said. "If she were unable to control herself –"

"– she could destroy everything in her path." Liliannia added for her brother. "I'm interested to see whether Alice can control her power, or allow it to consume her."

"Then we go back to what I suggested earlier, elimination." Xavier jumped from his throne, his bare feet taking the impact with little effort. He prowled forward, black stripes appearing on his skin before Rex reached forward and held him back. After a tense moment, Xavier sat back down, curling his legs beneath him.

"Let us first see what Alice can do, then we will decide." Valentina nodded to continue.

"The first trial, is energy," Frederick explained from his seat. "It's simple. Win."

CHAPTER 29

aba waved, gesturing for Alice to step forward. From inside her dress she pulled out a long, thin wand. When Baba flared her chi in greeting, Alice flared back.

What the fuck is she?

The sensation was a million needles prickling across her skin.

"Prinimat'."

Alice hesitantly took the wand, feeling the wood vibrate beneath her fingertips. Baba sneered, her mouth stretched so wide it showed off her lack of teeth. She pointed back to the circle, her smile not waning as her eyes followed Alice's every step.

"What am I supposed to do with this?" Alice asked when she was back in the centre.

"Vi pedesium!"

Alice turned just as the arcane scorched past. "Shit!" She rolled, her aura aching at the assault.

The female guard who had escorted her from the castle stood at the other side of the circle, her own wand pointed.

She had to win a duel.

"Well, isn't this fucking great," she murmured to herself. She had never used a wand before, the instrument way past her pay grade, nor had she trained specifically in arcane. *"ARDENTI TURRIS!"* Fire swirled from the tip, spiralling into a vortex that roared.

"What the..." Frederick inched forward on his seat, everyone's attention on the single flame.

Cracks appeared down her wand, the wood straining before it splintered apart. "Oh, bloody hell." The fire vanished.

The guards began to laugh as Alice stared at the remains of her wand. It had broken into three pieces.

"Impetus acritas!"

"ARMA!" Alice raised her arms, her aegis shield appearing around her with a second to spare. The arcane blast rippled across her aegis, strong enough Alice thought it could fall. "Shit. Shit. Shit." She grabbed at the wand fragments, trying to stick them back together as panic settled into her gut.

Another blast, diluting the green, blue and gold of the molecule thin shield created from her aura. A black began to creep across the dome, blocking out the light. It was going to fall, it was only a matter of time.

Alice clearly didn't know how to use a wand. But she knew how to win a fight.

Just before her shield shattered Alice launched herself forward, closing most of the distance between herself and the guard before she dropped out of the way of another spell. As soon as the flare soared over Alice was back on her feet, and threw herself hard at the guard. They both fell down in a tangle of limbs.

"Stay still!" Alice disarmed her with a twist. "I don't want to hurt you."

They scrambled for the wand, punching and kicking before Alice secured it in her right fist.

"*ADOLEBITQUE!*" Heat separated them, pushing them both apart just as the wand splintered once again in her hand. "Seriously, what are these made of?" She threw the wooden instrument to the ground as it sparked.

What were the chances that two wands broke?

Latin tumbled out of the guards mouth, a spell Alice didn't recognise. The earth beneath her feet died, creeping across the grass in search of Alice.

"Shit. Shit. Shit." Before the guard could finish the black charm Alice reared back and punched her square in the jaw, shutting her up. "What the bloody hell are they teaching you in The Magicka?"

Red cuts dripped from the guards arm, ones that looked self-inflicted. Black magic was banned, even the smallest spell requiring some sort of sacrifice. Yet, it was the second time one of The Magicka had threatened her with it.

"Stay down!"

The guard kicked up, knocking her to the side as she scrambled for her wand, her jeans riding up to show off a silver anklet.

She wasn't a guard, she was a prisoner.

"*VENTILABIS!*" Alice thrust her hand forward, her ball of arcane hitting the woman between the shoulder blades and striking her to the ground. She forced an arm under the woman's chin, clasped her hands together and crushed her forearm against her throat.

It took thirty seconds for the guard to stop flailing, and when Alice released her she gasped for a breath.

"Please," Alice whispered. "Stay down."

"I..." A cough. "I can't. If I win, I'm free to go." She pulled a knife, hidden in her jacket and thrust it up towards Alice's chest.

"Fuck!" The blade scored a line across her stomach, hard enough she felt warmth coat her skin. Alice felt a force pull her back before Baba Yaga appeared with a frown. She pointed to the woman, spoke in Russian before the guard began to convulse, blood dripping from her nose.

"This was an energy trial," Frederick bellowed across the green, anger vibrating his tone. "No weapons were permitted."

Alice clutched her stomach, blood seeping through her fingers. It hurt, but wasn't deep enough to do any lasting damage.

Where's the dagger? She spotted it in the grass beside the woman, but Baba Yaga was already removing them both from within the circle. *Fuck.*

"Where's this power you speak of?" Edwards asked with a tut. "She won by physical force, not arcane."

"It is —"

"— disappointing."

"Frederick," Xavier purred. "Are you wasting our time?"

With an annoyed huff Frederick gestured to Baba. "The second trial is memory."

"Memory? What has..." Alice stopped as Baba tapped her staff against the green, the marked grass lighting up as she sealed the circle around them both. Vines appeared from within the earth, growing up the circle until they formed a cage high above, trapping her inside.

Alice stared at the structure that surrounded her, even though her heart was a tattoo against her chest.

"Vy gotovy?"

"Err…" Alice looked past Baba for help, able to see The Council through the vines clear enough. "Okay?"

Baba chuckled as she lifted her hand before blowing a grey powder. Alice coughed, her eyes blurring as the particles swirled and filled the whole circle in a fine haze.

Alice rubbed her eyes, blinking them several times to clear her vision. Baba was back behind the vines, watching intently.

"Please. Please," a voice begged from behind her. "Why?"

Alice froze, her chest tight at the familiar voice. Her body responded, tears forming as a sob caught in her throat. Her mother knelt a foot away, her white nightgown spread across the grass. Her blonde hair caught in a phantom wind, whipping it across her tear stained face.

"Mama?" Alice choked out the word. She went to reach forward, her arm stretched before a shadow, his whole body the same shade of grey appeared behind her.

He slowly moved his arm, and slit her mother's throat.

CHAPTER 30

"**M**UM!" Alice reached her mother just as she slumped forward, her arms passing through her body as she disintegrated into dust. Her chi reacted, her core pulsating as grief overwhelmed her senses. She brushed her hands through the grass, the particles floating before they blurred into the haze.

The grey man stood over her, faceless as it breathed heavily, its chest rattling with each breath. It moved slowly, its fingers brushing across Alice's hair, removing it from her neck, the touch reciprocating across her throat, cutting.

"*ADOLEBITQUE!*" She turned and blasted it, the grey man letting out a high screech that set her teeth on edge. Her fire kept going, pouring from her arms as he tilted his head, and curled his fingers to the earth.

Tinkerbell appeared with a pop, happily dancing around her head.

Particles formed in the air, swirling lazily before they joined together as one. It soared through the short space, knocking her to the ground before a heavy weight pinned her hands.

"I'm sorry it has to be this way," Rex grumbled as his face formed, blue eyes, heavy with regret.

Alice felt a phantom sharp, short pain in her side. Warmth grew from her abdomen, bubbling through her bloodstream as her tongue became heavy in her mouth.

You're not real!

Alice crushed her thighs together, trapping Rex's as she pushed hard, forcing her knee into his side and rolling them both. As her weight settled Rex crumbled beneath her.

She let out a scream, her fists pummelling the ground as the little particles floated around. Her stomach sunk, a sickening feeling of loss and betrayal mixing with her sorrow. Tears dropped onto her hands, settling on the dust that coated her skin.

She had already cried too many tears over Rex. Yet she felt hate ignite a passion that heightened her chi.

This isn't me.

Alice stood, her muscles trembling as she fought the onslaught of emotions that weren't her own, at least, not completely.

Her flames crackled against the shield, almost overwhelming the large circle as her magic raged out of control. The trial was designed to break her, weaken her though amplified emotions she had long ago absolved.

In igne comburetis. Cinis in nos exsurgent.

One by one she was surrounded by the acolytes from her memory, their robes soaked in blood. They stared with eyeless sockets, their mouths sewn shut with a single pale thread.

"Ah, there she is." A hand brushed against her arm.

Alice refused to turn, even as the large shadow swallowed hers. She could hear his wing scrape against the concrete, even though she knew that it was impossible. Yet the sound was so clear.

"I know you're awake." An intimate whisper against the back of her neck.

She waited for fear to overwhelm her, the familiar taste of acid at the back of her tongue. But nothing, even when she finally turned to the creature that still haunted her nightmares, she felt... nothing.

She wasn't afraid.

With a deep breath she reigned all her magic back, leaving behind scorched earth wherever it had touched. The grey man rattled out a breath, a crack appearing across his chest that leaked light.

Master gave her a slow, satisfied smile. He was tall, over seven foot with two horns that curled down to his ears. His skin was marked by battles, his chest and legs ripped with muscles. But between his legs he was smooth.

He was a memory, and memories weren't always accurate. She remembered he was naked, but not the exact details. Which either meant she was too traumatised at the time, or his appendage wasn't impressive enough to remember.

Alice couldn't help her smirk.

"With your life force, we will Become. The blood of The Dragon, the blood of War," he said, fangs dripping with red as she felt a wet warmth cover her hand.

When she lifted her palm her scar was raw, a nasty bite that poured blood as if it was only made moments ago. She watched it drop to the earth, covering each blade of grass for a second before disappearing.

Master's hand snapped forward to curl around her throat.

"Pay attention," he growled.

"Fuck you." She repeated the exact same words as that night. "This isn't real. You're just a memory!" She thrust her palm upwards, her hand encased in blue flames licked with green. *"Ignis loquiturus!"*

His hand tightened, face shifting, changing as the grey man slowly walked around them, nudging the acolytes as they crumbled.

Grey eyes bored into her. "I can still feel you leaking energy. Has my son not taught you anything?" Mason asked with a dissatisfied tut. He released a slight pressure from her neck, his thumb hovering over her pulse. "You may look relaxed, but I can feel it beneath your skin, your chi's electric. All I would have to do is..."

She felt the memory of Mason trying to syphon her chi, but it was only an echo, like a river across her senses. One that was toxic.

"Your mother was a power your father craved," Mason said as she closed her eyes. "He chose her over The Order, even over The Council. They became dangerous, first when he didn't disclose who your mother was, and then when he refused to hand her over. So they both had to be neutralised."

Her pulse was loud inside her head, drowning out the murmurs of those watching and the crackling of her flames. She embraced the anger gladly, allowing it to overwhelm everything else that sought to cripple her. She was no longer weak, no longer a defenceless child who had watched her mother die, or a naive woman who had trusted the wrong man.

"It was a shame something as beautiful as your mother got in the way," Mason continued. "She would have made a great pet."

Alice opened her eyes, and Tinkerbell exploded into a burst of white light.

CHAPTER 31

B eneath Alice's feet the earth was blackened, the circle ruined as her power erased the anchor markings. The vines wilted as they died, some charred while others turned to ash that caught the wind.

"How is that –"

"– even possible?" the twins asked with a frown. "I've never seen –"

"– anything like it."

Alice was surprised herself. Tinkerbell had never done anything particularly helpful in the past. It was usually just a nuisance that liked to embarrass her in awkward situations. She wasn't even sure what had happened, but what she did know was that she felt... exhilarated. Her chi energised in a way she had never felt before. It had always been her emotions that held her back, her subconscious that caged her own power.

"Do you see what I mean?" Frederick said with a smile. "She is War."

"It's interesting," Valentina mused. "She seemed overwhelmed with her own emotions."

"She has the classic markings of a witch unable to control herself in stressful situations," Frederick explained. "Normally it wouldn't be an issue. But with someone with so much potential..."

"Stop talking like I'm not here," Alice snapped, pain heightening her already bubbling anger. "I have no idea what it is to be War, but that doesn't mean I'm suddenly going to try and destroy the world."

"It's said in the scripts..." Frederick began.

"Just because someone wrote it down, doesn't make it true," she interrupted. "I don't believe in fate."

"We shall see," he said as his frown morphed into an arrogant smirk. "While we're all here I would like to proceed with the prosecution of one Dread Grayson."

Valentina pursed her lips in thought before she nodded her agreement. "So be it. Dread Grayson of my blood, stand before The Council."

Dread confidently climbed to his feet, his hands raised to accommodate the chain around his throat. He paused to look at Alice, his dark eyes wet.

I'm sorry, my daughter.

"Wait!" Alice cried.

"Dread Grayson, you have been charged with attempted treason against The Council, the punishment for this is death."

"Agreed," the twins said in unison.

"Agreed."

"Agreed."

When Xavier vocalised his agreement, Rex met her eyes and she felt a violent urge to be sick.

He looked desolate.

Valentina gently stepped off her throne, reaching over to brush her fingertips across Dread's exposed cheek. "Ça ne devait pas être comme ça, mon ami. Je te verrai dans la prochaine vie." She kissed his forehead, leaving a red smear. "The Council have spoken."

"NO!" Alice screamed.

Danton stepped forward, his long sword glinting in the moonlight as he raised it above his head.

Alice tensed to run, flames rippling down her arms.

"*ADOLEBITQUE!*" Her chi pulsated as bright white lightning crackled out of her flames, shooting towards Danton before it was deflected with a bang. Wild magic merged with her own, the raw, chaotic energy amplifying her power beyond what she had ever imagined. Another spell teased her tongue, something darker, deadlier that she had read from her mother's grimoire.

But she was too late.

The sword came down, the blade separating skin just as a heavy weight hit her stomach. She collapsed to the ground, pinned to the earth as Rex settled on her hips.

"I'm sorry," he said, his voice deep as the wolf pulsed through his veins.

Sobs wrecked her body, her fingers digging into the earth as tears burned down her face. Her breath ragged, she gasped for each breath as her remaining strength vanished. She didn't care that she was falling apart, or that she was collapsed in the mud as her heart shattered. She had been too late.

She closed her eyes as Rex pulled her into a sitting position, his arms wrapped around her tightly as his face nestled into her neck. He murmured quietly into her ear, the words not registering as the pain blocked everything else out.

Slowly she relaxed into his comfort, her eyes void of

tears before she sucked in a big breath, and screamed. She screamed until her lungs burned and her throat hurt. Screamed until the pain was a little easier to handle, screamed until she couldn't anymore.

Power tingled her fingertips, so strong she thought she may explode as the wild magic protested, wanting to be used. It lived for chaos, for destruction.

And right then, with her sorrow still raw she could imagine herself as War.

She gently pushed against Rex, not wanting his heat as she felt the first drops of rainfall. He resisted, holding her tighter as she forced an arm between them, pushing them apart. As she lifted her face to the sky, she allowed the rain to wash across her skin, mixing with the tears and dirt. Her top had risen, her bare breasts brushing his chest. She tugged the fabric down, her hands shaking before she closed her fists so tight they turned white and her nails dug into her skin.

"Xavier, handle your pet," Valentina said with an eerily detached voice. Alice would have believed it to be grief if she didn't hate her in that moment.

She hated them all.

"You're not allowed to interfere," Edwards said with a sharp look to his right. "Remove your wolf before we continue the trial."

A clap of thunder in the distance.

Xavier growled, the noise almost like a sharp bark as Rex jumped to his feet, neck bent to expose his throat to the more dominant shifter. With one swipe Xavier scored three lines into his skin, slicing the flesh in warning. Blood began to trickle down, but Rex just resumed his position beside the throne, his gaze cast to the floor.

Alice couldn't stop as her eyes settled on the man who

had raised her, body slumped on the grass with his head severed beside him. He had already begun to wither, not turning to dust like Hollywood liked to embellish.

Baba slowly approached Dreads body, a look of sick excitement colouring her features.

Alice flicked out her hand, the energy cremating Dread without any effort. Breed didn't bury their dead, preferring to grieve the memory, not a corpse. It was the only peace she could give him.

Danton bowed his head before he moved to stand beside Valentina's throne. Alice couldn't look at him, not someone she had called a friend.

Another clap of thunder, louder but still distant.

Frederick glanced at the ashes then back up. "The last trial, is survival." He lifted his wand, a thin green beam shooting skyward before exploding into a sheet of energy that covered The Council.

Rain fell thicker, softening the earth.

Baba stood off to the side, her attention on the blood stain that remained of Dread. The rain was beginning to wash it away, but she gently bent until her fingertips were covered in red.

"Hey!" Alice warned, her palms heating up as the wild magic crackled from her fingertips. "Back the fuck off."

With a smirk Baba wiped it diagonally across her face before she began to speak in Russian.

"I said..." The earth began to shake beneath her feet. The splash of red on green darkened, turning black before it sank completely into the ground. The surface cracked, the lesion moving across the field until it ended in the centre of the ruined circle, beside Alice. "What the?"

A roar as the earth opened, forcing Alice to scramble

back before she was swallowed whole. A growl as something crawled out.

"Are you out of your mind?" Edwards moved closer to the barrier that protected The Council. "That Shadow-Veyn is highly venomous. Just one bite..."

"This is the trial of survival. Let's see how Alice handles this hellhound."

Alice froze when the creature turned towards her, its red eyes staring from deep within hollow sockets too big for its face. It snarled, showing off two rows of very sharp teeth. It was around the size of a large wolf, the head and body of similar shape. But that was where the similarity ended. The dark, matted fur didn't cover the head or ribs, leaving the bones exposed with a flash of white that unnerved her more than its lack of nose. Smoke floated between its visible ribs as well as its mouth and hole where its nose was supposed to be.

"Of course I get a fucking zombie dog." Alice stepped back, arms held out as the beast followed her movement. Its ears were flat to its head, twitching as The Council murmured between one another. "Good doggy." Alice slowly lowered her body, making her head lower than the hellhounds.

Skin was pulled tight to its back, highlighting each bump along its spine as well as its long, thin tail.

Shit. Shit. Shit.

The hellhound pierced the ground with its claws, legs tensed as it began to launch itself forward.

"ARMA!"

Her aegis strained under the force of the hellhound. Fangs and claws bared as it searched for a weak spot.

She was running out of options. She couldn't wait it out,

but she also wasn't prepared to deal with a creature straight out of hell. Literally.

Alice puffed out a breath. "I've got this."

She slowly edged back, ready to pop her shield.

"I've got this." The hellhound snarled, watching every small movement with complete focus. "Oh bollocks."

As soon as her aura rebounded from the shield she had thrown herself to the side, sliding in the mud as the hellhound jumped over her in one large bound.

"VENTILABIS!" She pushed up, searing the underside of the hound and throwing it onto its flank. It regained its footing faster than she could, the rain plastering her hair to her face as she slipped. *"ARDENTI TURRIS!"* A spiral of flames protected her for a second as she climbed to her feet, lightning striking out from her fingertips with a snap.

A weight settled into her right palm.

The hound yelped, but recovered quickly as her flames crackled along with the thunder high above.

"SHIT!" She dropped the heavy weight in panic.

Her attention shifted, confusion swirling as her sword sank into the wet mud. A sharp bark as she clambered forward for her sword, the runes pulsating and flames circling the steel as soon as her palm touched the hilt.

Alice spun just as two sets of sharp teeth sunk into her thigh.

CHAPTER 32

lice's blade pierced the hound's shoulder, deep enough that it let go. The sharp pain intensified, the wound bleeding profusely, her blood tinged a sickly green.

"Fuck. Fuck. Fuck." She tried to cover one of the holes, the skin cold to the touch. Alice struggled to her feet, just able to put her weight on her leg as it shook. She held her blade with both hands, calming her breathing as she waited for it to pounce once more.

The Council remained silent. She could feel their eyes, watching, judging her every move.

When the hound snuck closer, her blood decorating its snout she swung, slicing across its face.

An intense cold spread from her thigh.

"ADOLEBITQUE!"

The hellhound danced out the way with a wolfish grin, its long black tongue lapping up its own blood, as well as hers.

Her leg gave out, crashing her to the ground. She leant

heavily on her sword, the tip sinking into the earth as her arm shook uncontrollably. She looked up, through the wet strands of her hair and saw two red eyes a second before it tensed to attack.

Alice braced herself, the feeling long gone in half her body as she tried to hold her arm out, ready to burn them both to hell.

Riley shifted mid-run, allowing the sweet pain of his beast to take over. He collided with the hellhound just as lightning brightened the sky, sinking his teeth into its flesh just as he had hundreds of times before.

His chest ached, heart thumping as his beast took over, its own concern for Alice a surprise. They both saw her collapsed in the mud, her body weak, yet she held her head with such defiance in the face of death.

As a Guardian, he had been taught everyone was expendable.

Alice wasn't expendable.

Mine.

The declaration shot through his mind, just as the hound shook free of his grasp. But it wasn't his. His beast – which he liked to call it, very rarely verbalised its thoughts or feelings. It knew violence, hunger and sex. The most basic urges. They had been forced together since he was a child, the learning curve difficult for them both. Unlike shifters who were either human or animal, The Guardians were always both. His beast was always in the back of his mind, always scrutinising everything he did.

Mine.

The beast snarled, unveiling its tail just as he heard a weak cry.

Xander had moved Alice onto her back, his hands glowing as he tried to subdue the poison that pulsed through her body. The beast tensed, ready to fight his second for her before Riley forced himself to take back over.

They had a job to finish.

A sharp pain as claws carved across his chest.

His brothers hovered around, mostly shifted as he turned with a snarl. He warned them to stay away, their own growls and barks annoyed. This is what they were made to do, their sole purpose. Yet the hellhound was his.

The beast bared his fangs, one of his tails whipping out to cut alongside the hellhound when it got too close. He began to circle it, the hellhounds attention shifting between the beasts as it licked along the line that sliced through its face. The smoke that filtered through its ribs began to crawl across its fur, attempting to heal the wounds.

The beast tensed, hind legs pushing off the ground faster than the hellhound could react. Blood against his tongue as his fangs penetrated its throat, and ripped the hellhounds head off with one clean jerk.

He shifted, allowing the rain to wash across his naked skin as the earth opened up and swallowed the hound whole.

He made it to Alice with two strides, scooping her up and crushing her to his chest just as The Council approached. She shivered in his arms, her lips blue as she weakly settled her hand over his heart. His wounds protested at the contact, his chest sliced open, his glyphs glowing as they expelled the poison.

"L-l-l-ife isss like a dick," Alice stammered into his

chest. "It getsss hard for no reason, and isss mu-much too short."

He held her tighter, her skin ice to the touch.

Valentina warily cast her eyes across The Guardians, who had all flanked Riley. "That is the end of the trials."

"What?" Frederick gasped. "The last trial has clearly been compromised. I will have to take Alice back until she is well enough to repeat." He reached for Alice, pausing when both Titus and Axel pointed two Glocks at his head. "Edwards, control your..."

"Alice stays with me," Riley said with a snarl.

Mine.

Rex growled, the low rumble starting low in his abdomen until it poured from his mouth in warning. Riley met his eyes, watching as his wolf struggled to understand the dominance between them.

He wasn't simply an animal, wasn't a shifter.

"She must be returned to me." Frederick stamped his foot. "Only I have the anti-venom."

"It's definitely like you had this planned," Xavier chuckled. "Alice has already proven herself to hold power beyond even you."

"Yes," Edwards added, turning to his fellow Councilman. "There is no anti-venom to hellhounds."

"Of course there is," Frederick said, flustered. "I would never have subjected Alice to the trial otherwise."

"The trial has finished." Valentina slowly reached her hand to rest on Alice's arm, ignoring the weapons and warnings from The Guardians. "This was brought forward by Councilman Gallagher due to his concern both for her control, and future entanglement with the Shadow-Veyn."

Frederick stood his ground. "She *must* be returned to

me. Only I can help her with training. Clearly the druids have done nothing for her control."

"Alice showed no homicidal traits," Quention said, his head tilted to the side as he stared curiously at The Guardians who were still in beast form.

"She showed no connection with the Shadow-Veyn other than to defend herself." Liliannia edged back, eyes wide as she partially hid herself behind her brother.

"What about her control? She fractured and almost killed us all!" Frederick spat. "This is ridiculous! She's dangerous!"

"I'm dangerous," Xavier grinned, showing off his sharply filed teeth. "Did you want to try against me?"

Edwards glared furiously, jaw clenched as The Guardians ignored him. "Let us vote. All for Alice to pass?"

The Council looked between one another before everyone but Frederick nodded in agreement.

"Alice has passed the trials," Valentina stated, stepping back. "She will be released immediately."

"This is a big mistake. I will not allow her to roam around as a threat," Frederick said, storming away. "That's if she survives."

CHAPTER 33

The pain when it hit started in her thigh, a throbbing ache that radiated outwards until even her eyelashes hurt. She had suffered cuts, beatings and broken bones, but nothing came close to the over-whelming agony.

She was on the ground, and she could feel every glass blade, every drop of rain like acid against her sensitive skin

"Hold her down," a voice said as the pain intensified. "She's going to hurt herself."

Alice let out a cry, her skin burning at every touch.

"Fuck sake, she hit me in the eye!"

"Grow up you fucking wombat."

She was too hot, her clothes too restricting. She tried to pull at the fabric, her arms not coordinating.

"Shit, the venom has reached her heart."

Reached my heart? She thought through the confusion. *Yep, that makes sense.* The pain was in waves, matching every beat. But it was slowing, becoming less intense with every breath. Soon it would be over.

"She's going to die."

"No." Riley touched her skin, and she let out a hiss. "She can't die."

"Sire..."

"No, we have to do something."

"If we move her, we will kill her," Xander said as he crouched down, his hand covered in a weird glow Alice wanted desperately to comment on, but she couldn't feel her tongue. "She won't make it any further."

A gust of wind made her whimper, the sound escaping before she could stop it.

"What happened?" Kyle demanded, his eyes tinged with red as he held his wings high above his back. He had landed beside them on the green.

The Guardians pulled their weapons, ready to take him down.

"How did you find us?"

"Sam reached out when she was arrested," Kyle said, trying to approach before he was warned away. With a grunt he knelt, his wings twitching in irritation before he stretched out, holding one horizontal so she was protected from the rain.

"You didn't answer my question." Riley watched the spike at the end of his wing cautiously. Kyle may be new to them, but they were still a weapon and capable of serious damage, even by accident.

Kyle clenched his jaw, eyes narrowed. The red around his green iris' grew before he shook his head to clear it. "I can track her by the mark. It's like a beacon for daem... for people like me." His eyes settled on the crescent scar on her palm.

"If you can track her, what took you so fucking long?"

Kyle ignored the question, instead turning to Xander. "What happened?"

"She was bitten by a hellhound," Xander answered without hesitation. "She hasn't got long."

"Let me take her."

Riley snarled, lifting Alice into his lap.

She would have cried, except there was no pain anymore. She could feel the pressure of his arms, of his hands as he cuddled her close, but she couldn't feel his heat.

"I have experience with hellhound bites," Kyle said. "Let me help her."

"Sire, she won't make it to our healers."

Alice tried to stroke Riley's chest, but her hand wouldn't move. All she could do was stare above, counting the pretty feathers of her shade. She was so tired, her heart slowing.

It was almost peaceful.

"If she dies, I will hunt you down," Riley growled.

"She should be dead, you know."

Alice woke, her face crushed into a pillow made of fur.

"What did you give her?"

"Oh, you do not want to know." A deep chuckle. "Hellhound bites are a biiitch. If it wasn't for that fucking faerie thing on her wrist she would have been dead before you even drifted."

"What about the tattoo?"

"Out of everything that I had to do, you're going to complain about that?"

Alice compressed the fur beneath her fingertips, an overwhelming happiness as she could feel every fine hair.

Her bones ached, thighs burning but she was grateful to be alive. With a heavy sigh she rolled onto her back, taking a second for the dizziness to subside before she attempted to sit up, her arms shaking at her weight.

She was on a circular bed, one covered in several different colour furs and skins and draped messily across her legs. The wall behind her was covered in black shelves, clearly DIY as they seemed placed at the wrong angles. Each held an array of pearlescent bottles, jars, grimoires and scrolls. The walls seemed made of stone, and there was no door, just a hole which had a pentagram carved into the threshold.

Where was she?

"Oh look, it's sleeping beauty." Lucifer grinned from the doorway. His leather squeaked when he walked in and sat on the white chair opposite, a pink frilly apron tied around his waist. "That wasn't a happy fairy-tale by the way. It was actually damn right fucking sadistic, just how I like my children's stories."

"Is she awake?" Kyle hesitated at the door, his eyes sunken and tired. His iris' glowed yet, the colour matching Lucy's.

"Erm, where am I?" Alice coughed, her throat dry. She reached for the glass of water on the bedside table, taking a sip before she spat it dramatically over herself.

Lucy slapped his knee, body shaking as he laughed. "Yeah, water sucks down here. Too many gases. We can't seem to purify it enough."

"Yeah..." Alice placed the glass back down with a grimace. "Where exactly is down here?"

"Hell," Kyle said with a straight face.

"Stop calling it Hell you cheeky fucker," Lucy snapped, pointing his long nails at her brother. "That's a human concept. It's not as simple as Heaven or Hell, or even good or evil. We're just down here, and they live up there."

"Fine." Kyle crossed his arms. "We're in The Nether."

"What am I doing here?" Her mind was hazy, her memory sluggish. "Wait, Dread?"

There was a pause.

Kyle looked uncomfortable, his eyes darting to Lucifer then back again. "I'm sorry."

Alice nodded, her throat thick with emotion. "Why am I not dead?"

"Well, it looks like this little thing helped." Lucifer held a gold bangle in his hand, the glass bead broken. "It leaked all over my bloody sheets. It's going to be a bitch to wash out."

Alice hesitantly reached for it, the metal light in her hand. "What was it?"

Kyle shrugged. "We're not sure, but when your heart stopped, the glass bead broke and it began to beat again."

"I also sucked all the poison out of your bloodstream, which was one of the most unpleasant things I have ever done. And I have done some nasty things." Lucifer stood, adjusting himself. "You're welcome, by the way."

Kyle moved out the way as Lucy walked out the room, muttering to himself.

"Lucy has healed your leg as much as he could, but he had to tattoo you to help your body fight the poison."

His hand reached forward, hovering over her arm until she flipped it over. On the inside of her forearm was a line of glyphs, starting from her wrist and ending just shy of her elbow. The black lines were raised, the surrounding skin red.

"You need to recover, but I can take you back tonight if you want."

Alice clutched her arm to her chest. "What do I owe him?" Daemons didn't do anything for free.

"Nothing." Kyle hesitantly took the seat opposite, sitting forward until his arms rested on his knees. "I've agreed to stay with him a while."

"What? Why?" Alice forced herself forward, her thigh burning at the movement. With a hiss she pulled back the fur blanket, the wound beneath raw but clean. "You need to come home."

"Alice, look at me. I am home." He held his hand up, halting her protest. "I'm... settled. Lucy and I have a mutual understanding."

A bellow from the other room. "YOU USED UP THE LAST OF THE CEREAL YOU MOTHERFUCKER!"

Kyle gave her a slight smile. "He's helping me, believe it or not."

"But..."

"It's for the best. Down here... I can learn more."

"Learn what exactly?"

Kyle ruffled through a drawer, pulling out several large notebooks and a few pieces of paper. "I've been trying to find more on The Knights, figure out what they want, who they are." He held out a single sheet. "They wrote this as a warning..."

"What?" Alice looked at the paper, confused with the writing but recognised the sun symbol printed on the top. "What does it say?"

"Roughly translated, it states The Elementals, when ascended would become The Horsemen that could destroy the veil between the worlds. Fire would rain from the sky, the sea would carry disease, the air would destroy the worlds crops and earth would crumble and fall."

It was like the poem, a premonition of what was to

come. "They were scared The Horseman would destroy the world..." Alice looked away, breath caught in her throat. "The reason I'm born, can't be to start the apocalypse."

"It's not just that," Kyle continued. "If the veil between the realms fractures, it could allow creatures not meant for this world to escape through the cracks."

Her head snapped back. "Like Shadow-Veyn?"

Kyle nodded. "They're not native to this realm, they were forced from their home by the Fae. It was part of an agreement to keep peace between Far Side and Earth Side. So between them they created The Nether, or Hell as I like to call it."

"Then why are you staying here?" she asked. "Are you trapped?"

Kyle stood, settling the paper on the table. "They call themselves The Originals. They're the first druids who were tempted by the darkness, and are bound here as part of their curse. There's a ritual that involves one of The Originals, and many don't make the transformation. The ones who survive are bound to The Nether, unable to leave without the use of their summoning name."

"And you?"

"My change was... different," he said, voice quiet. "But down here is the best place for me to be. According to Lucy, only one druid every three-hundred years or so chooses the dark, not understanding that they bind themselves to live an eternity trapped. It was why Master was trying to create a hybrid, force the change on any Breed he could capture so he had an army, one who would be ready once the veil falls."

"And he succeeded with you, without the ritual?"

"Hmmm." Kyle hesitated, his back to her.

"What's this all got to do with The Knights?"

"From the limited information I could find, The Knights were one of the first protectors of the veil, protecting Earth Side from whatever passed through back in the late fifth century. They've made it their sole purpose to stop the prophecy from happening, but that isn't even the start of it."

"What else is there?"

He clenched his fist, gaze trained to the floor. "Ali, Daemons have their own version of the prophecy. Master failed in his army, but that doesn't mean there isn't increasing unrest." He looked up, eyes glowing. "There are some that will do anything to help shatter the realms, even if that means the end of everything."

A lice tried desperately not to touch the headstone, even as she swayed on her feet. Her leg ached, protesting at her weight as she carefully stood in the moonlight.

"A cemetery? Really?" she said with a sigh. There was nowhere to rest without sitting on the dead, and knowing her luck she didn't need some clingy ghost following her home. She had already trained her eyes forward, ignoring the white glows in her peripheral vision as the stubborn spooks vied for her attention. Ghosts were at their strongest where the dead lay to rest, able to project themselves without the assistance of necromancers.

"I know right?" Sam laughed, bumping his hip against hers hard enough she almost stumbled. "And under a full moon. So cliché."

Alice squeaked, jumping forward much to the objection of her thigh. She was sure something brushed down her back, phantom fingers lingering on her skin.

"Don't tell me the one who's supposed to end the world

is afraid of ghosts?" Sam snorted, wiggling his fingers. "Path-et-ic!"

Peyton shot them both a disapproving look, mouth pursed as he sat cross-legged on a random burial vault, the name long worn off. "You shouldn't joke about that."

"Daeizan Raeron," Elduin grunted from his guard position by Peyton. "The moon mourns, we must hurry." His hand clenched his curved blade, attention concentrated on Jordan who sat between them in a hand-drawn circle.

"How can a moon mourn?" Sam whispered, chuckling at her shrug.

It had been a week since Peyton discharged himself from the hospital, well, disappeared from his hospital bed much to the distress of the doctors and Brady. She hadn't asked him where he went, but he looked a lot better than he did before. Alice, on the other hand, looked like she had been hit by a truck. Which pissed her off more than the weakness in her leg. Elduin seemed to be his over-protective shadow, as Sam was hers.

"Your glass is broken," the unfriendly elf murmured, his words thick in accent. "You did a terrific job."

"He means terrible," Peyton added, shaking the bottle in which she had attempted to capture Jordan's consciousness. She wasn't even sure why she had brought it with them, the dark cloud was long gone by the time Kyle returned her home.

"Wow, rude." Alice couldn't help her smile at Elduin's confused face, his mouth shaping the word as he tried to understand what she meant. Her spell might have failed, but Jordan had been stuck recovering in her kitchen rather than eating her neighbours, so she called it a win. "Is this going to take long? This place is creepy and I'm hungry for burgers."

"It will take as long as it takes," Peyton shot back, adjusting his circle by adding a large diamond around Jordan.

"What is this burger?" Elduin asked.

"You've never had a burger?" Sam chuckled. "Oh my man, you haven't lived until..."

Peyton began to sing, the strange lyrics washing over her aura just as the wild magic danced to life inside her. He hadn't opened their connection, the warmth missing yet she felt wild magic caressing her chi. It longed for him, wanting the shared connection that he refused to open.

Elduin growled, his attention shifting as he took a threatening step forward.

"Alice... control yourself..." Peyton gasped, his muscles tense as perspiration broke out across his skin.

Oh shit! "I'm sorry!" She reigned back her power, not realising it had stretched to encompass him. It was as if her magic had actively searched for him, knowing he was her familiar. They really needed to sever that connection.

Peyton shook his head, hands coming around in a loud clap. The ground jolted, and Jordan cracked open with a burst of light.

"Fuck me!" Sam cursed, shielding his eyes as a dark ball vaulted into the sky, projecting a high-pitched screech.

With a last word Peyton held up a new bottle, one with patterns drawn on the glass. The dark ball jerked, stretching as it was sucked inside before Peyton screwed the lid tight.

"Now that was cool," Sam said. "What is it?"

Peyton shook the glass, staring inside with a frown. "Looks to be a wraith. A type of dark spirit that feeds on souls. It attached itself to the gnome for some reason and used it as a conduit, moving it around to find its next meal."

"Well, isn't that lovely." Sam stretched, arm dropping to

wrap around Alice. "Now let's go get some burgers." He sniffed, a shiver going down his spine. "Peyton, seriously though, why a cemetery?"

Peyton turned, his face serious. "Because even though they're dead, the spirits and ghosts watch over us in protection. They're never far away."

Alice felt her heart ache, the loss still raw. With a nod she looked away, fighting the tears that threatened to spill. Her leg shook, exhausted.

"You aching?" Sam asked quietly. "We can skip food if you just want to go home?"

"It's fine." It wasn't, it hurt like a bitch. "I wouldn't recommend petting a hellhound though."

"Well, maybe you shouldn't go around poking dangerous things."

"But he was so cute and fluffy," she said, putting on a girly voice.

He just rolled his eyes in return. "What you thinking about?"

Alice sighed, resting her head on his shoulder. Dread may not have been his father figure, but he loved him all the same and his death hit him hard. They were a family, albeit a messed up one.

"Overlord." She deliberately used the nickname Sam liked to call him.

"I hope he's found peace." Sam kissed the top of her head, a purr vibrating his chest.

Alice smiled. "You think?"

"Oh aye, with lots of necks for him to suck on."

She elbowed him in the ribs. "You're an idiot. If Peyton's right, he would probably be watching, judging us against his old ways."

"Oh bloody hell, don't say that. I'm never going to sleep again knowing that bugger is watching me wank!"

"SAM!" Alice laughed, tears breaking through to trickle down her face. She had loved Dread, he was her father in every way but blood. But it was the Breeds way to remember the good memories of the dead, and not dwell on the pain. She would never forget him, just like she never forgot her parents, even if those memories were faded with age.

She was no longer upset at his death, just angry. But she wasn't sure what to do with that anger yet.

"Oi, your highness," Sam smirked, waving at Peyton while Elduin snarled. "We done here? This place is starting to give me the creeps."

Peyton dropped the bottle into a bag, turning to glare. "Let's go get some bloody burgers."

Xander watched from downwind, conscious that the leopard would smell him. He wasn't sure why he was there, why he was following her. But he couldn't seem to help himself, was almost curious. She should be dead, but there she was cuddling a leopard.

"It's not over, you know."

Xander knew he was there, but had tried to ignore him. "You should go into the light, you know, the big fucking white thing." He assumed it was white, he had never seen it for himself.

Dread clenched his jaw, a vein in his head pulsating. "She shouldn't be punished for her heritage."

"Not my problem," Xander grunted, turning to the

vampire while all the other ghosts howled for his attention. He fucking hated cemeteries.

"Then why are you here, Aes-Si Seer?"

That was a name he hadn't heard in years, not since he was ripped out of his mother's arms as a child and forced into training by his bastard uncle. "I watch over her."

"Why?"

Xander paused. "Because he loves her, and that's against the rules." Every time they shifted, they lost a part of themselves to their beast. It was something they had accepted a long time ago, the inevitable that one day they wouldn't come back and would have to be taken out like the monsters they were.

They had trained to control them, but strong emotions forced them to shift more. So they couldn't fall in love, couldn't soul bind without giving in to their spirit beasts.

Yet Riley, the leader of The Guardians would risk everything for her.

"I wanted her to lead a normal life, but I realised early on that would be impossible," Dread said, looking at Alice in the distance. "She's extraordinary, and would have made her parents proud of the woman she has become."

Xander shifted onto his other foot, wanting the vampire to leave him in peace. "Why are you bothering me?"

Dread shot him a warning, his eyes impossibly darker in death. His skin was pale, even for a vampire and a red line sliced his neck in two.

"There's a secret I've hidden from her, about her legacy."

"How original, a vampire with secrets," Xander grunted.

"Careful," Dread growled. "There's a coin, a seal, that

once broken she would officially ascend into War. If that happens... she can't be saved."

"Why does this seal matter? She's hardly the homicidal type."

"Because it's part of the Elemental's Curse. She inherits the magic of her ancestors, all of it, and risks destroying everything."

"I don't believe in prophecies."

Dread smiled. "You sound like her."

He began to flicker, becoming transparent before recovering.

"If her coin touches the blood of another Elemental and breaks, it would unlock her full power, and inevitably create a fissure in the veil, opening up the realms to a war between those above and below." Dread paused, turning his face to the sky as the full moon shimmered high above. "It's why they're coming, and they won't stop until she's dead."

The End of Book Four

This series continues with Knight's War: Buy here!

A personal note from Taylor

I hope you enjoyed Elemental's Curse! If you want to show your support, I would really appreciate you leaving a review from the store you purchased. Reviews are super important and help other readers discover this series!

Check me out on Facebook, Instagram and TikTok!

Continue reading for an excerpt of Knight's War, Alice Skye book five.

KNIGHT'S WAR

I t didn't take her long to find the clearing, a large flattened circle that was surrounded by trees for privacy. To the left was a handmade wooden obstacle course, while the rest of the space was used for sparring. Both Titus and Axel were running through, trying to beat each other's time in a blur too fast for her to distinguish. Riley met her eyes as soon as she appeared, a slow smile curling his lips.

"Appointment go well?" he asked, arms crossing to drop her attention down to his naked chest. Small bursts of sunlight broke through the canopy of leaves above, glittering across his skin.

"Am I interrupting something?" she replied with a smirk. "You seem to be all in various stages of undress."

"We run hot," Axel chuckled, smacking his palm over his own naked chest while Titus shook his head.

"I assume your appointment with D.E.A.D overran, so we don't have much time," Riley began, his head subtly shifting to face his men. "You know what to do."

Alice knew he wanted to ask her how it went, but he also knew she wouldn't want to discuss it in front of Titus or Axel. Not something so personal.

With a sigh she dropped her bag to the earth before she held out her arm.

The warmth in her hand was familiar and strong. It crackled as it grew with barely any effort until her arm was completely encased in blue flames licked with green.

"Do it again," Riley said with a sensual smirk that caused her stomach to knot in excitement.

Unable to stop her tongue from darting out to lick her dry lips she released her energy, only to repeat the same motion of the fire climbing up her arm once again. Riley's eyes narrowed, following her tongue at her accidental tease.

"Do it again," he growled, voice deepening.

"This is becoming uncomfortable," Titus murmured, arms crossed against his chest. He leant against a tree, his knee bent as the wind played with his pale shoulder-length hair. "It's clear her powers are developing far quicker than we anticipated."

"No shit," Axel chuckled beside him. "She can hold onto that arcane longer than any witch I have ever seen. Fuck, I bet she can give you a run for your money, Tit."

Titus snarled. "Call me that again, pretty boy," he threatened. "Just because she has the power, doesn't mean she has the experience."

"Is there a reason they're here?" Alice asked when she flicked a glance to her right.

"You need to be trained by different styles of instructors," Riley replied. "And they need to learn patience."

"Patience?" Axel muttered. "Patience my arse."

Patience? she mentally added. *That's a bit bloody rude.*

Riley chuckled as if he knew exactly what she thought. "Axel, you ready?"

Axel stretched, then immediately jumped into the makeshift circle. "Ready to eat dirt, my little doomsday?" He grinned, holding his hands out as arcane coated his fingertips.

"Bring it on, pretty boy," she said, using the same nickname Titus had just used.

His grin tightened, his dark eyebrows coming low over deep green eyes. In a flash he threw a bolt of arcane, the purple sphere dissipating at her feet as she jumped out of the way with a gasp.

"So slow," he taunted, readying another.

Alice steadied her legs just as he threw a larger sphere, the arcane burning across her flesh before she was able to rebound it back.

"That's more like it," Riley clapped.

A high pitched hum in the distance, beating in intervals like a drum.

Bom. Bom. Bom. Bom.

"Watch out!"

Alice moved out of the way of the bolt just in time, the purple ball hitting the tree directly behind her.

"Sorry," she said, shaking her head to clear the noise. "Let's go again."

What the bloody hell was that?

She managed to dodge every bolt, returning some with her own blast of arcane. Her chi pulsated, energised as she tested its strength. Witches were restricted in their magic, their chi's only able to stretch so much before they needed to recover. Alice was different, the closest to the original Elementals who each brandished a single element. Over time and a millennia of breeding, witches once singular powers mixed amongst the elements and diluted. Yet, Alice still held the strength from her ancestors power. It was supposed to be a gift, yet it felt like a curse.

Who really wanted to be in a prophecy for the end of the world?

Buy Now!

ABOUT THE AUTHOR

Taylor Aston White loves to explore mythology and European faerie tales to create her own, modern magic world. She collects crystals, house plants and dark lipstick, and has two young children who like to 'help' with her writing by slamming their hands across the keyboard.

After working several uncreative jobs and one super creative one she decided to become a full-time author and now spends the majority of her time between her children and writing the weird and wonderful stories that pop into her head.

www.taylorastonwhite.com

Printed in Great Britain
by Amazon